THE IRON PHOENIX

Visit us at www.boldstrokesbooks.com

THE IRON PHOENIX

by

Rebecca Harwell

2016

THE IRON PHOENIX

ISBN 13: 978-1-62639-744-6

This Trade Paperback Original Is Published By
Bold Strokes Books, Inc.
P.O. Box 249
Valley Falls, NY 12185

First Edition: May 2016

Credits
Editor: Ruth Sternglantz
Production Design: Susan Ramundo
Cover Design By Jeanine Henning

Acknowledgments

I am blessed to have many wonderful people in my life without whom this book would be only an idea. Thank you to my parents, Jane and Mike, for your unending support. John, for your insightful feedback and excellent music recommendations. Mandy, for reading many, many rough drafts. Other Becky, for poems. All my wonderful Knox friends, for 2 a.m. milkshake runs and continued encouragement. The Creative Writing department at Knox College, and in particular Cyn, Monica, Robin, and Sherwood, for pushing my writing to new depths. And finally, the amazing team at Bold Strokes Books, for making this book a reality.

Dedication

For Amanda, who believed in Nadya's story
from the very beginning.

CHAPTER ONE

Night sank into Storm's Quarry. With it came the eerie stillness that fed off the shivers of those traveling alone on cobblestoned streets. Elaborate manors of the citystate's fourth tier loomed overhead, guarded by wrought-iron gates and gargoyles carved into roofs, gutters forcing rainwater out of their silently shrieking jaws. In the darkness, they looked like demons from another realm.

Gedeon did not fear the dark.

He leaned up against the wall, waiting. The night wasn't cold, but he wore a full cloak as he watched the deserted road from the shadows. They were his kin; they were all he'd had for a long time now. Even the gas lamps that bordered the street, their pale light battling against the night, could not touch the shadows.

Between breaths, Gedeon felt the power stir in his bones. Whispering. Coaxing him to draw upon it and bring the man who had shamed him to his knees. In time, he told it. Even he, who had little to fear from the Duke's Guard, couldn't be foolish about murdering one of Duke Isyanov's favorite courtiers in the middle of the city's wealthiest neighborhood.

The clattering of hooves against stone broke the silence. Gedeon straightened as a lone carriage wound around the corner. It stopped before the ornate gate. One man jumped out of the driver's seat and, with a hurried glance over his shoulder, opened the carriage door and helped a stooped figure down. Another figure, smartly dressed in the livery of a private guardsman, surveyed the area.

Gedeon pulled farther back into the shadows. The guardsman opened the gate for the older man: Master Jurek, a bard and a courtier, beloved by the native Erevan people of the city. His silver hair gleamed as he moved slowly but surely along the curved walkway up to the double doors of his manor. His guardsman, one of the Nomori people by his dark skin and black hair, trailed behind him, eyes sharp for intruders. The driver led the horse and carriage away.

Gedeon stared at the courtier. It had been twelve years since he last saw him. He had been a young boy, a Nomori in the wrong place, stumbling into the wrong man, and that man, Jurek, had ordered his servant to make an example of him.

Concealing a thin smile, Gedeon took a step out of the shadows and onto the path. Both men stopped, and the guardsman reached for the rapier belted at his waist.

"Please, I ask for sanctuary," Gedeon said softly in Erevo, the harsh-sounding language of Storm's Quarry and its Erevan inhabitants. He spoke it well enough that his Nomori accent did not slip through.

Master Jurek frowned. "I do not take beggars in. I make my donations to the ration lines in times of floodwaters like any good citizen. Go now, and find rest elsewhere."

The Nomori guardsman stepped forward to carry out his master's words, but Gedeon let his cloak fall back to reveal a richly embroidered tunic of black silk. With his own Nomori features muted by night, he could pass for an Erevan courtier.

The older man's eyes widened. "Forgive me, sir. I thought you were one of the beggars from the second tier, or a Nomori layabout from the bottom." His guardsman flinched, but the courtier did not notice. "Please, what happened to you?"

"My name is Petro," Gedeon said. "My manor is in the arts district, on the other side of the tier. I was headed home earlier this evening when my carriage was seized by thieves in masks. Apparently, my driver had been bought off. I barely escaped with my life." He realized he sounded too calm, so he added some sporadic breathing for effect. Inside, he could not have been more pleased. Finally, this rat in fine silks would answer for how he'd humiliated

Gedeon all those years ago. "I ran until I found myself here. I do not know this part of the city, and no carriages run this late. A bed for the night would be most appreciated. I can pay you." He put a hand to his belt and jingled a bag of coins. If Master Jurek had doubt regarding his status, it vanished.

"Come in, sir, and I'll have my maid show you to our guest room. A warm bed and hot cup of tea will take away the shakes, and in the morning you can go to the Duke's Guard and report the thieves. Nomori, were they?"

Gedeon nodded, hiding a smile. How easy it was to manipulate this man, and he didn't even need to draw on his power.

Jurek sighed as he led him to the doors. "If the Duke weren't so besotted with those witches, this city would have nothing to fear except the storms. Peace, I tell you. That's what prevailed in Storm's Quarry in my day." His words turned to a low murmur as he unlocked the heavily barred door.

Gedeon kept one eye on the Nomori guardsman. The man's mouth drew into a tighter and tighter line until it looked like his face might crack. "I will go check the perimeter, sir," he said curtly.

"Good, thank you, Duren." Jurek waved a hand. The guardsman jerked a bow and left. Gedeon watched him go. Yes, this guardsman would do nicely. Perhaps he wouldn't get the satisfaction of killing Jurek himself, but it would conceal his involvement entirely.

"Come, come," Master Jurek said. He waved Gedeon through the doors into a softly lit reception hall. Paintings hung on the walls between gleaming candelabras, meticulously maintained to avoid the ever-present damp of the city. Gedeon noted the doors that led off the main hall and began creating a mental picture of the manor floor plan.

"Lana," Jurek called up the stairs, "we have a late guest." He turned back, saying, "I'll have a bed made up for…"

Gedeon had already vanished.

He swept through the manor, darting around corners as he followed the approximate map in his head. It was wrong about a few of the turns, but soon he reached the back door of a humbly furnished kitchen. Gedeon opened it and entered the night.

The Nomori guardsman was checking the locks on the rear gate of the manor's grounds. His back was turned. Gedeon stole up behind him. He waited, half concealed by shadows, as he readied the power. When Duren turned, the guardsman's hand flew to his rapier.

Gedeon smiled. He might share the same Nomori heritage as this man, but Duren was about as close to him as a dog was to a king.

Before Duren could draw his sword, Gedeon pulled at the well of darkness lurking in the edges of his consciousness. It flowed through him, electrifying every nerve, and out into Duren's furious eyes. The power latched onto the guardsman's anger, and it became the doorway into his mind. He shook with spasms; his eyes flickered open and shut. When the power had come to rest, he opened them to reveal a pupil-less stare as black as Gedeon's own.

Gedeon clamped down on the power with a mental fist, cracking the whip of control. Warmth settled in his chest. He leaned forward and whispered into Duren's ear, "Kill him."

❖

The citystate of Storm's Quarry was named for both the torrential rains that plagued it every few months and the precious gemstone mines it built its fortunes upon. When the Nomori people were invited in by the Duke to use their gifts to save the city from a Great Storm twenty years ago, they gave it a different name. They called the city *Natsia*, Nomori for *long journey home*.

Seated upon a rugged island in the center of an inland sea, Storm's Quarry was a pearl amidst gray waters. Marble walls, fifty paces tall, surrounded the city, keeping the waters of the Kyanite Sea at bay. In the times of flooding, when the storms of old would overwhelm the island entirely, the gates were sealed shut. The waters rose so high that the city would be trapped for weeks, cut off from the traders who provided its sustenance in return for jewels. Five tiers, each separated by a wall, arose to form the city. The Duke's palace sat at the top on the fifth tier, watching over the city like a kindly sentinel. This Duke was sympathetic to the plight of the nomadic Nomori, far more so than the Kingdom of Wintercress to the west or the South Marches, and when the chance presented itself to bring them together with the Erevan inhabitants of his city, he did so.

Despite the Nomori Stormspeaker's warning of the Great Storm of the Veiled Moon, as it was named, Storm's Quarry never truly became the home they had dreamed of. The Erevans feared them for the psychic gifts their women possessed and the preternatural fighting ability of their men. The Nomori in turn feared the Erevans for their numbers, their muskets and gunpowder, and their anger. For twenty years, they had managed to live together with no small amount of tension, but mercifully few attacks or murders. The two peoples kept to themselves, and life in the city went on.

For seventeen-year-old Nadya Gabori, life in Storm's Quarry was never that dull.

She had a secret.

When the day's duties were done, and she had finished the last delivery for her mother's jewelery shop, she sneaked out the back window into the night. It was late spring, and the faint breeze carried a heavy heat that spoke of another oncoming season of storms. A half-moon glowed overhead. As the tier's gas lamps wicked out, the moon's light cut soft shadows between stone buildings. Nadya made sure to stay within their darkness as she scrambled up the side of her two-story home. Her fingers dug into the lines of mortar; her boots kicked at bricks. The night smelled faintly of damp and mold, but in Storm's Quarry, such scents were a way of life. The near-constant rainstorms meant that everything was always wet. Perhaps those in the higher, wealthier tiers of the city could afford to have their mold scoured away, but here at the bottom, in the Nomori tier, such a thing was luxury. Just another thing the Nomori gave up in order to live close to the Kyanite Sea. They were a river-people at heart, once nomadic, traveling the coasts and tributaries, never staying in one place for long. That is, until Storm's Quarry. Although the safety the citystate provided drew them in once the Great Storm had ceased, whispering promises of *Natsia*, the water still pulled at them, its nearness a comfort born into their blood.

Gripping the edge of the roof, Nadya hauled herself up. She balanced carefully on the slanted stonework. The last of the afternoon's light rain ran down, condensing into iridescent droplets, then dripping down to the culverts below. During storms, those carved culverts directed all the water down to the basins along the inside of the great wall of Storm's Quarry.

It was only weeks now, perhaps less, before the new season of storms would be upon them. *And I doubt even I could stand being out in the torrential downpour that's coming.* She listened for any disturbance in her house. Even through the stone, if she was very still, she could hear the rattling of her mother's breath as she slept.

I have few nights like this left.

She scanned the horizon. Clustered rooftops of Nomori dwellings and shops in every direction, leaving small gaps for roads and even smaller for drain culverts. The mass of buildings went right up to the wall, fifty paces high, that ringed the entire city.

She backed up a few steps. Then, bending her knees, Nadya leapt across the four-pace-wide alley to their neighbor's roof.

The moment her boots touched stone, she was off. Running, skidding when she hit a patch of rainwater, she pushed herself to the limits of her speed. This was well-known territory to her. In the past months, the Nomori tier had become her playground at night. She thrust off skyward with her left foot, and then came down on her right. Her muscles knew the movements well, within the sturdy contours of her own body.

Since she had discovered she was not like the rest of her people, Nadya had always felt ungainly, awkward. She had to carefully watch herself, watch her strength, make sure to hide the unnatural part of her that had surfaced. The memory of her first encounter with her abilities surged forward in her thoughts, and bile burned her tongue. She thrust it back, along with the near-reflexive prayer to the Protectress that rose in her throat. No prayer of the cursed would be answered, that she was sure of.

Now, with the only witnesses the stars, the moon, and the city itself, Nadya let all that go. Each tier rose up before her, separated by great walls of white marble that glowed in the moonlight. Shadows punctuated the brilliance, dark veins of gutters splayed out from the city's heart. In them ran the blood of Storm's Quarry: rainwater, pouring down to the culverts and pumped back out into the sea. A city of tempests and ghosts, and she was a wraith, stealing through the darkness.

During the day, she was the picture of a dutiful Nomori daughter. Except for how she talked back to her mother and ignored her grandmother's speeches about marriage and upholding the family name. She worked for her mother, whose psychic gift with gemstones made her the best jeweler in the city. She pretended to have her own gift, as all Nomori women did. A bit of sight beyond sight, a ruse her enhanced senses, keen enough to hear the quickened heartbeat of a liar, helped convince everyone of.

At night, however, Nadya was herself. And now, clambering to the top of the wall that separated the fourth tier from the lesser parts of the city, she had never felt more whole.

Well, perhaps in a quiet moment with Kesali, hands threaded together, leaning into one another, watching the bustle of the tier go by, leaving only the two of them in its wake, an island to themselves. Even then, she had to be in character, to hide what made her different.

The fourth tier of Storm's Quarry, home to the wealthy elite, sat just one step below the palace. Its buildings were nearly four times as high as those in the Nomori tier and as she stood on the wall before it, she felt dwarfed by them.

Here, the Duke's Guard patrolled often. She could not linger, no matter how breathtaking the view. Backing up until her tunic touched the opposite parapet, Nadya kept her eyes and ears keen. For the moment, all was still. She took a deep breath. It filled her lungs, her body, bolstering the excited energy that buzzed in her limbs.

Like a bullet released from its musket, Nadya shot forward. Going up and away, she made an arc over the wall and down onto the lower roof of the nearest manor. She landed on one knee. Pain shot through her leg. It would bruise, but it'd be healed by noon tomorrow. Nadya climbed up the wall to the top. Here, she stood higher than everything except the upper wall and the palace. Here, she thought, puffing with excitement and exertion, she could truly push her limits. It was a distance of nearly one hundred paces between where she stood and the next manor. A distance she had never before attempted.

Nadya backed up, then sprinted forward, launching herself off the edge.

In that moment, she had wings.

The nearest she'd ever felt was the warm buzzing in her collarbone when she drank a bit too much of the second tier's sweet potato ale, but it could not compete with this.

No one could leap across rooftops and not feel...

Invincible.

Another, and another. Nadya found her rhythm. Each time she took off, she didn't know if she'd land with a solid thump strong enough to rattle her bones or cling to the edge by her fingers or even to come up short and fall without ever touching stone. But she gave herself over completely to her abilities. It was moments like these when Nadya could forget the grave consequences of being found out, the struggles of hiding her unnaturalness from her family, her friends. Here, she owned the skies and she reveled in what her body could do.

She landed on the roof of the tallest manor on the block. She teetered on the parapet for a moment, her stomach performing a few circus flips. It was such a long way down. The loose hair around her face whipped about in the wind. Her eyes watered.

Below, the courtyard of the neighboring manor was illuminated by ghost light, turning every stone bench, every gable into a specter. Shadows of two figures standing at the back gate stretched all the way through the garden to the brass manor door. She could not see much besides that one was taller than the other. It was the shorter one, however, who seemed to be advancing on the other—a Nomori man, she thought as she peered down.

Nadya was about to turn around and leave, as no good would come of being seen, when the scene below shifted. The Nomori man suddenly faced toward her. Before he ran back inside, rapier in hand, Nadya saw his eyes. Pure black, not a speck of any color.

She shivered, and looked to the other figure. He stood in shadow, nothing about him giving any hint as to who he was. His head tilted up, and she saw eyes as dark as midnight.

A scream split the stillness of the night. A man's voice. Nadya covered her ears, wincing against the shrill terror. The man below darted away. The Nomori guardsman stumbled out the back doors of the manor. His rapier gleamed red, and Nadya wished her eyesight were no better than everyone else's.

She didn't know what had happened, but no sooner had the scream died away that the faint sound of many running boots—the Duke's Guard—echoed through the neighborhood. She could not be found here. Not by the Guard, or worse, her father, a captain of its ranks. Tripping over her rush to get away, she sped to the opposite side of the roof and made an ungraceful leap to the next one. It would be nearly dawn by the time she returned home. She had a feeling that what she just witnessed was no small matter. *Murder*, her mind whispered as she sped down through the city. Hopefully, Protectress willing, she would avoid any consequences from it.

After all, Nadya Gabori had a secret. And if anyone found out, she would lose everything she held dear.

CHAPTER TWO

Nadya slipped into the back window of her home just as the first rays of sun hit the great marble wall. She landed softly in the loft where her pallet lay. Quickly, she stripped off yesterday's clothes and pulled on a fresh pair of blue trousers and a cream shirt. Her seal of the Protectress remained fastened around her upper arm, a metal band with a five-petal flower—a river lily—imprinted into it. She brushed it with a finger. Warmth blossomed in her arm. It could have just been her imagination, but she liked to believe it was a response to her unspoken prayer.

After taming her wind-snarled hair into a braid, Nadya climbed down the ladder to the main house, careful not to let the rungs squeak. She couldn't do the same for the growling noises her stomach was now making. Her nose had already picked up the scent of cinnamon flatbread.

"You weren't in your bed last night."

Nadya froze, her hand halfway to the ledge where the flatbread lay cooling. Before she could say anything, a grating cough echoed throughout the small dwelling. Her mother covered her mouth, but her body shook with the effort to stop it. She leaned against the stone wall. "Where were you?" she asked hoarsely.

Mirela Gabori was a small woman. Once she might have been called lithe, but now she looked frail. Her trousers and vest hung off her frame. Silver streaks peppered her black mane, which she kept plaited back in a knot on her head as was custom for a married Nomori woman. Still, she had an air about her that would allow no one to question her as the heir to the Gabori family, nor as one of the more powerfully psychic of the Nomori women.

Nadya met her eyes for a moment. "Nowhere."

"Am I expected to believe that?" Mirela asked. Her voice regained its strength, as it always did when she found fault with Nadya.

"I just needed some air." She turned around and grabbed a piece of flatbread, scoffing half of it down in one bite.

"Do not lie to me, Nadezhda."

It's not as if I can tell you the truth, Nadya shouted in her mind. *You would disown me and throw me out of here before I could give you two words of explanation. So what exactly do I owe you?*

They were toxic thoughts, and she knew it. But Nadya ignored the prick of her conscience and the tired lines in her mother's face. She grabbed her second-best vest off its peg on the wall. It was light blue and embroidered with a desert scene of quick-footed deer being hunted by a feline predator. Her grandmother might be many things, overbearing being the nicest of them, but she was unrivaled when it came to creating such pieces of art. She slipped it on and fastened the buttons. "I'm going out."

"So soon? It's as if you hardly live here anymore." Mirela stepped away from the wall to block her path. "You are not leaving this house until you've finished your chores. There is mold growing in the corners, and it'll only get worse as the season of storms approaches."

"It isn't that bad," Nadya said. She tried to keep her tone even, but that was hard. "I'm going to walk Kesali to work, all right? Nothing forbidden or scandalous. I won't even leave the tier. I'll clean tomorrow."

"I have heard that before." Mirela crossed her arms. "You think I don't understand, but I do."

No, Mama, you do not. You could never.

"You are young, and it's hard to think beyond today. But you are nearing your eighteenth birthday, and you must start taking on more responsibility, Nadya." Mirela sighed. "You are a Gabori, and you need to start understanding what that means."

"I know what it means," Nadya said sharply. She pushed past her mother, carefully. "It means I'll have to get married to a man I hardly know in the coming year. It means I won't be able to go anywhere in the city because I'll be the next head of the family. It means I'm going to lose all my freedom." She clenched her hands into fists and made herself breathe deeply. Losing control now would do no good.

"Nadya…"

She whipped around, and her mouth almost betrayed her: *It means that if my secrets were ever found out, I would no longer be part of this family.* But she caught herself in time. Her anger was dangerous, and her mother meant well, at least. Even if she would never understand, and Nadya would never be able to confide in her.

About anything. Not her abilities, not Kesali.

"Sorry," she mumbled. "I'm just…tired."

It was the perfect opportunity for Mirela to comment once again on her nighttime absence, but she must have decided it wasn't worth another argument. Instead, she nodded and said, "At least bring you father his lunch. He's at the Guardhouse this morning."

"Okay." Nadya grabbed the cloth sack from inside their icebox and left through the curtain that parted their living quarters from her mother's shop. The shop was messy, with tools and bits of wires and cuttings of gemstones strewn across the worktable. This wasn't like her mother, to keep things in such disarray. Maybe coming home early to help tidy up would be a good idea. Her mother wasn't feeling well after all, and hadn't been for a while.

"Be safe," Mirela called.

Nadya muttered, "Good-bye," and left the house.

Her family was luckier than most. With her father a captain in the Duke's Guard and her mother one of the best jewelers in all of Storm's Quarry, they could afford to live in one of the nicer districts of the Nomori tier. It was still plain and waterlogged compared to the finery she had seen last night in the fourth tier, but Nadya had spent plenty of time running through the more impoverished parts of the Nomori tier, and she knew how much the Protectress had blessed her family to not have to endure that.

The air was thick and damp, a sure sign of the coming storms that would leave the city surrounded by floodwaters. Nadya was barely out a few minutes before sweat was running down her face and pooling in the depressions in her neck. Damn, it was hot! She almost wished for winter again, and the cooling breezes it brought through the streets of the city. She passed dozens of other Nomori, but no Erevans. The Nomori men were in uniform, ranging from the crimson of the Duke's Guard to the white of a personal guard to a courtier or a trainer to that same courtier's obnoxious children. The women wore everything from the thick smocks of engineers for the city's pumps to the bangles and headbands of a palm reader or fortuneteller. The Erevans of Storm's Quarry didn't like or trust the Nomori for the most part. That did not stop them, however, from employing the natural gifts of the Nomori: the psychic talents of the women and the preternatural fighting abilities of the men.

"Such a long face for such a beautiful day. Did you lose your smile while you were running all over the city last night?"

Nadya grinned in spite of herself as Kesali hopped off her doorstep. "And were you spying out your window to see me drop it?" Suddenly, the morning's argument seemed far away, as if chased off by Kesali's presence. She frequently had this effect on Nadya, calming whatever storms currently raged in her life with nothing more than a glance, a word or two.

"No. I, unlike some layabouts"—she poked Nadya in the arm—"have duties to perform, so I can't be up half the night. It's the bags under your eyes. They always give you away. Buy some cream from the third tier, the stuff those ladies use to cover their faces. It'll stop your parents from being able to tell."

Nadya shook her head. "They would know even if I paid a doppelgänger to sleep on my pallet. Do I really look so tired?"

"Try sleeping. You will be amazed at what it can do." Kesali laughed and dodged Nadya's friendly jab. Nadya was careful to let her. Kesali knew about the nighttime excursions because she had caught Nadya once. She didn't know about Nadya's secret, and Nadya planned to keep it that way.

"Let's go, hmm? I can't be late. The Head Cleric is a man devoted to his studies, and woe to anyone who doesn't share the same commitment." Kesali tugged on her arm. "Coming?"

Nadya smiled and started forward. "Can't have you being late, can we?"

Kesali's only response was to tug harder, and they proceeded down the narrow street toward Miner's Tunnel. There, a carriage waited to take Kesali up to the palace for her training as the Head Cleric's apprentice. Before her, that role had been an honor reserved only for Erevans.

She was the Nomori Stormspeaker after all, inheriting the title from her mother, the woman who had saved both peoples from the Great Storm of the Veiled Moon nearly twenty years ago. Her psychic gift in predicting the weather was passed to her daughter, and Kesali now bore that responsibility.

But Nadya tried hard not to see all that. She was just Kesali, and she was her dearest friend.

"Something is wrong, though, isn't it?"

Nadya shook her head. "It's nothing."

"You can't lie to me, Nadya. I read you as easily as I do the skies. Is it your grandmother?" Kesali asked, the humor gone from her voice. Her large, deep brown eyes looked down at Nadya, who caught her breath. Kesali was beautiful in a timeless way that would make any sunrise hide in shame. She wanted to touch that smooth skin, to brush a wisp of hair that had escaped her braid behind Kesali's ear.

She blinked and turned away. Such things couldn't be done in public, especially in the Nomori tier.

"My mother is beginning to talk like her. Responsibility and the Gabori name and all that." As soon as the words were out of her mouth, Nadya realized how pathetic they must sound to Kesali, who had the fate of the city riding on her shoulders come every season of storms. Storm's Quarry only survived because the storms and consequent floodwaters would be predicted and prepared for. "I'm sorry, I don't mean to complain."

"Nonsense. I understand, believe me," Kesali said.

Nadya wanted to believe her. But there was still a part of her life that no one would ever be able to enter, not even Kesali, whom she had known since they were babies wrapped in swaddling cloth and set beside one another while their mothers worked.

"I'm lucky she didn't bring up marriage, but it surely will come up again." Nadya ducked around a young man pushing a cart of rapiers, the preferred weapon of Nomori guardsmen. He was probably a trainee, tall and strong-looking, with dark hair cut to his earlobes and a nice enough chin. Someone her grandmother Drina would be thrilled to pair her up with, no doubt. She rolled her eyes.

"Be nice. You could be betrothed to someone wonderful. He'll be smart and strong, at least, for your grandmother to think him worthy."

Nadya stopped. "That's not what I want." Her heart pounded. How could her body feel the same way now as it did last night, when she leapt from building to building, defying the stars?

Kesali gave a small, resigned smile. "People like us, dear, rarely get to do what we want." She started walking again.

Nadya watched her for a moment before catching up. She wiped at her eyes, blaming it on the sun glinting off the windows of the storefronts they passed. It didn't matter, she told herself, if Kesali knew or not, if she felt the same way. It wasn't just her duty to the city and Nadya's duty to her family that made it impossible. It was the secret between them, the secret that made her hold Kesali at an arm's length when she wanted nothing more than to embrace her and smell the sweet spice of her hair.

She remained quiet through the rest of their morning walk. If Kesali thought something was amiss, she didn't press her.

The crowds grew thicker as they reached Miner's Tunnel. All roads in the tier converged into one chaotic street that led up to the hole in the earth. The dark road pierced straight through the heart of the mines Storm's Quarry sat on, built to allow its miners a quicker commute to and from their work.

A red carriage waited at the corner, with an Erevan footman holding the reins of two horses, a rare, expensive, and unwieldly resource in Storm's Quarry. He wore a frown and kept looking up at the sky, following the sun's path.

"I must go," Kesali said. "Thank you for walking me here. You know that you don't have to do this every day."

"And you know that I want to," Nadya replied without a pause.

Kesali bent down slightly and gave her a quick kiss on the cheek before bounding off to the impatient footman. Nadya stood there, rooted to the spot by the weight of that small good-bye, until the carriage vanished into the darkness of the tunnel.

The sack in her hand finally reminded Nadya that she did have things to do this morning. She carefully made her way through the crowd to the opposite edge of the tunnel's mouth, where the pedestrians trod through. She took a deep breath and entered.

Nadya hated the tunnel. With only lamplight to illuminate the gloom, not even her eyes could see very far. She would have much preferred to run around the outer wall of the city, but only guardsmen were allowed up there. Of course, that hadn't stopped her from running its length several times over the past months at night.

The tunnel let out on the south side of the Nomori tier, where a faint hammering could always be heard coming from behind metal doors that led deep under the city. These mines were the reason Storm's Quarry existed as more than a barren rock in the middle of the Kyanite Sea; the precious gemstones brought up kept the hundred thousand people in the city fed. A fence ran around the entire area and guardsmen patrolled the outer perimeter, keeping a wary eye on the crates of material sent up to the palace and its refiners. Just outside the wall, the squat two-story prison of gray stone stood like a watchdog over the mines.

From there, Nadya left the suffocating darkness of the tunnel behind and climbed the stairs that led up to the palace. It was a daunting climb that would take a normal person over an hour to reach the top tier of the city, where the palace, its storehouses, and the headquarters of the Duke's Guard lay. Most people opted to pay a coin and take the rail that ran on either side of the marble stairs. Nadya elected to walk, going faster than perhaps was wise in public, but no one she passed had any cares but their own. When she reached the top, her breath came heavily.

Ignoring the crowds going to the Duke's open forum, Nadya headed straight to the Guardhouse. She did not miss the dirty looks cast her way. Not many Nomori came up here, and those who did usually wore the uniform of the Guard.

An imposing building of white marble, as old as the city itself, it was not as tall or as ornate as the palace, but it had an impressive presence nonetheless. A ten-pace wall surrounded the grounds, with two guardsmen at each entrance. Nadya walked up to the gate that was guarded by two Nomori men in the crimson uniform of the Duke's Guard.

"Business here?" one asked curtly in accented Erevo, but the other held up a hand.

"The captain is one lucky man, having a beautiful woman visit him," the other guardsman said with a wink. "Good to see you again, Miss Gabori. Go on in." He stepped aside and motioned for his companion to do the same.

Nadya couldn't remember his name, but she had been coming here her whole life and knew most of the guardsmen by sight at least. "Thank you," she said with a smile and went inside.

The actual Guardhouse took up less than half of the area. Most of it provided training grounds for new recruits. Nadya passed several Nomori men sparring with rapiers. Beyond them, some Erevan guardsmen practiced in a firing range with muskets. In the sparring court closest to the Guardhouse, two men squared off. The taller of the two was older, early forties, with graying hair that stood out starkly against a dark Nomori complexion. He wore a sweat-stained uniform, but he moved as if he was fresh.

"Keep your legs moving, Marko!" he shouted. "You are giving me more opportunities than I could find on my own."

"Ay, Captain," the redheaded younger man said, puffing. He did not have the preternatural speed and reflexes of the Nomori men, but he moved with a grace that bespoke years of training with the best. His rapier flashed, seeking an opening.

Nadya stopped just outside the sand sparring circle. Neither man noticed her, engrossed in their bout. Her eyes followed every movement, noting strike positions and where they balanced their weight. The Nomori captain clearly had the upper hand in the fight, and always would. No one could defeat a Nomori with a rapier.

Especially not her father.

"Now, show me that you've been drilling the crescent moon sequence," Shadar Gabori called out.

The younger man stepped back. He brought his blade up, then charged, swinging it down in a backward crescent pattern so fast it was a silver blur.

Shadar wore a small half smile. He spun, brushing off the blow and bringing his blade up to his opponent's throat.

Lord Marko Isyanov, son of the Duke and heir to the citystate, bowed his head in defeat. As soon as the blades were lowered, he broke out into a grin and slapped Shadar on the back. "Sometimes I wonder why I continue to put myself through this." He winced and rubbed his side.

"Because you're not an idiot," Shadar said, wiping his forehead.

Nadya was afraid to speak for a moment. She couldn't help the feelings of jealousy that roiled in her chest whenever she watched her father train Marko. She wished it could have been her in that ring. Shadar could teach her so much about control, about balance, about channeling just enough of her strength. But Nomori women were too important for their psychic gifts to learn the way of the weapon.

And revealing her secret to her father, bound to the law of the Elders as well as the Duke's Guard, was impossible.

"Nadya," Shadar said, seeing her for the first time. "I wasn't expecting you." He spoke in accented Erevo out of respect for Marko. Even in his deep voice, it lacked the musicality of their native Nomori tongue that Nadya was used to hearing him speak. He greeted her with a kiss on the forehead. When he saw the linen bag in her hands, he smiled even wider. "What did I do to deserve a daughter such as you?"

"Protecting the city is a start," she replied.

"Miss Gabori, it's nice to see you again," Lord Marko said, nodding to her. Nadya returned his nod. He didn't like people bowing to him, something she'd learned when he first became her father's pupil, many years ago now.

"Milord," she said, trying not to let any of her lingering jealousy toward the Duke's son into her tone.

Anything further was interrupted by heavy footsteps. A man wearing the copper badge of an official messenger hurried up to them. It must be something important, Nadya thought, for them to send a man and not a pigeon. Immediately, she began sweating ice. It couldn't be about her...No, she hadn't been spotted. And even if she had, it wasn't as if anyone but herself had the eyesight to identify her.

"Come," Lord Marko asked, stepping forward. He gave an apologetic look to Nadya as he, Shadar, and the messenger retreated to just under the roof of the Guardhouse. Official business and all, and she wasn't exactly cleared for such things.

It helped that she could hear it all anyway.

Nadya kicked at the sandy edges of the sparring circle as she listened. The messenger began, "There's been a murder in the fourth tier. Egor Jurek."

Nadya froze. They couldn't be talking about the incident she had witnessed the night before. But how many murders went unreported among the wealthy of the fourth tier?

By the Guardhouse, Marko said, "One of my father's closest friends. How? Are you sure it was murder?"

"There can be no doubt. A patrol of the Guard took a suspect into custody. They will be here soon. Master Jurek's house has been sealed, waiting for your word, and messages have been sent to his relatives."

A pause, and then Marko spoke, "Captain, I want you to handle the interrogation. Draw on any resources you see fit. I will head to his house and gather what I can. This must take precedence over everything except flood preparation. My father will be devastated, and he will want answers."

"Ay, milord."

Nadya pretended to be absorbed in her boots when her father returned. He touched her shoulder. "Tell your mother I will be late tonight. There is much that needs to be done."

Before she could think better of it, she blurted out, "I can help you."

"Nadya." His tone brooked no argument. Here, he was Captain of the Duke's Guard, and that duty must come first, before even that of a father.

"I heard something about an interrogation," she said quickly. Risky, but it was fairly quiet, and there was nothing to suggest that she couldn't have picked up a few words. "I might be able to determine if he's telling the truth."

Last night, Nadya had run while a man died. If she could make up for that, she would. She needed to.

Shadar sighed. "I was planning to call your grandmother. She'll be able to help us."

Being in the same room with Drina wasn't something Nadya usually did voluntarily. But she persisted. "Two psychics are better than one. It will bring a tighter case before the magistrates, at least. Please, I want to be useful. For more than running packages all over the city and delivering lunches."

Shadar looked at her for a long moment. Nadya's heartbeat thudded in her ears. Finally, he inclined his head. "All right. But you must do exactly as I say."

She nodded. Becoming more entwined with the inner workings of the Duke's Guard wasn't perhaps the smartest idea for someone with a secret, but she would see this investigation through.

CHAPTER THREE

Shadar made her wait in the courtyard until her grandmother arrived. Nadya kicked at the sand. She didn't make eye contact with any of the guardsmen, even when they called out a friendly greeting.

"Nadezhda, what are you doing up here?" her grandmother barked as she walked up to the Guardhouse, flanked by men on both sides. Proud as she was, Drina did not lean on either one of them.

Nadya uttered a quick prayer to the Protectress and willed her emotions to settle. She was upset enough about the incident in the fourth tier last night that if she was not careful, Drina would pick up her anxiety and start to question her. Lying to Drina Gabori, regarded as the most powerful psychic of all the Nomori, was not something anyone got away with.

"Grandmother," she replied, trying to speak with the proper level of respect for the head of the family, "I am to join you in the interrogation."

Drina's dark eyes were hawk-like rather than liquid like her daughter's. Not a single wisp of hair escaped her silver braid as she looked over Nadya, frowning. "Well, as glad as I am to see you taking interest in something that is not childish or overwhelmingly Erevan, your...skills are not needed."

Heat rising in her cheeks, Nadya stared at the ground. "I can't get better without practice."

"Very well." Drina sighed. "Make sure to behave yourself."

"Yes, Grandmother."

When Nadya entered the interrogation room behind Drina and the guardsmen, any confidence she pretended to have immediately vanished, leaving her with the desperate desire to run out. Two pairs of eyes turned on her. The all-encompassing damp threatened to choke her as her sensitive nose picked up the scents of fear, sweat, and blood. The last came from the rust-colored stains on the handcuffs chaining a Nomori man dressed in fine livery to the room's only bench. As his hollow eyes met hers, she looked away. She knew this man, Duren, a friend of her father. Shadar stood off to one side, noticeably paler, but his gaze was strong and his expression clear. He was a guardsman before all else, Nadya knew.

Shadar gave Drina a deferential nod. She acknowledged him with a sniff. Clearing his throat, he spoke to both of them once the other guardsmen had left. "His name is Duren. He was personal guard to Egor Jurek, one of the Duke's courtiers. His master was found slain early this morning by a rapier strike."

Nadya knew what that meant. While the Erevan guardsmen favored pistols and muskets, Nomori men with their inborn fighting talent preferred the thin blade of a rapier. In the years since the Nomori settled in the city, the Duke's Guard had turned it into a deadly strategy. The Erevans shot, and while they reloaded their muskets, the Nomori moved in with their blades. Despite the Erevans' distrust of Nomori guardsmen, even the most stubborn admitted it was an effective way to bring mobs under control. The only Erevan Nadya knew of that used a rapier was Lord Marko.

"You think one of our people murdered him?" Drina asked sharply.

Shadar's face was carefully blank. "We are following the evidence. Nomori are not above the Duke's justice. If we let personal feelings cloud this investigation, the city will not easily forgive us."

The Erevans in the city, you mean, Nadya thought silently.

Duren was staring at the ground with the expression of a man who knew his time had come. He was Nomori and he was suspected of an Erevan's murder. It would take more than a Nomori gift to get him released.

Nadya swallowed. Shadar nodded to Duren to start talking.

"Master Jurek was coming back from the palace last night. He was met by another courtier, who he offered sanctuary to. I saw them to the manor's door. Then I went to check the perimeter of the grounds. It is the duty of the personal guard to see to that every evening and morning."

"Ay," Shadar said softly.

Duren continued, still staring at the floor, "As I was testing the locks on the rear gate, someone stole up behind me. Before I could react, I must have been hit with something, because I blacked out. I'm not injured, though. I can't explain that." He sighed. "When I came around, my weapon was gone. I rushed inside to see to my master." His voice choked slightly. "Master Jurek was lying as the base of his staircase, dead. There was a puncture wound in his chest. His guest was gone. Perhaps this is the man you should be looking for."

Duren went silent. Shadar looked to both Drina and Nadya. "Well?"

Drina turned to Duren, face colder than icy wind. "You have disgraced the Nomori people. You will be cast out for your crimes."

Duren's eyes widened, but Shadar intervened both any more could be said. "Forgive me, but this is not a Nomori tribunal. He will face the justice of Storm's Quarry." He turned to Nadya. "Do you concur?"

His words hit her hard. She wished part of her gift included disappearing, because she would have done it then and there. Her grandmother was never wrong. She looked to the floor, biting her lip. She wasn't a true psychic like the rest of Nomori women, who each had their own unique gift. Drina perceived the emotions of others, and Mirela read people through the gemstones they owned. Nadya had not developed a psychic talent of her own. Instead, she grew stronger and faster with quicker reflexes and uncanny physical senses. Those were not the abilities of a Nomori, and Nadya did not know what they made her. She was able to masquerade as a weak psychic, however. Her sense of hearing was acute enough that she could sometimes tell when someone lied to her. Their heart rate sped up, and she could smell sweat and fear on them. She was a perpetual disappointment to her grandmother, but it was enough of a ruse to throw off suspicion that she was anything more.

As Duren told his story, his heart began hammering. It wasn't the pounding blood of a nervous man, either, for he had been calm until the words came out of his mouth. He was lying. He killed his master. Nadya knew it.

But that is not what I saw. The cloaked man with black eyes, he didn't attack Duren.

Drina's conclusions were always ironclad. But damn it all, Nadya had been there. She had seen this man go into the manor, heard the scream, yes, but he hadn't been alone. And there was something about the other figure that unnerved her in a deep way.

Nadya couldn't bring herself to look at Duren. She could not come to his defense. No one could know she had been there. Unbidden, her thoughts went to Shay, a Nomori girl she had played with as a child. When she was twelve, instead of developing a psychic gift, Shay began calling up flames from her fingertips. One day, Nadya went to her house to find her friend gone. What was more, her parents denied ever having a daughter. *There is no Shay that lives here. There never was.* The coldness in their voices had seeped into her bones and remained, chilling her to the core whenever she thought of what might happen if she had been in Shay's place.

There is no Nadya here. There never was.

Whatever happened to her childhood friend, Nadya could not stand the thought of her family, led by her grandmother, denying their familial bond, exiling her, perhaps even trying to kill her.

"He's lying," she whispered.

"Are you sure?" Shadar asked, a slight desperation in his voice.

Nadya stared at the ground. She had seen proof that Duren killed Jurek. And yet, she could not shake the image of the other man. He did something, had some part to play in the murder.

It was an accusation she could never make out loud. "Yes," she said more firmly.

"Very well." Shadar turned to Duren. He kept his tone formal. Here, they could not be friends. Here, he was a captain in service to his Duke. "You will remain here until I notify Lord Marko. Then you will be tried according to the laws of Storm's Quarry. If found guilty, you will be sentenced accordingly." He glanced back at his family. "Many thanks to both of you. You can see a clerk on the way out for your payment."

Nadya swallowed and turned toward the door. Drina's eyes drilled into hers, and her throat tightened. Her grandmother slowly strode over to her. Drina stood with a stoop, but she walked with the gait of someone used to being respected. Even the Duke could not claim that kind of presence.

When they entered the corridor, leaving the dank interrogation room behind, Drina spoke. "That was good work, Nadya." She spat on the ground. "Imagine such a disgrace, with Nomori blood. It makes me sick."

Nadya remained silent, following her shuffling grandmother though the winding halls of the Guardhouse. Her chest had gone cold, and she wondered if there was ever going to be a time when she wouldn't have to worry every moment that her secret would be revealed. Or how many other choices she would have to make, how many scruples she must sacrifice, in order to keep it.

❖

She couldn't escape her grandmother as they left the Guardhouse. Drina latched onto her arm with a viselike grip. It was a welcome distraction, however, from the chest-tightening thoughts of what she had left unsaid during the interrogation.

"Do you know why a good Nomori man would turn into a monster like that?" Drina was rambling in Nomori. "It is from living in this cursed city, I tell you. We are not meant to be encased by walls, and between these walls and those damned Erevans, our people are being driven mad."

"I think he is the exception," Nadya said patiently. It was all something she'd heard before. She had calmed down enough that she didn't think there was a danger of Drina reading anything suspicious. Besides, her grandmother was working herself into such a nice froth that Nadya was sure her own emotions overpowered anything she might have picked up from Nadya about her abilities.

"I cannot accept what our people are coming to," her grandmother muttered and got into the railbox waiting for them. "Maybe it was more dangerous out on the water, but at least we kept our traditions, our hearts."

"No one is tearing out Nomori hearts," Nadya said under her breath.

Once they boarded, Nadya steadying Drina since there were no empty seats, the whistle sounded. She held on to one of the wooden beams that stretched across the tight box as the engine began to churn. It vibrated through the woodwork. Made of the same technology as the steam pumps that pumped water out of the city and over the walls during storms, it provided a quick, if bumpy, ride down to the lower tiers of the city. Nadya felt the air change as the railbox continued down at its harsh angle to the second tier. It grew heavy with the scent of waste.

"We must fight against the demons that have taken hold of our beloved city," a voice shouted from the rail stop.

A man, Erevan and pale with brown hair and wild eyes, stood atop a stone bench. His clothes were filthy, but he didn't seem ashamed as he yelled in Erevo to everyone who passed him by. "The storm gods are angry. The Nomori witches, they are allowed to live among us. Eat our food. Play with our children. We have let them poison our ways. Death to all the Nomori! Their presence in our city has brought on the wrath of the storm gods. Death to them, or this season of storms will be our destruction."

Nadya remained rooted to the spot as the man's eyes found her. He pointed, shrieking with froth at the mouth, "Death to you, Nomori whelp. Death to all of you!"

"Ignore him, Nadya." Her grandmother gripped her arm as the whistle blew and the railbox began moving again, its powerful engine pistons pumping up and down.

"What—"

"Nothing but a zealot trying to stir people up." Drina spat out the window. Her right hand reached for her neck, where she wore her metal seal of the Protectress.

"A zealot?"

"Pay him no mind," her grandmother said again. "The Erevans, they don't even believe in their storm gods. Once they might have, when the city was first built and they believed their nameless gods had to be appeased to stop the wind, rain, and lightning from destroying their home. That old belief is gone. They sacrifice a bit of bread here, a fowl there during the dry seasons, but none think the gods actually exist. That man was crazy. Fear makes people do unnatural things."

Nadya glanced down at her upper arm, where her seal of the Protectress was hidden beneath her shirt. "Why have gods you don't believe in?"

"I don't try to fathom what goes on in Erevan minds."

Finally, the railbox made its stop on the second tier, and all of the Erevans exited. Only Nadya and Drina remained. The beaten wooden benches that lined the sides of the box were now open, but Drina, in her stubbornness, did not sit down. She stood stiffly, leaning against the side, until the railbox came to a stop in the Nomori tier.

The whistle sounded. Nadya helped Drina off. The rail stopped at the bottom of the great staircase, just in front of the Nomori public square. Behind the crowds of Nomori people running errands, their children tumbling through the street, a great marble fountain gurgled and splashed. Unlike the rest of the city, it was built of a dark gray marble, nearly black. The water arched up in a smooth curve, raining down with a sound like a hundred stone pigeons. Since Nadya had come into her abilities, she always thought it smelled faintly of peppermint. Dozens of one-story shops bordered the square. It was toward one of these that Nadya began walking.

"I need to stop for a moment," she said. Their larder was growing empty, and it was always good to begin stocking up early for the season of storms, when food became scarce very quickly. Ration lines could not always be relied on. Perhaps bringing home a few groceries with her pay would placate Mirela a bit.

Drina huffed but followed her into the corner shop. It stood next to Brishen's bakery, a friend of their family and the most masterful baker on this tier. The scent of his boysenberry scones penetrated this shop's walls and made Nadya's mouth water. Then she remembered that he was Duren's father, and the scent turned to brine.

"Good morn," the shopkeeper called.

Nadya gave her a quick nod. She looked over the clay shelves of dried foods and selected a pack of dried corn and another of flour. She was reaching for a bundle of greens when her grandmother asked, "Have you considered which Nomori boy you'll take to be your husband?"

"What?" Nadya almost dropped the food she carried.

"You turn eighteen next dry season, my dear. You'll be a woman under Nomori custom, and you'll need to take a husband in order to carry on the Gabori name."

Nadya swallowed. She avoided her grandmother's eager expression and continued to pick food off the shelves. There was no guarantee this selection would be here much longer, so she wanted to buy as much as she could. It was dried; it would keep.

"Do we have to talk about it here?" she asked, looking through the bin of carrots and picking a handful.

Drina put a hand on her shoulder, forcing her to turn around. Nadya swallowed. That look in her grandmother's eye meant she was analyzing Nadya's emotions. Drina sighed.

"Your mother hasn't been feeling well lately, you know."

"I know," Nadya whispered. She detached herself and busied herself in the far corner of the shop.

"And I may be loath to admit it, but I am no spring chicken. We must look to the future. You will be the heir to the Gabori family, perhaps sooner than you would like."

"There's nothing wrong with Mama, nothing more than a cough," Nadya said a bit too loudly, causing the shopkeeper to glance at them. She lowered her voice. "It doesn't do to dwell on maybes, not with more than enough of the present to keep up with."

"No need to lecture me, Nadezhda. But, pray tell me, what have you been keeping yourself so occupied with?"

She couldn't reply, and when she did not even turn around to face her grandmother, Drina sighed. "I thought as much. You must start thinking beyond your nose, and soon. The head of the Gabori family can't walk around with her mind in the clouds."

Nadya put a hand against the cool stone wall of the shop. In this back corner, there were used clothes, gaudy fake jewelry, and anything else the shopkeeper thought he could make a coin selling. She looked down at the ground. What kind of leader of her family would she make, a Nomori woman with no psychic gift?

"You need to carry on our bloodline. Picking a husband from the sons of another good family is your duty."

Her shoulders tensed. She hated that word.

"Nadezhda, are you listening to me?"

Nadya turned around. "Yes, Grandmother, I am. I just don't want to think about it now, not with the season of storms so close…"

"Well, you need to. Storms are a way of life in this cursed city, and so we must continue through them."

Nadya turned back to the shelf of odds and ends. Drina ceased her questioning, for the moment at least, and she was able to breathe. Her eye caught a piece of gray sticking out of the barrel of cloth. Drawing it out, she gasped.

The cloth was old and worn, but sturdy. A hood melted into a floor-length cloak. What brought a little buzz to Nadya's chest, however, was the scarf attached to the hood. It was fastened on either side of the hood with metal clips. An old fire cloak, she realized, as its thick scent of resin hit her senses, made sturdy and flame resistant for those who fought against the rare fire outbreak in the tiers.

Old and used it might be, but it was perfect.

If I'm to go out at night again, she thought, glancing over her shoulder to where Drina chatted with the shopkeeper in rapid Nomori, *I'll need a disguise. I can't risk getting recognized when I use my abilities.*

With her grandmother distracted, Nadya slipped the cloak in with the packages she carried. She hurried up to the sales counter. "Just these."

"Stocking up for the storms? Better fill your pantries while you can," the shopkeeper said. "I don't expect another shipment for at least a week. Food is already tight, and it'll only get tighter."

Nadya thanked her and paid from the pouch of palace coins the clerk at the Guardhouse had given her. The round bits of copper, stamped with the Duke's seal of a shining sun, clattered on the stone as the shopkeeper counted them.

Nadya grabbed her parcels and left the shop.

But Drina wasn't done. She followed her granddaughter through the busy streets, embarking on her usual rant of the mistake the Nomori people had made when they permanently moved into Storm's Quarry. Nadya wisely kept silent. She had never known a life outside the city, and though she valued her Nomori heritage greatly, she couldn't see the utter evil her grandmother did in every facet of Erevan life.

Suddenly, Drina changed the subject. "Now, you've avoided my question. Why do you resist marriage?"

Nadya had hoped she had forgotten about it. She opened her mouth to lie when her grandmother nodded.

"You're in love."

"No!" She faced her grandmother, heart racing. She was not in love. She had never been in love. She didn't want to marry, but that didn't mean she—

"I won't ask you who the lucky Nomori boy is, because you won't tell me anyway. I hope to meet him one day." Drina continued down the street.

Nadya stayed where she was. A lie that blatant could not fool her grandmother. The lucky Nomori boy, however, was a tall girl with eyes like deep wells. It was the woman with whom she had grown up, who could make her laugh like no other, and who made her feel as safe as if she was in the arms of the Protectress herself. For all that, it was a child's dream that anything could ever come of such love. She didn't know what the Erevans thought of such a relationship, but for the Nomori, it was forbidden.

Nadya pushed the image of Kesali from her mind and hurried after her grandmother.

CHAPTER FOUR

A few days had passed since the interrogation, and Nadya's father barely spent more than a moment at home. The trial was to be expedited, by order of the Duke. Apparently, he had taken Jurek's death very badly, and he wanted his killer to see justice before the storms came. When Shadar came home for a brief sleep or a meal that wasn't hard ration bread, he and Mirela spoke about the murder, and so Nadya took to spending even more time out of the house. Whenever she heard Duren's name, her stomach began churning. She knew she should say something, that her testimony might completely change the trial. Of course, she kept quiet and excused her silence by telling herself it was too late anyway to speak up.

Tonight, she would not be leaping over rooftops. It was Arane Sveltura, the Festival of Crossing Stars. Nadya remembered tales she'd heard told by the Elders as a child, of two Nomori who fell in love and killed themselves rather than be pulled apart by their warring tribes. Their deaths many centuries ago inspired all Nomori to come together for one night then, and now on the night where the two brightest stars in the night crossed paths, a celebration was held every year. All the Nomori in Storm's Quarry would gather in the public square for music, food, and communion with the stars and their beloved Protectress.

It wasn't just the festival that made Nadya's chest buzz with crickets. It was that Kesali had asked to spend the evening together.

Nadya shut the door to her house behind her. She'd spent all day running around the fourth tier with packages of the jewelry orders her mother had fulfilled.

"Finished?" Mirela asked. She sat at her workbench. Her deft fingers strung mounted emeralds, smaller than mustard seeds, onto a wire.

Nadya set the delivery notices on the workbench. "Every one of them into the hands of a trustworthy butler or house mistress. Worry not, those poor courtiers will soon get their jewels."

"Someone already has the Arane Sveltura spirit." Mirela turned to look at her, eyebrows knitted. "Either that, or you stopped by a tavern in one of the Erevan tiers. If it's the latter, I'm afraid I cannot keep you from your inevitable fate. Drina will have you roasted along with the boar."

Nadya giggled. "I'm just excited for tonight." She hesitated, and made her voice as neutral as possible. "I am planning on spending the festival with Kesali."

"Good, good." Mirela turned back to her work. She twisted off the end of the wire, creating a perfect loop of tiny, sparkling emeralds. Laying it carefully on the table, she then pulled out an opal as big as an eye from a velvet pouch. "Ever since she took that apprenticeship, you hardly see her except a quick stroll some mornings."

Trying not to blush and failing, feeling the heat in her cheeks, Nadya was very glad her mother wasn't looking at her. "Yes, I am looking forward to it."

"And, of course, you will pass the light with your parents."

"Of course," Nadya said quickly.

"Good." Mirela was focused intently now, looping wire around the opal in order to create an intricate silver basket to hold it in, with a clasp to attach it to the body of the neck piece. "Now, make yourself busy. I have work to complete." She coughed, her steady hands wavering just a touch.

Nadya remained still, watching her mother. "Is it telling you anything?"

"It belonged to a courtier's wife. On the day her first child, a beautiful daughter, was born, she died. It is his day of greatest joy and deepest sorrow. He intends to give this to his daughter when she comes of age. She looks like her mother and has her kindness." Mirela smiled softly as she worked.

"Amazing," Nadya whispered. Her mother could read gemstones, their past, their owners. It gave her unsurpassed skills as a jeweler. She never said anything, but Nadya couldn't help but believe she could actually speak to the stones, coaxing them to her will.

"He'll be pleased with the piece. Now, let me work and take your thousand questions elsewhere." Mirela reached over and gave her an affectionate squeeze on the shoulder.

As she retreated through the curtain and into the house, Nadya wished it was always like this, light and cheerful between her and her mother. No secrets. No frustration. Perhaps, she thought, digging through her bunk for her best vest, she could be a better daughter. If not a more truthful one, a better one. She resolved to try.

The vest she chose had been a gift from her grandmother. Whatever she might say about Drina and her backward thinking, she was kind in her own way, and her skill with a needle outshone anyone else in the Gabori family. The vest was deep blue, the night sky just before the sun reached the horizon. Brought alive in silver stitching, a great winged horse flew over the tiny umber mountains at the hem. Every muscle was detailed and seemed to move when Nadya did. She ran her fingers over the horse's wing. Tonight, she would forget about what made her different, pretend to have no more worries than the season of storms and the colors of her faraway wedding.

❖

For perhaps the only time all year, the public square was silent. Thousands of Nomori gathered, spilling over into the surrounding streets. Everyone stood. Nadya closed her eyes. Her sensitive ears picked up only the breathing of those around her and, in the distance, the fountain's gurgling.

A nudge in her shoulder, and her eyes flew open. Her father beside her now held a lit candle. He nodded to her candle. Nadya quickly held it up to his, tipping it so its wick dipped into the flame and lit. On her other side, Mirela silently did the same thing with her own candle.

Slowly, the entire square lit up with candlelight. Every person held one. The eldest of the Elders, a frail woman of nearly ninety named Aishe, had lit the first candle by sparking two shards of rock together, one said to be a shard from a meteor that fell the day the two lovers died, the other a piece of stone from the original Nomori homeland. The passing of the light had begun, and Nadya was just glad she hadn't accidentally broken her candle yet.

The light was slowly passed throughout the ranks of standing Nomori until the entire western side of the tier looked as if it was on fire. The Elders began chanting in unison in an ancient form of the language only they still understood. Nadya looked up and her breath left her as the night sky, filled with stars not an hour ago, was completely black. Around her, everyone stared toward the heavens with the same awed expression. Shadar reached down and grabbed her free hand, squeezing lightly.

In common Nomori, the Elders said, "Now we give back the light which the Protectress has bestowed upon us. May she hold our people close to heart until we return home to the stars. Arane Sveltura!"

"Arane Sveltura!" the crowds rumbled in response and, as one, blew out the candles.

In an instant, the stars reappeared. The light had been passed.

Mirela embraced her. Shadar planted a kiss on the top of her head. "Go," he said. "Your mother told me you have plans. Be blessed, and have a good time. We will see you at home before dawn, yes?"

"Yes," Nadya said, grinning. She skipped off, heading to the meeting place she and Kesali had picked.

Now that the passing of the lights was over, the celebration part of the festival could begin. On every corner, people handed out sweets, hot bread, and brewed cider to all who passed. Despite the upcoming storms, Arane Sveltura was a time for sharing, to reflect the generosity of the Protectress. Many of the shops were open, giving away their wares. In turn, those on the receiving end did not take more than they could eat or drink tonight.

Nadya grabbed a cranberry tart from a tray held out by a smiling woman, mumbling, "Thank you," before she stuffed half of the oozing, butter-covered treat into her mouth. Flavors exploded in her mouth.

"Don't worry, it's not going to disappear," a teasing voice behind her said.

She whirled around and held out the other half of the tart in front of Kesali's nose. "Taste this."

Instead of using her hands, Kesali opened her mouth and took a bite. Her eyes went wide. "Amazing," she said, mouth full. She took the rest of the tart in a more ladylike fashion using her fingers and quickly finished it. Before she could wipe the butter residue on her vest, Nadya grabbed her hand.

"Family heirlooms are not handkerchiefs," she chided. "Come. Let's go to the fountain." Kesali's vest was as richly embroidered as her own. It was the light pink of cherry blossoms, embroidered with a purple firedrake twining around a dead serpent. Kesali had once told her that it belonged to her mother.

"I wouldn't think you'd want to be anywhere near your grandmother," Kesali said, looping her arm with Nadya's, who felt a sudden burst of warmth in her side.

"She'll be too busy making sure none of the young ones are acting too Erevan. She's been on a one-woman crusade to keep our culture pure ever since she set foot in Storm's Quarry, and if you speak to her, the situation is getting more and more desperate."

They reached the main square. Around one side of the fountain, the Elders sat in a circle, singing songs in ancient Nomori, some so old that even they did not know the meaning of the words. Texts and scrolls were not things a nomadic people could afford to carry, so the history of their people was sung down through the generations. Though most of the festivalgoers had left the square, off to celebrate with good food and drink, a few stayed, eyes closed, to listen to the words of their ancestors. The crooning voices of the Elders always raised chills on Nadya's arms. It was as if the stars themselves sang of times past.

Quietly going to the other side of the fountain, Nadya splashed some water on Kesali, who retaliated. It was only a glare from Drina, seated among the Elders, that stopped all-out war.

"I have a favor to ask of you," Kesali said as they walked off to the edge of the square where people sat on benches, sharing food and warmth. She sat and pulled Nadya down beside her. "Tomorrow evening, the new ballet opens in the grand theater on the fourth tier. Will you go with me? I don't want to go alone."

Nadya frowned. "The theater?" Nomori rarely went to the fourth tier, and they certainly never went to the theater or art galleries or museums. "But a ticket must have cost a month's pay. And when did you become so interested in such things?" Her tone took on an accusatory edge near the end, much as she tried to hide it. The two of them often made fun of the fancy diversions of the wealthiest in Storm's Quarry. It didn't sit well in Nadya's chest that Kesali now sought out those same activities. She had only been going to the palace for her apprenticeship for three months. Had it changed her in ways Nadya hadn't realized?

Kesali looked away. "I had hoped to spend the evening with you. If you're just going to make snide remarks about it…"

"No, I'm sorry." Nadya swallowed. "I just was not expecting that. Sneaking out to the wall or into the bathhouse or going to the gates of the mines, maybe. The theater is not something I think of when I think of you."

"And what do you think of?"

A question she could not answer truthfully, and Nadya's chest ached for it. *I think of your smile and the way the firelight reflects off the amber flecks in your eyes. I think of your hands and their warmth and how I wish for you to hold me and never let go. I think of everything that could be and everything that won't be, and it hurts.*

Kesali spared her the lie. "It wasn't my idea, I'll have you know. Marko invited me a few weeks ago. He stopped by the Head Cleric's office yesterday to let me know that he won't be able to make it. There was a murder in the fourth tier that needs his full attention." She smiled. "I think he'd rather play soldiers than sit through a performance. He told me I should still go, and I don't want his kindness to go to waste, so…?"

Nadya's mouth turned bitter as Kesali spoke. "I did not know you and *Lord* Marko"—she emphasized the title Kesali left out—"were so close."

"I think he likes having someone his own age to speak to. He says the courtiers are boring and his guardsmen too formal."

"But you're…"

"Just a peasant, and a Nomori at that?" Kesali laughed, but it was hollow. "Yes. But my mother wasn't, and I have her gift. Being the Stormspeaker is the reason I'm apprenticed in the palace, and I think I may have greater ties there soon. There has to be some kind of bridge between our people and Storm's Quarry. Something to bring understanding. It's eluded us for twenty years." She took a deep breath. "In my lifetime, I want to see no animosity between our people and Erevans."

Nadya wanted that too, of course, but she was still hung up on Lord Marko inviting Kesali to the theater. She didn't realize she was frowning until Kesali poked her in the side.

"It's a theater performance, not a death sentence. Don't make me face all those stuffy-nosed courtiers alone. Please?"

"All right," Nadya agreed, relenting.

"Thank you." Kesali turned toward the Elders as they began a new song, this one featuring small skin drums that a few held between their knees. The beats reverberated through the marble square.

Nadya was content to sit there together, listening to the music, but Kesali got a mischievous look in her eye. She jumped up and pulled Nadya with her, who was so surprised that she almost forgot to let her.

"Come on, it's Arane Sveltura," Kesali said, twirling Nadya around her. She began swaying to the beat of the drums and the voices raised in ancient song. Nadya stood still for a moment before she realized Kesali was dancing. More than that, she expected Nadya to join her.

The Nomori did not dance. They sang. Dancing was a frivolous Erevan pastime, as her grandmother would say. In fact, Drina noticed

Kesali twirling around on the cobblestones, clicking her heels in time with the music, and began glaring.

Nadya closed her eyes. Tonight, she had no secrets. Tonight, she had no worries. Then, staring directly at her grandmother, she began to follow Kesali's movements.

Under a star blanket, they leapt and twirled. They were air, starlight, and the beat was the only thing that kept them anchored to the ground. Kesali's forehead glistened with sweat as she beamed, swinging her arms. Her boots clicked together and added to the music. On the benches, those watching began clapping in time.

Nadya wanted nothing more than to let herself go into the dance, into Kesali's embrace, but she restrained her movements. She was far more mechanical than her partner, not as brazen with wide leaps and complicated foot movements. The last thing she wanted was to reveal herself in front of an audience. Or to hurt Kesali with a misplaced swing of the arm.

Still, her seal of the Protectress burned hot, and Nadya imagined herself alone, dancing across rooftops, leaving nothing but wind in her wake.

"See," Kesali said, panting. "You *are* having fun."

"Always, with you," she murmured in return.

Drina's snort brought her attention up from the intoxicating scent of Kesali, and for a terrible moment, Nadya thought she had given something away.

But no, it wasn't that. They were no longer alone in their courtyard ballroom. Other, mostly young people had joined in. Soon, the fountain sat in the center of a whirlwind of movement. The Elders' song faltered for a moment. She feared they would throw down their drums in protest. Then Aishe, the oldest with the most warbling voice, struck up the song again. The rest soon joined in, and Arane Sveltura became a night of true celebration.

"Isn't it beautiful?" Kesali said, waltzing around, Nadya holding onto her waist. "Look what we've done."

"What you've done." It was a small thing, but perhaps her earlier talk of bringing the two peoples together was not as fanciful as it seemed.

"Not without you. I'd have been terrified. You give me strength," Kesali said.

Nadya looked away, not knowing what to say. Warm fingers slid under her chin, bringing her face up to look Kesali in the eyes. Then, swiftly before either of them could think better of it, Kesali kissed her.

Warmth rushed to every part of Nadya's body, lifting it up as if she were nothing but air. Kesali tasted like cranberries and waterfalls. Her hand ran down Nadya's side, leaving warm chills in its wake. She wrapped her own arms around Kesali's waist and pulled her closer. Underneath the song and dancing, she heard a soft grunt.

Instantly, Nadya pulled away. "Did I hurt you?"

Kesali slowly shook her head. "No, of course not."

"Oh, okay." She swallowed. "I—I have to go. Meet my parents at home." The festival was not nearly close to over, but Kesali didn't question her.

"I will see you tomorrow night," she called as Nadya pushed her way through the dancers to the edge, where she broke into the fastest run she dared.

Fool. Thousand times a fool.

What if I had I hurt her?

What if someone had seen? Such relationships were not condoned in her world. Perhaps in the upper tiers, but not for her and Kesali.

She dodged festivalgoers as they sampled food and laughed and held hands. On a corner, a few set off golden firecrackers, much to the delight of all who passed. It was better this way, she told herself. As much as she wished it, such a relationship was impossible for numerous reasons, and she was saving herself a lot of pain.

So why did the pain seem so unbearable now? She had longed for this for months, and in the moments it lasted, the kiss was the fulfillment of everything she desired. With the ghost of their kiss lingering on her lips, she knew she would risk the pain of a thousand lifetimes for just one with Kesali.

Angry shouts brought her out of her own torturous thoughts.

The racket came from a shop on the corner of one of the tight cobblestoned streets. Nadya tripped to a stop across from it. Five men, Erevan from their light skin and the varying shades of brown in their close-cropped hair, piled into the squat stone building. One carried a wooden club.

Children ran screaming out the door. Their panic was lost in the general chaos of the festival. Only her sensitive hearing picked it out from the cacophony of laughter and firecrackers around her. Nadya's breath caught in her throat. It was Brishen's bakery, open to give out his boysenberry pastries to the children of the tier. He was Nomori, but age and lung rot from the perpetual damp of the city had dulled his inborn fighting skills.

He was also Duren's father.

The air around her froze. Had news of the murder spread so quickly? It certainly seemed so, for what other reason would these men have to come down to the Nomori tier during Arane Sveltura with weapons. Planned well, as the Nomori men were all occupied with their families and would not come to anyone's rescue.

Those men would beat Brishen to a bloody mess for what his son did.

Guilt rose in her throat, threatened to choke her. Maybe it would have all turned out this way if she had been completely honest during the interrogation. Maybe seeing the second man meant nothing. She could not, however, know for sure, and what happened here was on her head.

Brishen screamed. No one on the street heard.

Her thoughts went to the gray cloak she had stashed in a gap between the outer wall and roof of her house. It was too far, and Brishen did not have a lot of time. She resolved never to go anywhere without it again. Nadya took off her vest and handed it to a wide-eyed toddler who sat on the side of the street, sucking a caramel apple. She managed to smile at him, and then she took the sash from her waist and tied it around the lower half of her face. Its gray expanse covered her chin, mouth, and nose, leaving only her eyes visible. She'd move fast enough not to be recognized.

Nadya sprinted for the bakery. Her hand flashed out, and the door of the shop flew open.

Behind a stone counter, Brishen grappled with two of the Erevans, knocking the last of the pastries to the floor where they were trampled into mush. The Erevans smelled of piss and mud: inhabitants of the second tier, Erevan scum who scavenged at the edges of Nomori neighborhoods. Why would such people care about a courtier's murder?

In two bounds, Nadya vaulted over the counter and stood between the Erevans and Brishen as a third attacker brought his wooden club down on the shopkeeper's head.

It hit Nadya's shoulder and shattered, splinters flying across the small shop and burying themselves in hard loaves of bread. She didn't flinch. The impact only stung.

The five Erevans stopped for a moment, and Nadya hoped her sudden appearance would be enough to scare them off. Brishen backed away from her. His eyes were dark, wide, and scared. They roved over her, but they didn't carry the spark of recognition.

The man who had held the club backed away. His face was pale, and his hands bled with cuts from wood splinters.

The others weren't as cowed. "It's another piece of Nomori filth," the tallest said. "Are you an Erevan killer, too? Show us your face, so we can break it."

Nadya shook her head. Her voice would give her identity away, so instead of responding, she darted forward and pushed the man. He flew backward. Brishen yelped, but he seemed to realize that this mysterious Nomori was on his side, so he remained in the corner.

She nodded to him, and he returned the gesture. A moment later, the color drained away from his face, and she turned to see a pistol pointed between her eyes.

The tall man smiled. The arm that held his pistol was steady. Gunpowder was unreliable in the damp air of the city, but something about his smirk told her not to hope that would be the case now.

"Your people need to learn that you don't own this city. You don't even belong here. Give us a reason, and we will kill every single one of you. You may play at being a hero, boy, but you can't hide this scumbag from justice. He whelped that piece of shite."

He thinks I'm a man. Nadya was short, sturdy rather than thin, and built like a rock. Her loose shirt hid her breasts, and women, both Erevan and Nomori, did not fight.

Two men grabbed Brishen. The other, hands bleeding, slugged Brishen across the temple. The shopkeeper fell. A coughing fit, grating and horribly familiar, took hold of him, and he was helpless to fight off the Erevan's kicks.

Their leader was still smiling. "You Nomori dogs need to know your place. Don't think one of your kind can kill ours without consequence."

Anger rose in Nadya's gut. She grabbed his arm and wrenched the pistol away. It clattered to the ground at the edge of the shop. In the same motion, she yanked down on his arm. Bone snapped, and his scream pierced the air, digging deep into Nadya's ears. Blood dripped over her hand as she held the limp arm. Bone peeked out of his torn tunic.

The man's face was as white as his bone. Syllables blubbered out of his lips. Nadya didn't hear them. He attacked the Nomori. He put a pistol to her head. She was not going to let him walk away.

She brought her other hand up, fist tight, and slammed it into his ribcage.

He flew across the shop. Bones shattered and cracked as he hit the wall. The stones shook with the impact. He lay crumpled on the ground, blood leaking out the corner of his mouth. He didn't move.

The sounds of Brishen's cries and the yells of the Erevans immediately faded away until Nadya heard nothing but her own heartbeat. Her hands lowered. His blood dripped off her fingertips.

Her vision blurred, and she was no longer in Brishen's bakery. She was fifteen years old, standing in a culvert in the Nomori tier. Her hands were coated in warm blood that the rushing water slowly eroded away. The broken body of the Erevan boy who had attacked her lay against a stone wall. His life slowly seeped away through the gash torn in his back by a broken spine.

Nadya snapped back into the present. Her limbs shook. The other men backed away from her as she stared at the broken body of the man. He twitched. At first she thought she'd imagined it. *Oh, Protectress, please.*

Slowly, he groaned and moved his legs.

That was enough. Nadya was done. She shouldn't have come here in the first place. She knew she couldn't control her unnatural strength in combat. She should have realized that someone would get hurt, maybe even killed. She'd wanted to help Brishen, to alleviate her own guilt, but murder was a steep price to pay.

The remaining men unfroze. They scattered like mice before a hawk, tripping over one another to get through the broken door. Out in the street, cries went up from the crowds as they scattered around the crazed Erevans. A few men shouted. Nadya knew she and Brishen wouldn't be alone for long.

"Are—are you going to let them get away? What about him?" Most of the fear had left Brishen's voice as he staggered to his feet. He pointed to the moaning man.

Nadya gave him a long look over her mask. She slowly shook her head once and turned and ran out the door. She nearly barreled into four Nomori men, all member of the Duke's Guard.

She didn't stop at their surprised cries. She didn't stop at all, not until she fell to her knees, sobbing, in the culvert next to her house. Tearing the sash off her face, Nadya tried to calm her roiling emotions, repeating over and over, *He's not dead, he's not dead.* She shouldn't have gotten involved at all, should have just called for help, but Brishen would be fine. *He's not dead.*

How could she ever conceive of a relationship with Kesali when she could do such things with her bare hands? Nadya too often dwelt in the shadows, in the dark corners of Storm's Quarry, and Kesali should never have to leave the light. She deserved someone who was not cursed, someone who could share their heart with her without deceit or fear. Someone to stand by her side. How could she consider herself worthy of being that one?

Nadya didn't realize how much time had passed until she felt a tap on her shoulder. She leapt to her feet, and Shadar jumped back.

"Whoa, there, I'm a friend." When Nadya didn't answer his levity with a smile, his expression grew concerned. "Are you all right?"

"Yes." She wiped her eyes.

"Glad to hear—" He stopped, and his dark eyes roved over her. "Why is there blood on your clothes? Are you injured?"

She looked down and saw dark red splashes sinking into the cream-colored cotton of her shirt. "I—I..." She decided on the closest version of the truth she could. "There was something going on at Brishen's bakery. A bunch of Erevans came out, covered in blood. One fell into me."

"I heard as much. There is a lot of hate in this city, and I'm afraid it doesn't take more than an unjustified murder to spark it. Those men couldn't have known Master Jurek, and yet he was the reason for their attack. More likely an excuse than a reason, though." He sighed. "I am glad you're unhurt."

"Thank you." Nadya brushed off her trousers.

"Oh, and I found this with a very confused child." He held out her vest. "Drina would be livid if she found out." He paused. "And she's already in a hot temper, with the way the festival is going."

Nadya managed a small smile.

"Come, I would like to spend the rest of Arane Sveltura with my daughter, if that's all right. Unless you still had plans with Kesali?"

"No." She swallowed heavily. "I'd love to spend it with you, Papa." She held out her arms as he put her vest back on, covering the bloodstains. Then he took her arm in his and they headed out together, and she could pretend that she was a child once more, with nothing but a child's cares.

CHAPTER FIVE

Perched on a low-lying roof, hidden by shadows, Gedeon watched the festival of Arane Sveltura with narrowed eyes. Children ran unhindered through the streets, clutching candied apples, shortbread, and other sweets in their fists. The adults were no better. Laughter grated on Gedeon's ears. He snarled as a group of young Nomori men, all in the Duke's Guard from their formal walk, passed under him, holding beakers of cordial.

This is a mask you wear, nothing more. You let me wear the same one when you still counted me among you. I know what you are capable of. Now, however, I need not fear it. He smiled to himself. *One of you is already awaiting execution because of me. You think any are safe?*

During the passing of the light, Gedeon had averted his eyes from the miracle of the disappearing and reappearing stars. Long ago, the Protectress had forsaken him, so he no longer acknowledged her. His seal lay decaying in some gutter somewhere. But now, he watched the crowds with a mixture of anger and cold appraisal, as if seeing a group of jackdaws dancing around a dropped biscuit.

Shouting roused him out of his thoughts. Gedeon peered across the street, through the crowds, to the door of a bakery. He cocked his head, interested.

Something threw the door open, moving so fast he could not tell if it was a person or not. The shouting grew louder, but he could not hear any words, the noises from the revelers below too noisy.

Three Erevan men tumbled out the door. They spat and threw slurs at the surprised Nomori that surrounded them. "Unnatural freaks!"

One wiped blood from his face. "You kill more of us, and you'll pay!"

A few Nomori men moved to restrain them, and the Erevans took off running. In the chaos, something left the shop. This time, Gedeon was sure it was a person, though he could not make out more than that.

On this street, much of merrymaking had stopped. Gedeon paid it no more heed. He slipped back into his thoughts, though this time they were considerably more cheerful. To think that he had not used his power on those men. Not in the slightest. He'd never seen them before in his life.

And yet, they were as much under his spell as the Nomori guardsman had been.

He looked over the scene, taking in the crying children, the stiff-jawed older folk who had heard too many similar things, the overenergized youths whose urge to take rapiers and invade the second tier was only tempered by a calm hand on their shoulders.

Puppets. His puppets. As easy to play without his power as with.

He smiled. Perhaps, it was time to see how much he was truly capable of. To show those who dreaded him and his kind that there was truly something to fear.

He climbed down from the roof, staying in the shadows of the culvert. His knees jarred painfully when he dropped the last few paces. Gedeon ignored the pain. He melded into the crowd, searching every face he passed.

A young Nomori man, no older than twenty-five, passed him, and Gedeon nodded to himself. He tapped the man on the shoulder. When he turned around, Gedeon pounced, reaching for the well of blackness, taking out his will and shoving his own mind in.

When it was done, he leaned in close and whispered his instructions.

❖

The next day, despite it being only a bit after the noon bell, Nadya's house flickered with the light from the glowing embers in their kiln. The sun hadn't come out from behind the clouds that morning, and Storm's Quarry awoke to a thick fog that tickled the surface of the Kyanite Sea. The storms would come soon, and hard.

She sat in her loft. Below her, the small living area swam around, unfocused. Her pallet felt hard, unfamiliar. Knees drawn up to her chest, Nadya focused on breathing. In and out. Slow but strong.

Shadar had left her to return to the Guardhouse at dawn, and without her father's solid presence, the overwhelming memories of last night would not let her mind be. Kesali's kiss, a sensory overload Nadya didn't know what to do with, especially since she was committed to seeing her again tonight. Then Brishen's bakery. The feeling of bone snapping beneath her fingers. The smell of blood. The roar of bloodlust pounding in her ears.

You are lucky no one died. Do not be fool enough to believe things will turn out that way again. Her chastising thoughts took on her grandmother's voice.

Mirela coughed from the next room. Nadya stared at the hanging rug that separated their home from her shop. She wished she could talk to her mother about this. None of it made sense, and she needed some wisdom. Should she not see Kesali again, for fear of what she could do to her? Should she never use her abilities again for the same reason? As noble as that sounded, Nadya was not ready to give up all she enjoyed in life in the name of fear. Did that make her a fool?

"Nadya, come here please," her mother called.

She knew she looked a mess as she slowly stretched out her legs. Ignoring the ladder, she jumped down. She padded across the stone floor, parted the hanging rug, and leaned on the stone counter.

Mirela sat at the stone bench on the other side of the small space. Above her sweat-soaked brow, a myriad of tools hung from metal hooks. She held a pair of tweezers over a piece Nadya couldn't see. Jars of enamel and various instruments were scattered around her mother in her usual finishing-up-a-piece mess.

"How is the work on the neck piece going?" she asked finally, just to break the silence.

Her mother didn't turn from her work. "Nadya, I need you make some more deliveries today."

Nadya gritted her teeth. "I can't. I am sorry, but I'm busy this afternoon and evening."

"This is important," her mother said. Her eyes did not leave her work. Despite their thinness, her hands moved deftly. The many calluses that marked her as a master jeweler—to the embarrassment of many Nomori, including Drina—danced as she worked the opal onto the chain.

Nadya watched with a bit of jealousy. She could not make such beautiful things. Her abnormal strength meant she snapped the tools if she tried. "I know, but I can do it tomorrow. I promise." Today, she could barely handle getting into fresh clothes and dealing with the Kesali situation.

"Your promises mean less these days."

Nadya swallowed. She didn't know how to respond to that.

"The storms will come any day, and the tiers will flood with rain, faster than the pumps can work. I need to finish and deliver all of my commissions before then."

"But Kesali—"

"You must look after your own family first, Nadezhda. I thought I'd taught you as much." With a clang, her mother dropped her tweezers and picked up the finished neck piece. It was breathtakingly beautiful, shimmering in the low light of the workshop.

"You sound like Grandmother."

"Your grandmother may be many things, but she is loyal and unwavering when it comes to what means the most. A lesson you need to learn." Mirela sighed, shaking her head. "I'm not feeling well today, so I won't argue. If you are so unwilling, then I will deliver this to the fourth tier, as well as the rest of the packages."

Nadya bit her lip. "Mama, let me go. You shouldn't be going alone, not when you're not feeling well. I am sorry. I'll try to do better."

Mirela's dark eyes met her own. They were of the same height, but while Nadya was sturdy and thickly built, her mother looked like a storm wind could blow her away. Nadya tried to smile, but the disappointment etched on her mother's features melted it.

"No, I will go. Nadezhda, you have no idea how much I want to believe you. I have not been able to fathom what's going on in your mind for some time, and you tell me nothing." She sighed again. "I pray to the Protectress that changes one day." Donning a cloak, her mother shut the door behind her.

I wish I could, Mama. I feel like I'm losing you. But if I told you the truth about everything, I would lose you and Papa. And I couldn't bear that.

❖

The six o'clock bell chimed at every tier, echoing throughout all of Storm's Quarry. Seated with her back against the warm kiln, Nadya heard it and sighed. She leaned forward to peer into her mother's workshop. Mirela had not yet returned.

Her mother's deliveries usually took a while. Wealthy courtiers and merchants would invite her in for a cup of tea to talk about the Nomori and their unique customs. Mirela would answer every question patiently and with a smile to ensure a future commission. Yes, this was nothing to be worried about.

Of course, if Nadya had been a good daughter and had just taken the packages, she wouldn't be worrying at all. She wished Mirela hadn't insisted on doing it herself after Nadya's refusal, but a prideful streak did run in the Gabori family.

Nadya levered herself up and looked down at her clothes. She would need to leave soon if she was to arrive at the theater on time, and she needed to put on something other than dust-covered trousers and a nightshirt.

She spent ten minutes rummaging through her meager wardrobe and selected a pair of sky-blue trousers, a white undershirt, and a maroon vest. Kesali had once remarked that the deep red made her face glow. At the time, Nadya had frowned and given her a good-natured jab, but now she found herself picking up the richly colored vest. She dressed, then grabbed the depleted pouch of palace coins and stuffed it into her belt pouch.

She hesitated at the door. The thick, damp air of evening soon raised a sheen of sweat on her forehead and under her arms. After last night, should she even go?

Biting her lip, Nadya left her house and sealed the door shut. Perhaps it was foolish and selfish of her, but she would rather spend an evening with Kesali and their uncertain future than an evening alone at home wondering what-if.

It would have been much faster to don her new disguise and leap across buildings to reach the arts district in the fourth tier. However, Nadya did not want to be spotted or to arrive windswept and sweating like a miner in summer, so she elected to walk. A faint breeze blew through the streets of the lower tiers, tossing her hair gently and providing some respite from the humidity. She walked through the three tiers and climbed each set of marble steps, taking the better part of an hour before reaching the fourth tier. The guardsmen glared at her as she entered, but it was not technically restricted to the Nomori. They searched her carefully before finally letting her pass.

Nadya sucked in a deep breath of fresh, sweet-smelling air. Here, the wealthiest citizens of Storm's Quarry lived in manors that lined the scrubbed cobblestone streets on either side, separated by small gardens of ferns and flowers. Ornate freestanding buildings filled the tier up until the tall wall that separated the Duke's palace at the top of the hill from the rest of the city. It looked different from the ground. She kept her eyes down. Most of the tier's inhabitants who were out and about that evening rode past her in carriages. Others strolled, a parasol in one hand and a leash with a tiny barking dog in the other. Nomori did not belong up here, and even if they weren't precisely banned, the dark looks and cold mutterings were enough to tell Nadya she was not welcome.

The city's theater stood four stories tall and proud in the middle of the arts district. A museum sat on its left, a gallery on its right. People milled about in front of the marble columns, waiting for the doors to open and the evening's show to begin. Nadya's chest began to squirm as she saw all the beautiful ladies in their dresses, jewels, and overcoats. She heard them chattering about inane things. Where conversation in the lower parts of the city rarely turned from the oncoming storm, here it were barely acknowledged.

She was still on the other side of the street when the gnawing feeling in her chest became too much. Nadya turned to bolt. She nearly bumped into a man wearing a fine coat. He muttered something about *Nomori bastards* and walked around her as if she had been a tree or a bench.

I don't belong here. I'll go home, find Mama, and hire a pigeon to be sent to Kesali with an apology and an excuse...

"You look like a cat caught on driftwood in the middle of a flood." Kesali skipped up beside her.

Nadya mumbled a hello. They stared at each other for a moment, before Kesali stepped forward and embraced her lightly. Nadya caught a whiff of cinnamon before she pulled away. "Thanks for coming. You look wonderful."

"Not half as much as you," Nadya said, pulse racing. It was true. Kesali wore trousers and vest. Ornate embroidery brought a phoenix and flames alive, red against stark black. The vest might have been a traditional Nomori cut, but there was nothing familiar in the fine clothing. This must be something new, something made in the fourth tier, paid for by the palace.

"Are you all right?" Kesali asked softly. "Last night—"

"Is something I really do not wish to talk about," Nadya said. It came out harsher than intended. "Sorry, I am just tired, and..."

"I understand."

There was something different between them, a new awkwardness that Nadya could practically feel rubbing up and down her skin. Was it because of the kiss, or because she was pulling away?

"Shall we go in? I'm sure between the two of us, we will be able to raise some eyebrows and challenge some notions of propriety." Kesali offered Nadya her arm, and she took it before she could think of what she was doing.

The ticket master frowned as the two Nomori women approached him. "This is not a charity show. No tickets, no admittance."

Kesali did not flinch. In flawless Erevo, she said, "Lord Marko has two tickets reserved for us in his family's private box."

His face whitened to the color of old porridge, and Nadya tried to keep herself from giggling. He bustled through his notes, muttering to himself. "Ah, yes. Milady," he said, somewhat forcefully, "our humble theater is glad you have graced us with your patronage. We have the private box for you and Lord Marko ready."

"Marko sends his apologies, but his duty draws him away. My friend Nadezhda Gabori has deigned to accompany me in his stead." Her words were polite, but the gleam in Kesali's eye dared the man to argue.

"Of course, milady. Welcome, Miss Gabori. I will have an usher show you to your seats at once." He called over a sweating boy in green.

Kesali turned to Nadya. "First dancing at the festival, now Nomori at the theater. Twice in as many days. Look at us, causing pandemonium wherever we go."

Nadya stifled a laugh as the usher led them through the ornate metal gates and up a flight of carpeted stairs.

"If you keep your mouth open like that," Kesali whispered, "a bird will come and nest in it."

Nadya blushed and clamped her mouth shut. She could not stop staring, however. The walls were covered with frescos depicting scenes from the stage. Their brilliant colors almost hurt her eyes. Her boots plodded up the soft steps, and Nadya wondered how many laborers it took to keep the finery free from the perpetual damp of the city.

The stairs opened into a small balcony with four satin-covered chairs. Its air smelled slightly of incense, filled with the soft chatter of courtiers and merchants in the seats below. The usher helped each of them sit, and both Kesali and Nadya had to restrain their laughter at being treated as if they were fragile courtier ladies. He bowed and left.

The stage consumed her view. Polished wood gleamed in the gaslights that hung along the walls. Huge blood-colored curtains cut across the center of it. Beneath them, dozens of seats crowded up against the edge of the stage. Men and women, wearing elaborate jewels and hats with feathers, slowly filled them.

Kesali whistled softly. "Several times I've been here, but I'm still not used to this. I could never have imagined such a beautiful place while I ran through the alleys of the sea-scum tier."

Nadya winced at the Erevan name for her home. *Several times?* She hadn't mentioned that. Kesali didn't seem to notice her choice of words. She was watching the people who trickled into their seats below. Nadya wondered if Kesali would want to be counted among them.

Finally, she said quietly, "Please do not call our home that."

Kesali put a hand to her mouth. "Oh, Nadya, I'm sorry. It slipped out." When Nadya had no response, she continued, tripping over her words. "I spend most of my time at the palace now, and you should hear how they talk. Even the well-meaning ones. I had to talk like one of them to fit in. I was already an outsider there."

"And what would your mother say, leaving your people behind to fit in?" Truthfully, she did not know if she directed the question at Kesali, or at herself.

"She would tell me to do whatever I had to in order to save our peoples." Kesali straightened in her seat. "And I will. I have my mother's gift. She saved everyone with it twenty years ago. We weren't welcome in Storm's Quarry, but she had a vision of a storm, the likes of which even this place had never seen. No matter how much kinship we felt with the water, even our ships would've wrecked had we tried to escape the sea. Storm's Quarry was the only sanctuary from the storm, so she met with the Duke, and together, they saved everyone. When she died, she told me that because I inherited her psychic gift of storm sight, it was now my duty to protect the city."

Nadya swallowed. "That's a lot to place on the shoulders of a twelve-year-old."

"I'm not twelve anymore. I apprentice at the palace because it furthers that end. I am sorry if you don't like it," she said, not meeting Nadya's gaze.

Biting her lip, Nadya slowly reached over and clasped Kesali's leg ever so gently. "I'm sorry for my words. I'm just tired, and things with my mother have not been good for a long time. I...I share your vision. And I have no doubt that when the time comes, you will protect the city."

Kesali smiled at her. Before anything else could be said, the lights dimmed and the curtains pulled back. When the first dancer came onto the stage, the magic of the ballet made her even forget the woman sitting beside her.

The dance told the story of a pair of lovers across time whose love was doomed to fail. Women in elaborate costumes rose on the points of their toes and moved with a grace and balance that Nadya did not think even her abilities could give her. She sneaked a glance at Kesali, whose eyes followed the movements below with fierce attention. Did she see their own story through the performance? Nadya looked back to the dancers, at the rigid muscles in their arms as they reached for one another. She glanced down to where Kesali's hand rested on the arm of the chair. Her own fingers twitched. Could she be so bold, as brave as Kesali had been with the kiss? She wrestled with herself, preoccupied.

Kesali shifted in her seat, drawing her hand away. "There's a guardsman down there. They don't visit places like this without cause."

She looked to where Kesali pointed. A young man in Nomori trousers and vest wove his way through the final rows of seats and jumped onto the stage with the precision and balance of a Nomori fighter. Her stomach dropped as the man turned, drawing his rapier, and Nadya saw his face.

His eyes were completely, seamlessly black. Just like Duren's.

CHAPTER SIX

The black eyes that surveyed the crowd with a palpable disgust latched on to Nadya. Her mouth went dry. Again, it was happening again. Exactly like that night in the fourth tier. Instead of spurring action, the thought spun a great lethargy around her. She couldn't move. She was shackled by the nightmare that was coming to life before her. She barely breathed. Next to her, Kesali rose. She spoke to the usher, pointing to the man on the stage. Nadya didn't hear her words. The wooden armrests of her chair cracked under her grip as she tried to reconcile what she was seeing.

The black-eyed man raised his rapier. Around him, the dancers stopped, uncertain of what was happening. Ushers began to push through the crowd of patrons in order to get this man off their stage. He smirked at them and bellowed in accented Erevo, "Death to all Erevans. Soon, the Nomori will rule!"

He turned around with startling speed, sinking his blade in the chest of the lead ballerina. Her eyes opened in a voiceless scream as the beautiful white silk of her dress slowly turned red. He withdrew his rapier, and she crumpled to the ground.

The theater stood in shocked silence for a moment before patrons began to scream and run from their seats. The doors were soon clogged with courtiers trying to escape. Several Erevan men tried to tackle the Nomori man to the ground, but they were quickly felled by rapier strikes. No one else dared try.

Only one figure, a man by his height, still stood before the stage. He wore a dark cloak that shielded his eyes. Nadya's breath froze. It was the same man.

She hadn't seen any identifying characteristics when she was up on top of that manor, but the way this man carried himself, a half swagger that showed no fear, no deference to anyone, mirrored the figure from that night.

"Why in the name of the Protectress…" Kesali looked down for a moment, shaking. Then her head rose, and she turned to the pale-faced usher behind them. "Get word to the Duke's Guard and Lord Marko. I want guardsmen here now." Her voice carried authority Nadya did not know she had.

He bowed and hurried off.

The black-eyed Nomori was not finished. With a smile born of madness, he reached inside his shirt and pulled out a small parcel. A fine gray powder sprinkled from it, covering the now-bare stage. The strange man had disappeared.

The scent of gunpowder touched Nadya's nose. The thought of Kesali in danger was enough to overcome her paralysis. She stood so fast the chair flew back and hit the wall, shattering.

Kesali turned around to see Nadya grab her hand. "What are you doing?"

"He's going to blow himself up, along with anyone who stays here," Nadya said from between clenched teeth. She hustled Kesali down the stairs, keeping herself between Kesali and the chaos of the theater.

At the bottom, dozens of people packed in, sealing the exit shut with their bodies. Panicked shrieks echoed through the lobby. The air was hot and thin, filled with Erevan breath. The scent of blood trickled in as people kicked and clawed at one another to get through the madness. Pretty dresses tore, jewelry was thrown, and parasols thrust out like swords. Nadya dodged a strike from a white-haired woman.

She had to get Kesali out of here. With one hand holding Kesali's arm, she shoved her way through the masses of people and out into the street. They kept going until they were on the other side, pushing through the gathering crowds.

"We must help them," Kesali said.

Nadya was loathe to leave her, but even more hesitant to start an argument she could not win. She sat Kesali down on a bench. "Stay here." Before the Stormspeaker could protest about duty or some other ridiculous excuse, she added, "You are no use to this city dead. I'll go."

Kesali nodded. Nadya ran back toward the theater as a group of guardsmen, led by Lord Marko, arrived on the scene. She ducked her head to avoid recognition. If she could make it to the doors, she could tear them off their hinges, creating more room for escape.

An explosion rocked the street. Bits of stones and wood rained down on carriages and people alike. Nadya swore as a chunk of rock hit her in the back. She stumbled forward.

The ruined remains of the theater smoked in the evening air. Stone foundations jutted up, their edges sharp and blackened. The stairs Nadya had walked not an hour ago spiraled up into nothing. The once-beautiful carpet smelled like burning hair and smoked. Soot-stained courtiers crawled out of the rubble, calling for loved ones and servants. Nadya fell to her knees.

All her abilities, and she couldn't stop this.

Tears stung her eyes, squeezing out of the corners and trickling down her cheeks. She shook silently. Each breath grew harsher until it felt like she was swallowing sand. First Jurek, then Brishen, now this. It was as if the city's storms gods were taunting her, gutting and slaying as she hung helpless like a puppet on strings. Nadya had always wanted to believe her abilities were a gift from the Protectress, meant for something, but the past week suggested the Elders were right. She was cursed, and she was a curse. Who would die next because she wasn't strong enough to save them?

A soft hand on her shoulder roused her from the downward spiral of her thoughts, and Nadya wiped her eyes. Kesali knelt down beside her. "It's all right to be scared, to feel for others' pain. There's no shame in tears."

"You're okay?" Nadya said, voice crackling. Blood dripped off a cut in Kesali forehead. She couldn't see any other injuries.

"Because of you. I don't know how you moved so fast, but we are alive because you acted and I did not." Kesali touched her wet cheek. "I owe you my life."

Nadya didn't want there to be debts between them. "Believe me, I owe you a lot more. So I think we're even."

Kesali looked past her, expressionless. For a moment, Nadya feared she had said something wrong. But the other girl remained impassive. She stared out beyond the wreckage of the theater, the weeping courtiers, their satin singed and bloodstained, to the horizon where the slightest bit of sunlight peeked out from behind gray clouds.

"Kesali?" Nadya put a hand on her shoulder. "What's wrong?"

She didn't respond. Nadya looked around for a medic to call for help or a guardsman, or even Lord Marko. She bit her lip and shook Kesali slightly. "You're scaring me. Please..." *Please let it not be something I did to you.*

Abruptly, Kesali stood. She did not look down at Nadya but instead walked forward slowly and deliberately to the center of the street, in the midst of the crowds. Lord Marko saw her and called out. She ignored him. Her glassy eyes surveyed all present as if they were nothing more than dumb animals to be led to water. Nadya stood up, wary. Had the strange man also gotten to Kesali? Her eyes were not black, but there was something...not mortal about them. Something ancient.

More people noticed the lone Nomori girl in the middle of the street. They watched, waiting, as Nadya did. She did not know what else to do. She rocked back and forth on the balls of her feet, ready to spring the moment something changed. If Kesali was under someone's control, she would stop her from doing anything dangerous, even if it meant exposing her own secret.

"*Hear me,*" Kesali said. Nadya jerked back. It wasn't Kesali's voice; it was darker, heavier. She did not shout, yet the sound seemed to carry to every corner of the city. It commanded silence, and all who heard, from servants to courtiers, complied.

"*In seven days hence, the sun will fall back into shadow and the rains will come.*" Kesali paused, and it was quiet enough that a single breath felt like the beat of a drum. To Nadya's ears, she was speaking in Nomori. But the rapt attention of all the Erevans that surrounded them gave her the uncanny feeling that what Kesali said rose above the boundaries of language.

"A Great Storm such as this generation has not seen. Day and night will become one. Air will turn to water. Stone to silt." Her gaze moved through the crowd. *"When the rains end, the water will remain."*

Behind her, Lord Marko stood surrounded by his guardsmen, and though he stood strong, Nadya could see his hand shaking on the hilt of his rapier.

"Hear me. On the day of the solstice, the day of the Blood Sun, the sea will settle, the floodwaters gone."

The final word rang out in the stillness. Kesali dropped to the ground.

Nadya couldn't quite process what had just happened. It didn't seem to be the work of the strange man who turned the eyes of men black, but it was equally powerful. Perhaps more so. She could not rid herself of the feeling she had been in the presence of something greater than the mortal world.

Rooted as she was, she did not realize Marko had already made his way to where Kesali fell. Nadya swore and rushed over, grinding debris to dust under her boots. She stopped just short as the Duke's son took Kesali in his arms. Such a look of concern on his face. He brushed the stray hair out of her eyes and ran his hand down her face in a way that said there was much more between them than a casual invitation to the theater.

Kesali's eyes flickered open.

"Do you remember anything?" Marko asked, helping her sit up.

Kesali took a long breath. "Yes. I just predicted the next Great Storm." She glanced up at Nadya, who tried to look reassuring.

"Can you move? We must tell my father before it spreads panic in the city."

"Yes." She levered herself up. Nadya reached out to steady her, but Marko was there.

"I have a horse here. Come, we must hurry," Marko said. He barked a few orders to his guardsmen, who dispersed through the crowds. Some would continue to help here. Others would work to ensure there was no panic.

"I have to," Kesali said to her. "It's—"

"Your duty." She tried not to make the words sound bitter. "Go."

As angry as she might feel toward Lord Marko, who in truth had been nothing but kind to her, a Nomori girl far beneath his station, she understood the urgency. Tensions had always been high between the Erevan and Nomori inhabitants of Storm's Quarry. The attack on the theater was enough to ignite a lot of rage, and perhaps even more reaction like what happened at Brishen's bakery. But with the impending threat of a Great Storm, the city might tear itself apart in anger and fear. Nadya had never witnessed a Great Storm, but the stories told by her parents and the Elders were enough to scare her.

She glanced back to see Kesali surrounded by a dozen of the Duke's Guard. She gave her a quick nod, and before Kesali could call out to her, Nadya shoved through the crowd toward the stairs and home.

The trip down to the Nomori tier was a blurred haze of white, brown, and damp. Nadya didn't know how much time passed before she descended the stairs to the bottom of the city. There, she pushed through tired-eyed workers as they returned home, still worn out from the festivities the night before. How would they look when news reached them of Kesali's prediction? Relief caught in her throat when the squat stone building of her home came into view. She skirted around a merchant hawking cloth from a cart and saw a figure lying in front of their doorstep.

Mirela coughed. Her body, pitifully small before the door, shook. The scent of blood carried through the air.

This time, Nadya did not freeze. This time, it was her mother.

She sprinted through the street, knocking people over without a backward glance. "Mama!" Nadya skidded to a halt. A few cobblestones cracked under her feet. Falling to her knees, she cradled her mother's head. Another coughing fit tore through Mirela's body, and Nadya held her until it subsided. She hadn't realized the illness was this bad. It had only been a cough.

Mirela spat out blood, then turned to look up at her daughter. "It's all right. I am all right. It just came over me all of a sudden."

More tears threatened to choke her, but Nadya held them back. She gently picked her mother up and carried her inside. Once Mirela was nestled in a cocoon of blankets on her pallet with a spitting bowl beside her, she sealed both doors shut and lit the coals in the kiln. Her actions were automatic, copying what she had seen her grandmother do in countless Nomori households when she was little. Before long, the room glowed with warmth, burning the damp out of the air.

Her mother coughed again. The harsh hacking sparked against Nadya's nerves. Each one sounded like it could be a last breath. She swallowed hard, forced a smile, and then turned around.

Mirela smiled weakly. "You don't have to do this, Nadya. I can take care of myself. It was only a little fall." Another coughing fit stopped her from saying anything else, and Nadya glanced away as she spat phlegm into the bowl she had placed there.

"It was more than that. You could have…been really hurt." She could not bring herself to say *died*. "Has that happened before?"

Mirela's hesitation before her quiet no was enough for Nadya to know the truth.

"I may not be Grandmother, but I know that's a lie." She sat beside her mother. "I am so sorry. It should have been me doing the deliveries. What can I do?"

"Tea would be nice."

"Of course." She put a kettle over the coals. As it heated, she paced back and forth, trying to find words to tell her mother what had happened on the fourth tier.

"Should I fetch someone?" she asked, stalling. "Grandmother, maybe?"

"I don't want her to worry. I just overexerted myself today." Mirela sighed. It ended with a harsh hack. "It was as much my fault as anyone's."

"I should have taken the packages." Nadya walked over to the bed and gently took her mother's hand. "I should not have let you go. I should—"

"What's passed is past." Mirela squeezed her hand. Nadya nodded, throat dry. Her mother was not just speaking of today, but of the past weeks, months, that Nadya had put herself before the family. There was not necessarily forgiveness in her tone, but a chance to be better.

"Mama, something happened today. At the theater." Before Mirela could say anything about Nadya skipping her duties to attend a frivolous courtier pastime, she added, "A Nomori man let off an explosive. I think a lot of people were hurt."

"Protectress watch over us all. There will be blood to be paid for such an act. I cannot begin to fathom what drives a soul to that." Her gaze ran up and down Nadya's body. "Were you there? Are you hurt?"

"Yes, but I'm fine." Nadya swallowed again. She could not seem to get any moisture into her mouth. "Mama, there's more. Kesali— she made a prediction in the middle of it all. There's another Great Storm coming next week."

Mirela looked past Nadya to the small tapestry that hung on the far wall, depicting the mountains of legend that their people came from. "Yes," she whispered, "Protectress save us all."

The kettle whistled, but its sound was far off, buried beneath the weight of things to come.

Chapter Seven

Early the next morning, a gong rang through the damp air, rattling the teacup in Mirela's hands. Five short trumpet blasts followed it. Nadya winced. It had been a long night of tending to her mother. Instead of feeling exhausted, her limbs buzzed with excess energy. Too long had passed since she'd left the confines of their small house behind and ran across rooftops, leaving nothing but wind. She rapped her fingers against her leg.

"A gathering," Mirela said, her voice hoarse. "No doubt to announce the Stormspeaker's prediction."

Nadya flinched at the title. She didn't like to think of Kesali as the Stormspeaker. That was Kesali's mother. But, she supposed, after what happened in the fourth tier yesterday, the city would think of her no other way.

"You must go." Mirela set her tea down. "I feel much better, and you look like you are ready to tear a hole in the wall."

If only she knew how accurate that was. Nadya shook her head. "I know what will be said. I am not leaving you alone."

The door opened, and Shadar staggered in. Nadya heard him unbelt his rapier and hang it up before he parted the curtain and entered the room. Dark circles made his eyes look hollow. He only managed half a smile as he greeted them. "I wish I came with better news for the two most beautiful women Storm's Quarry."

Nadya snorted. What must they look like, her hair knotted, her clothes a day old, Mirela thin and pale. "Papa, we know."

"You were there, with the Stormspeaker?"

That title again. She nodded.

Shadar sat down, groaning. "I have been on my feet all night. The Duke and Lord Marko had me running through the tiers, preparing the Guard. They'll make the announcement today, starting up in the palace, and then moving down through the city."

"We heard the summons," Mirela said. She coughed into her hand, and Nadya smelled blood. Her mother tried to hide it, but Shadar stood. He walked over and gently took her hand.

"What's this?" He turned to Nadya when Mirela started to protest that it was nothing.

"She fell," Nadya said quietly. "I found her outside the door. It was a lot worse last night."

"Exactly. I am better this morning," Mirela said. It ended with a cough that sprayed tiny red droplets across Shadar's chin. "Oh, I'm sorry," she said, covering her mouth.

Shadar wiped it away with a sleeve. "My dear, you need a physician." He looked at Nadya. "Go to the third tier. Do you know the Cinnabar district? Good," he said when she nodded. "There is a doctor there who works part-time in the Guard's infirmary. His name is Arkady Maslak. His practice has a pestle and diamond carved into its sign. Tell him I sent you, and to come here as soon as possible."

"It is really not nece—" Mirela could not finish the sentence for coughing.

"Nadya." Her father's tone, calm and unemotional, scared her. "You must be quick."

Something she would not fail at. "I'll be back as soon as I can."

❖

Dr. Maslak wasn't all too receptive to a strange Nomori girl knocking on his door, even when Nadya told him who her father was. He looked down his long, thin nose at her, scrutinizing, she imagined, everything from her wrinkled vest to her red-rimmed eyes.

"What are the symptoms, again, you say?" he barked.

She cleared her throat. "She's had a cough for a long time. Yesterday, she collapsed. Now she's coughing up blood. I think she may also have a fever." Her voice trailed off. Laid out like that, it sounded so serious. She hoped Dr. Maslak could just give her mother one of the potions she smelled through the doorway, and Mirela would be fine.

He nodded slowly. "Tell the captain I will be down this evening. Until then, keep her in bed. Try to soothe the cough as much as you can, and if she does have a fever, use cool rags to keep it contained." He shut the door in her face. Behind it, Nadya heard his mutter, "First of the floodwater cases. Bit early, but not the last, not the last."

Wondering what he meant, she turned to go. The Cinnabar district was unusually quiet—only a few people out and they seemed to be hurrying, heads bent low. The damp was less pronounced up here than back home, but it hung in the air like an oppressive curtain. People were struggling to accept another Great Storm. They had prepared for a season of storms no harsher than usual: a few days of storms, then a few weeks of being trapped by the waters of the Kyanite Sea. But Kesali had predicted the floodwaters would not recede until summer solstice, over two months away.

Nadya began to run down the stairs. If anyone saw her, no one paid any mind. It was as if the news of the Great Storm turned the city's inhabitants into walking automatons.

A final gong rang out when Nadya reached the second tier. The Duke's gathering in the Nomori square had begun, and she was missing it. Her parents as well, since Shadar would not have left Mirela's side. She might already know about the oncoming Great Storm, but she did desperately want to know what the Duke was going to do about keeping peace after the storm, when the gates of Storm's Quarry would be sealed by floodwaters.

She sped up. If she was lucky, she would be there for the last of it.

The Nomori square was nearly as full as the night of Arane Sveltura, but a distinct somberness pervaded the crowd. Nothing good could come of the Duke, his son, and a contingent of the Guard calling a meeting in the Nomori tier.

Nadya strained to see the figures beyond the red uniforms of the Guard, but she was too far away to make out anything. She heard the strong voice of the Duke, though. "We have all been shocked by this news, but we will not let shock turn into fear. Storm's Quarry has faced worse in its history, and these walls still stand." His grasp of Nomori was slow, halting, but clear.

Biting her lip, she looked around. Pushing through the crowd wasn't an option; she might hurt someone. Instead, she headed toward the closest building, the Nomori public bathhouse. Scents of spices and beeswax soap drifted out of its cracked door as she slipped behind it. No one stood near the alley, and everyone's attention was on the Duke. Nadya began to climb.

In the square, the Duke continued, "True, in times past, there was greater cause for worry. Such storms could not be predicted, and the city was often caught unaware and unprepared. That is no longer. Since you have joined us and become part of Storm's Quarry, the gifts of your men and women have only strengthened our city." She hopped over the wall and onto the roof with a small thump. Keeping low, she made her way to the other side of the roof.

Duke Isyanov stood on a makeshift stage. He wore simple clothes that would blend in on the third tier, if it were not for the jeweled collar around his neck—the signet of the leader of Storm's Quarry. Beside the Duke, Lord Marko stood with his arm wrapped around Kesali's shoulder.

Nadya stared. Her hands, gripping the raised edge of the roof, began to shake.

"Like her mother before her, Kesali Stormspeaker has given us a blessing. A forewarning of the storms that will come down on our city within the week. I thank her and the Protectress for the time they have given us," the Duke said solemnly.

Whispers rose among the gathered crowds, most people nodding. For the Erevan ruler of Storm's Quarry to acknowledge the power of the Protectress went a long way to bridging the chasm between him and the older Nomori.

Underneath her fingers, the marble of the roof began to crack. She could not pull her eyes away from Kesali, who looked out over the crowds with a calm, confident expression. She still wore traditional Nomori clothing, but that was not all. A chain of rubies encircled her neck. Every so often, she would reach up and touch it, as if reminding herself it was there.

"The Guard will be readying the city for this storm. They will assist in any way that you require—you need only ask. In six days, there will be a citywide lockdown. Stay in your homes, seal the doors, and wait out the rains. If we remain strong, this storm will pass easily." For the first time, the Duke broke his somber expression with a smile. "Life goes on despite storms of any size, and I am grateful to give you a piece of glad news, something to hold on to through the coming weeks." He nodded to Marko and Kesali, who both stepped forward.

Each heartbeat roared in Nadya's ears, yet she felt lightheaded. She knew what was about to be said, she knew it in the very core of her being, because she was cursed by the Protectress, and someone who is cursed was not allowed to be happy.

"It has been twenty years since we welcomed you into our city, and I think it is past time that our peoples are bound by stronger roots." Duke Isyanov put his hand on Marko's shoulder. "I am happy to announce the betrothal of my son, Marko Isyanov, to Kesali Stormspeaker."

The stone under Nadya's hands turned to dust with a crunch as she curled her fingers into fists, knuckles white.

"It was the vision her mother and I held for the city when the first Stormspeaker saved us, and now it will bind our people together as one." The Duke continued, but Nadya's senses were slowly replaced by a dull roar.

Betrothed. Tears leaked down her face. She shook. So long in the planning. Kesali had known. *She knew all this time, and yet she still allowed me to believe...*

Anger so great that it frightened her built through her chest. Nadya stood up suddenly and sprinted off the back of the roof, leaping and coming down with the thud on a neighboring building. She had to get away before she did something she might regret.

Not paying attention to her step, she missed the edge of a roof and slipped into an alley. Her body hit stone with a crack, and Nadya bit back a scream. A hundred hot coals burned into her side. Gingerly, she got to her knees. She tried to stand but fell back.

The tears flowed freely now, and she couldn't tell which pain caused them.

Nearly an hour passed there, in that alley among the stagnant drain water and rats, before Nadya struggled to her feet. She meandered through the streets of her district, not seeing anyone. No one saw her. The Duke's announcement of a betrothal might have been an attempt to cushion the news of an oncoming Great Storm, but the Nomori were a practical people. When your family was down to the last piece of stale bread, your children crying from hunger, and your coin useless, a wedding mattered little more than a than a falcon wheeling its way across the sun.

Finally, her house was in sight, but there was someone standing on the stoop. The air rushed out of her like she had been punched in the stomach. She turned around quickly, but before she could run away, a voice called, "Nadya!"

Kesali's voice.

Slowly, she turned. Kesali ran up to her. The ruby necklace, a betrothal necklace she realized with a taste like old salt filling her mouth, bounced with each step. "Nadya, I didn't see you at the gathering."

"I was there," she mumbled, not meeting Kesali's gaze.

"Oh." Kesali started twirling the necklace again in a way that made Nadya want to throw up. "I just spoke to the captain. I'm sorry about your mother. I will pray to the Protectress that she gets well and soon."

"Thank you."

"Nadya, I am sorry I didn't tell you before today, but everything moved so fast after I saw the storm coming, and—"

"Don't lie to me." Her hands at her sides were clutched into fists. She took a step back, just to be safe.

"What?" Kesali shook her head. "I'm not meaning to, I—"

"You've known. For a long time. You knew, and you still..."
She couldn't say the words.

"You mean Arane Sveltura? I...I did not know things would
progress so fast. It was never certain. I was always told, one day."
Kesali reached out for Nadya's hand. "Please, I meant everything
that night."

Nadya snatched her hand away. "It doesn't matter."

"You know the struggles our people face. This might be the
solution, to one day have a ruler who is half Nomori. We cannot
keep up the walls we've built between us and them. I am a tool
for that peace." Kesali's voice shook. "Don't you see? I have to do
this, just as I have to predict the storms. It's for a better future for
everyone. It has nothing to do with love. It cannot. I...I could not
love Marko, not..." She stopped. "Nadya, I—"

"No!" Nadya practically shouted. She drew a deep breath.
The sadness that crept into Kesali's liquid eyes burned her, but she
shoved that pain away. "You cannot have both. You chose this. Yes,
you're very noble, and that is fine. But you cannot come here and
think you get to have both. That is your path. So take it back up to
your palace, *milady*." Nadya stormed passed her, to her front door.
Behind her, Kesali did not speak.

❖

The Protectress was punishing her.

For as long as Nadya could remember, the name of the Nomori
deity, the ever-loving, ever-watchful spirit that kept her people
safe, brought warmth to her chest. When other children teased her,
she would hide in her loft, not letting either of her parents up. She
huddled in a corner and held her seal close to her chest, praying. At
the time, she never thought of it as praying. It was speaking to an
older sister, a guardian, a friend.

Those days were long gone. Ever since she discovered her
abilities, ever since the accident and her first deadly encounter with
her strength, Nadya struggled to believe that she was not some kind
of monster in Nomori skin, a curse unleashed upon the city. Now,

she knew. The Protectress had given her a test those years ago when her abilities appeared. She'd failed. She continued to fail, then with the Erevan boy, now with Duren, with the gang in Brishen's bakery, with her mother.

"Lung rot," Dr. Maslak had said. With those words, the world of the Gabori family shattered. Shadar held Mirela tightly, as she tried to keep a brave face. Nadya stood off in the corner. Her tears were used up for the day.

"I am sure of it," the doctor continued. "Too much exposure to damp. The coming storm will only worsen it. I don't need to tell you how dangerous it is. Hope remains, though. There are medicines, but they are expensive, now so more than ever. I can give you an address, but I cannot promise anything."

That was five days ago. In five days, Nadya saw lines in her mother's face she hadn't noticed before, and gray hairs and hollow cheekbones. In five days, Storm's Quarry turned from a city of life to one under the oppressive shackles of the sky. She finally understood why Erevans used to worship storm gods. The storms truly controlled the city. Store shelves grew bare as everyone stocked their larders for what was coming. The doors to the mines were sealed shut to keep the rainwater from pouring in; the same was done for Miners' Tunnel and the outer city gate. The Guard instituted a harsh curfew and mandatory district checkpoint. Shadar was barely home, so busy was he in the city, enforcing peace and quelling panic with raised rapiers and loaded muskets. Nothing had actually escalated to violence, but it did not bode well for the coming time of floodwaters, when the storm's recession would leave the city trapped by the sea for two months. No food could get in, and Storm's Quarry had little in the way of anything other than its gem mines. The city relied on trade for survival. No one could get out either. In the past, it was a peaceful, if tense time, with only a handful of disturbances. But a Great Storm was sure to be different.

In five days, Nadya slowly became numb to the news of Kesali's betrothal. She hadn't seen the Stormspeaker since that day. Instead, she spent her time damp-proofing the house, something she should have paid more attention to the past months. If she had, perhaps the doctor's verdict would have been different.

Now, with the morning skies still dark with clouds and stars, Nadya donned her new disguise and left home. The cloak did encumber her a bit as she leapt between buildings, running up to the fourth tier her own way to avoid any unpleasant encounters with the Duke's Guard, but the anonymity it and the scarf she pulled across her mouth provided was well worth it. Any who saw her from the street would only note a billowing, dark figure streaking above them.

Stone cracked under her boots as she landed on the roof of the practice of one of the best-known Erevan physicians in Storm's Quarry. Unlike Dr. Maslak, this one treated only those who could pay dearly for it. Manors rose up on either side of the modest building. Below, on the meticulously maintained street, few pedestrians were out before the sun rose.

With few people out, no one would know who was breaking into the offices of a physician. Any signs of a break-in would be attributed to looters, a growing reality as the storm approached.

She climbed down the slanted roof. Her fingers clung to the edge of the final row of shingles. Twisting her body, Nadya peered down at the stone wall. A window sat ten paces underneath her. She pressed her legs against the wall until her knees bent, then pushed off. As she swung back toward the building, Nadya let go of the roof. Her boots hit the glass-paned window, shattering it, and she tumbled through onto expensive carpet.

She jumped to her feet. The room was deserted. Plush chairs stood in tasteful patterns, interspaced with ferns and other potted plants. Nadya did another sweep to make sure some servant wasn't on duty, then went to the door. It was locked, but she broke it easily. The door creaked open. A hundred different scents hit her full in the face. She blinked away tears and looked up to survey the shelves of medicines in glass bottles labeled neatly. It took a moment for her to find what she came for: a vial stamped with an X divided by a line, the symbol of lung rot. She gingerly placed it in her belt pouch and left.

She hurried home, skidding across rooftops. At the edge of the fourth tier, just before the wall that separated it from the lower parts of the city, she paused. She was not far from Jurek's manor, and the murder that had taken place there. Was Duren still alive, or had news of the Great Storm hastened his execution?

A lightning bolt snapped down from the sky. It lit up the entire world for half a moment, not even a full breath, before it struck the roof of a manor not far from where Nadya stood. She leapt back. The air buzzed. Hairs on her arms stood up. Thunder boomed, shaking the city to its roots. Nadya clasped her hands over her ears.

The first raindrop fell on her bare hand. Soon, it was joined by many others. The sky darkened as a curtain of rain advanced over the city. The Great Storm of the Blood Sun had come.

CHAPTER EIGHT

In the thousand years that Storm's Quarry occupied a lone rock in the midst of the Kyanite Sea, every spring brought the season of storms. Torrential rains poured from heaven. Lightning split the sky as the storm gods ripped at the veil between the mortal world and the beyond. Over the years, the storms had lost a bit of their potency, with deadly onslaughts a rarity. According to the archives up in the palace, the realm of the Head Cleric and his apprentice, there had been twelve Great Storms in the history of the city. Those living now in Storm's Quarry more than two decades old were the first to see two in their lifetimes.

It rained. It rained like the heavens dumped out a bottomless bucket on the city, hardly a hair's breadth between monstrous drops. Water sloshed down through the culverts. It rose to chest height in the upper parts of the city. In the Nomori tier, no one could leave their home for fear of being drowned by waves of rainwater, higher than the tallest man. Any caught out in the storm died. There were probably a few drunken fools whose bodies would be found floating somewhere when the skies cleared. At the base of the wall, deep under the floodwaters, the steam pumps were the only things in the city working, tirelessly pumping the water out and over the walls. They hardly made a dent in the rainwater that filled Storm's Quarry to the brim.

Up in her loft, Nadya could hear nothing but the dripping of water leaking into the house and her parents' breathing, Shadar's quiet and Mirela's harsh and catching. The constant roar of the rain drowned out all else, but for sharp thoughts of Kesali. Nadya sat on her pallet. Her legs twitched with extra energy. She wanted nothing more than to burst through the stone wall and run until she could not run anymore. To let her feelings be swept away by currents, over the wall and out to sea. To purge the image of the newly betrothed couple from her mind.

Her family barely spoke. Shadar stayed next to Mirela, quietly stroking her hair as she tried to rest. The medicine kept the worst of the coughing at bay, but she looked pale and sickly in the light of the single lamp. On the fifth day of the rains, their final candle flickered out, and they sat in darkness.

The rain lasted two more days.

On the morning of the seventh day, Nadya dreamed of running. She raced along the rooftops of Storm's Quarry, wearing only her nightshirt. Everyone who passed her recognized her. Their shouts fueled her legs. She leapt, and her feet found air. She was running through the sky, over the floodwaters, tracing the rivers her ancestors had once sailed.

Silence woke her. She started, hitting her head against the stones. She smiled as she realized what the silence meant. *The storm is over!*

Nadya heard her parents' voices as she climbed off her pallet. She was surprised Shadar hadn't been called out by the Duke's Guard yet. Perhaps the city was not yet free enough of water for anyone to be out. She cursed under her breath as she stretched. Her body ached to get out of the house and run and jump and get away from the world, but there would be time enough in the next few days to explore the flooded city from its rooftops. Climbing down, Nadya nearly stumbled back at the bright smiles on her parents' faces.

Both of them sat on the stone floor around the knee-high table, illuminated by the morning light streaming in through the window. Nadya was relieved to see the color was back in her mother's cheeks, but she looked at the setup with suspicion. Was this an attempt to broach the subject of marriage again? Or—

Her thoughts stopped. "Apple jam?"

Shadar patted the ground next to him. "I don't envy that nose of yours when you go up to the second tier, but yes. Come and eat breakfast."

Toasted hard rolls filled a basket to the brim on the table, and next to it sat a small pot of jam that made Nadya's mouth water. She plopped down beside her father, who tousled her hair. Her mother patted her leg from the other side and set two rolls on her plate. Steam rose in the damp air of the room.

Nadya looked from one to the other. "This must have cost a fortune. Why—?"

"The storm is over," her father said, smiling. "When you get to be our age, you start celebrating the little things. We are still together as a family, our house did not fall, and we did not kill one another while we were cooped up in it." He ruffled her hair again, and Nadya dodged away.

The first bite was heaven in her mouth. The steaming bread had warmed and melted the jam until it turned into a sugary soup with chunks of apples. Nadya wiped her chin with her fingers, then licked them. Only then did she use the napkin. Her mother laughed, and she realized it had been a long time since she had heard that sound.

They ate, laughing and talking, and all of a sudden, they were a family again. The lung rot wasn't mentioned. The dire situation facing the city in the aftermath of the Great Storm did not enter their conversation. Nadya's mysterious absences were not brought up. This had been life when she was fourteen years old, and she wished it could return.

"You will be able to see Kesali again, once the streets are free of water," her mother said after Nadya finished chewing her fourth roll. "She has probably moved into the palace, but that shouldn't stop you from being able to go say hello."

The last of the bread stuck in her throat. "Maybe."

"I would have never thought a daughter of Jaelle would ever settle down, much less with an Erevan, but seeing the two of them together, you have to think it's for the best. For them, and for the city," Shadar said as he spread jam on his own roll.

Mirela nodded. "The Erevans may dread having to bow to a Nomori, but their betrothal fills our people with hope. For twenty years we have lived in a place that was promised as a home, and instead is a vipers' den. Kesali and Marko can bring our two peoples together. They can give us our *Natsia*." She looked up at Shadar, and they shared a smile born of the pain of years.

Nadya shifted uncomfortably and changed the subject. "Mama, you do look better."

"The medicine you brought me did a world of good. I only hope it will still be available, even with the shortages that are sure to come. How did you get it again?"

Nadya looked at her knees. She did not want to lie, but she could not tell the truth either. "A physician in the fourth tier," she mumbled.

Her father cleared his throat, and Nadya waited for them to accuse her of stealing it. She expected her mother to whisk the breakfast away. Her father would march her up to the prison, or worse, to her grandmother's house, in pursuit of the truth. The truth would come out, and their family would be broken.

She waited, eyes on her knees.

"Thank you, Nadezhda," Mirela said finally. "I don't think I would have done as well during the storm if not for it."

Her father nodded. "It is good for you to be looking after your mother. Your duties here will only increase, and I am glad to see you taking them so seriously. The medicine was—thoughtful."

The taste of the rolls and jams, delicious just moments ago, turned to ash in Nadya's mouth. Her parents did not meet her eyes, but neither did they pepper her with accusatory questions.

They knew she stole it, and they also knew, if asked, she would just lie.

She tried to swallow the ash down, but it would not go.

❖

It takes two sides to make a war. The thought had consumed Gedeon throughout the storm. He was holed up in an abandoned house at the edge of the second tier. He did little else but pace, only remembering to eat from his paltry store when he felt faint. The effects of his two attacks on the city's elite had provoked a physical reaction in the Erevans. Though the courtiers in the fourth might only sip tea behind locked doors and debate the ramifications of a civil war, Gedeon knew there were plenty of people in this city all too eager to make it a reality.

But it took two sides to make a war, and four days after the rains stopped, as soon as the streets were walkable, Gedeon found himself in the grimiest, piss-smelling district of the second tier after midnight. Erevans stumbled in and out of alehouses, vomiting on the filthy cobblestoned street. Their vomit floating away, swirling on storm water as if drained down a culvert through the Nomori tier and eventually to the deep trenches on the inside of the walls, where it would be pumped out and over to the sea on the other side.

He kept his cloak tight around him as he walked. The wealthy clothes of a courtier would be as much of a target here as in the Nomori tier. A man stopped in front of him to relieve himself in the middle of the street. Gedeon quickly skirted around him.

"They think they can murder us in our own beds?" a drunkard yelled to the handful of men drunker than he was who gathered around him at the mouth of an alley. He stood on a creaking wooden box and took a swig from a canteen every few words. "We're gonna make them see that Storm's Quarry belongs to us. The Duke's blinded by their witchcraft. We can't depend on his Guard. It's filled with Nomori scum. They caused this gods-cursed storm. We've got to take it into our own hands!" His final proclamation was met with a drunken chorus of approval.

Gedeon let himself have a small smile as he passed them. A few simple actions on his part, and he would watch as the city tore itself apart. It would have been fine without the floodwaters, but with them, the city was a war ripe for the prompting.

He kept his gaze sharp, looking for a good candidate. He lost track of the alehouses he walked past until a man stumbled out of one and practically into his arms. Gedeon recoiled from the stench. The man burped and looked up at him. "Got a bite to spare, mister?"

Gedeon opened his mouth to dismiss the cur, but paused. The man before him was tall and strong looking, even if he was swaying from liquor. His power could take care of that. This man had the air of a criminal about him, and Gedeon didn't think for a moment that anyone would have trouble believing him capable of some great evil.

"Ay. Come, I can take you to a place where you will be fed." Gedeon held out a hand.

The tall man, mind clouded with drink, took his arm and walked obediently as Gedeon led him through the narrow streets of the second tier, down the marble stairs, and into the Nomori tier, where the water remained ankle deep. They had to stop twice for the man to relieve himself. Gedeon put a hand over his nose each time and politely looked away. The drunkard hardly seemed to notice.

The Nomori tier was mostly empty this time of night. Gedeon wove through the neighborhoods, at times dragging his companion along. If any saw the odd pair, they made nothing of it.

"We there yet?" the tall man asked.

Gedeon stopped, steadying the man, in front of an impeccably kept house. "Yes, we are." He turned the man to face him, drawing up the power at the same time. It latched onto the hatred this man carried for the Nomori and burrowed in. He blinked, his black stare completely devoid of drink.

"There is a woman in this house. Kill her."

His eyes full of Gedeon's power, he nodded and turned. Gedeon watched as he broke the lock on the door and disappeared inside. He waited, half-concealed by shadows, until he heard the scream.

Gedeon nodded, then disappeared into the night.

CHAPTER NINE

After four days spent helping out around the house and anxiously waiting a chance to run through the city, Nadya could barely feign sleep. She tossed and turned. She wore only a long shirt, lying without covers on her pallet, yet the oppressive damp was thick as a down quilt. Several hours passed. Just when she was sure both her parents slept, she opened her eyes and smiled. Finally, time to run.

"Nadya."

She lurched up. Her forehead hit the slanted roof of their house once again. Wincing and rubbing it, she saw her father.

Shadar stood on the ladder. "Sorry to wake you, but we need to leave."

"Leave?" She couldn't help the disappointment that leaked into her voice. Would she have to wait another night before she could run?

"There's been another murder. Lord Marko sent a messenger requesting both of us. Shhh. Be as quiet as you can. Your mother is sleeping, and she needs her rest." Shadar patted her on the knee and then descended the creaking ladder.

For a moment, Nadya wrestled with herself. Seeing Marko would be almost as bad as seeing Kesali. She never begrudged him the power that came with being heir to Storm's Quarry, nor the training he received from her father, though that made her buzz with jealousy. This was different. He could marry anyone in Storm's

Quarry and beyond, but he chose Kesali. What would it be like, to have the fates hand you everything wonderful in the world, Nadya wondered, bitterness dripping from her thoughts. She sighed. Her deceit about Jurek's murder lay heavy in her thoughts, heavier than her resentment of the Duke's son. Perhaps she could make up for it. All plans of running tonight evaporated. Automatically, she grabbed trousers and a vest from the neat little pile of clothing next to the wall on the ledge. She swung her legs over and pulled on the trousers.

Her father nodded silently when she stepped off the ladder and put her other arm through the vest. They walked through the room, skirting around her parents' pallet. Nadya smiled at her mother's sleeping form. The medicine must have been helping. Before, most nights, her mother could not sleep for coughing.

When they padded out into the damp night air, Nadya was surprised to see her father turn west, away from the marble stairs and the rail that would take them up to the palace. He led her deeper into the Nomori tier. She followed without asking.

It was still some hours before dawn. The tier was lit only by the occasional torch and the starlight filtering through heavy clouds. A faint wind blew across the empty streets, scattering bits of discarded paper and ruffling the fur of scavenging rats. Water pooled in every depression, so she had to keep her focus on the ground to avoid soaking her boots. The steady buzz of the steam pumps filled the air. Nadya looked up at the wall as she walked a step behind her father over dirty cobblestones. In the darkness, the faraway palace glowed with an eerie ghostliness.

She wondered if Kesali was there in her rooms at the palace, sleeping untouched by all that transpired on the Nomori tier. Had she even heard the rains amidst all that finery?

Shadar said nothing as they walked. His mouth was a hard line, and Nadya suspected that he knew more than he let on about what they were about to walk into. He turned down a narrow street, his heavy boot tread echoing. Nadya heard the rustling of others before her father stopped in front of one of the nicer houses in the Nomori tier.

Lord Marko, surrounded by five Nomori guardsmen, stood before the house, speaking in low, angry tones to an Erevan man pressed up against the wall. His eyes were wild; he shook. His hands, clenched into white fists at his side, were stained an awful crimson. The smell of it nearly sent Nadya reeling, but she planted her feet and breathed through her mouth. It didn't help much.

A man unfamiliar to Nadya stood off to one side. He wore the heavy bangles and necklaces characteristic of Erevan courtiers. His right hand held a book and pen, and his left played with one of the jeweled bracelets on his wrist. He looked to be about thirty. Nadya's face grew red as she realized he was staring at her, his expression unreadable.

Drina was also there. She acknowledged her son-in-law and granddaughter with a weary nod. She still wore her nightdress, and wisps of silver hair had escaped her braid. She stood next to a still form lying on the damp ground covered by the purple funeral cloth of her people.

Nadya swallowed. The victim was Nomori.

A limp hand stuck out from the cloth far enough for her to see the glint of a bronze seal, and with a jolt, Nadya realized where they were. She had visited this house before, alongside her grandmother, when she was younger. That particular seal of the Protectress belonged to the matriarch of the Draba family. Her name was Jastima, and her psychic gift of sensing illness and poison in food and water was nearly as powerful and sought after as Drina's.

They had also been fast friends, this dead woman and her grandmother.

Nadya reached out and took her grandmother's wrinkled hand. It was cold, but Drina managed a tired smile for her.

"Thank you for coming, Captain, Miss Gabori." Marko also looked exhausted. His skin was especially pale in the lantern light. Nadya almost felt sorry for him. Almost. "Madame Gabori," he continued in near flawless Nomori, "would you like a chair to be fetched so you can—"

"I'm fine," she snapped. "Let's get on with this."

Marko gestured for Nadya and her father to come closer to the man pinned up against the wall. "This man was caught leaving this house with blood on his hands by a Nomori guardsman. The body of Madame Draba was discovered a few minutes later."

Behind her, Nadya's grandmother heaved a rattling sigh.

"We need to find the truth. Here. Now. The repercussions of this murder could be the spark that sets this city alight, and it must be contained. I do not want him taken to the prison, not without knowing some answers. This cannot be allowed to get out of control, so we question him here."

At a hand signal from her father, the guardsmen fanned out, blocking off this part of the street from any drunks or rebellious youths that might stumble upon the scene.

"Tell us your story," Marko ordered the man. He then turned to the well-dressed stranger who kept staring at Nadya. "Magistrate, I would like everything recorded and stamped with the seal of my father."

He nodded and sat right down on the damp cobblestones. He opened a leather-bound book on his lap, turned to a black page, and posed a pen over it, waiting. Still, he sneaked another look or two at Nadya. She shivered and focused on the suspected murderer.

The detained man's face screwed up in defiance, and Marko drew his rapier in one swift movement.

"All right, all right, I didn't do anything." The man's voice was harsh and raspy. "Name's Anzor. I live in the second tier. Look, I was out tonight, searching through garbage for something to eat. It isn't easy to earn a decent meal, 'specially when the only guards anyone is willing to hire are so-called superior fighters, those Nomori bast—"

Shadar shifted. His white-knuckled hand clutched the pommel of his rapier.

Anzor visibly swallowed. "Anyway, I couldn't find nothing up a tier, so I came down here. That's not illegal. Anybody's free to travel between tiers. I was rooting around here, and then I was attacked by that Nomori guardsman. I didn't kill the old lady. I don't know how her blood got on my hands. I'm innocent of murder, all right?"

Silence reigned for a moment, the only sound the faint scraping of the magistrate's pen as he finished putting down Anzor's words.

"But no one would suspect you guilty of decency," Marko said, spitting at Anzor's feet. "Madame Gabori, what is your reading of him? Please copy it exactly, Magistrate."

The magistrate nodded and joined everyone in looking toward Drina.

Her grandmother's eyes were sharp, piercing abysses of black. Her entire body shook as, through clenched teeth, she hissed, "I...I am not sure."

Nadya could not believe it. Her grandmother was as sure as the dawn.

Drina hesitated. "He killed Jastima. That I know. But he tells the truth about the rest of it as well. They are...confusing, his emotions. I recognize some of the same from the guardsman, Duren. At the time, I did not think of it, but...there is something similar here."

Shadar shook his head. "That cannot be."

She rounded on him. "Do you think I would lie to protect such a worthless piece of Erevan shit when Jastima is lying here, murdered? It took all my honor to tell the truth."

Her father murmured apologies as Lord Marko looked at Nadya. "Can you tell us more?"

Nadya swallowed. She had paid close attention to the man, noting his heart rate and condition before and during his words, and there had been no mistake. His heart began beating even faster the moment he said he did not murder Jastima. The scent of sweat nearly overpowered the smell of blood. He was lying, or at least his physical body was telling her so.

"I think I might have an idea."

Marko nodded. "You sense something different?"

Avoiding the gaze of her grandmother, Nadya looked directly at the Duke's son as she spoke. "It's...hard. I guess the only way I have of describing it is that his body knows he is telling a lie, but his mind is not so sure." She flushed. "That doesn't make much sense."

"It's something," Marko said.

"Hey, I ain't lying. That Nomori girl doesn't know what she's talking about, milord. You have to listen to me. I—*ugh*." He crumpled to the ground. Shadar stepped away, rubbing his fist from giving the man a solid punch in the stomach.

"Thank you, Captain," Marko said. "I believe we have all we need for now, Magistrate. My thanks as well." He looked to Drina as the magistrate closed the book, groaned, and stood. "Is what she says possible?" Marko asked in Nomori.

Nadya felt her grandmother's burning gaze. Slowly, she raised her eyes to meet hers. Nadya's heart hammered in her hand, going twice as fast as Anzor's had been. She clutched her fists at her sides, fingernails digging crescent-moon furrows into her palms.

Drina took another rattling breath. After what seemed like an hour, she nodded slowly. "It is possible. You speak of the manipulation of the mind, something that has never been a gift of a true Nomori."

"How would such a thing be done? Who could do it?" Marko pressed.

"I am not sure of the exact practice of molding a mind like it is clay. I only know that no one can do such a thing without a foothold, a weakness of the mind. Fear. Guilt. Hatred. This scum before you would have many such footholds. Greed, bigotry. Any could be used to turn his mind against him." Drina sighed. She no longer looked like the powerful matriarch of a Nomori family. She was a worn elderly woman. "As for your second question, I don't know the answer."

Nadya frowned. Her grandmother's slow heart rate jumped slightly with that last statement.

"Thank you for what you have shared." Marko shook his head. "Is it the Great Storm, or has something more come over this city? First, a Nomori guardsman murders his master, then another Nomori man kills several Erevans and proclaims his race's superiority. And now we have an Erevan who has killed a beloved Nomori Elder. Not only that, but we have hints of power beyond any this city has known."

"I am worried about what this might incite. We will not be able to keep Jastima's death a secret," her father said gruffly. "There will be Nomori who will seek revenge and play into the hand of whoever orchestrated her death."

"Double the patrols in this tier, and make them all Nomori. No need to invite aggression," Marko said. He turned to the magistrate, but Nadya couldn't help but speak.

"Is that all?"

Everyone stared at her. She bit her lip. "I just...shouldn't something more be done? I am no military expert, but it sounds as if someone is trying to spark war."

Marko spoke, and she hated how friendly his tone was. "Miss Gabori, we have a long period of floodwaters ahead of us. The Duke's Guard will have their hands full just trying to keep the peace. As much as I want to believe you, and know that part of me does, I can't waste resources on a theory."

He continued to speak with Shadar on strategy as two of the guardsmen came and dragged the unconscious murderer out. Nadya watched, still angry at the Duke's son for his casual dismissal. But she could not really blame him. She hadn't told any of them about the strange man and the black eyes. She peered around at rooftops, wondering if even now he watched.

"Excuse me."

Nadya started and turned. The man Marko called the magistrate was speaking to her.

"I was saying that we had not been properly introduced. My name is Levka Puyatin, magistrate to the Duke. And you are?" His expression was friendly, but something lingered underneath.

"Nadezhda Gabori. I...um..."

"A Nomori truthteller. Yes, well, on behalf of the Duke, I thank you for your work here tonight." He patted her arm. Nadya resisted the urge to flinch.

She managed a quick smile and turned to go. She kept her eyes on the ground, but she heard her grandmother's mutter. "Work of one of the *nivasi*."

When Nadya dared look up, Drina's eyes were hard, staring at the corpse of her old friend. Nadya wanted to ask, though she couldn't. What were the *nivasi*, and why did they scare her grandmother, the most fearless person she knew? Why did it bring chills to Nadya's chest that had nothing to do with the damp of the night?

CHAPTER TEN

If Lord Marko and her father weren't going to look into the murders much further, then Nadya resolved to do so herself. She already knew something they did not: the seamless black eyes that tied Duren to the Nomori man who blew up the theater. If she had anything to wager, she would bet the Erevan scum who murdered Jastima also had those eyes when he did it. There were plenty of puzzle pieces still missing, however. She hoped she might find one or two more in the Guardhouse.

Early the next morning, Nadya and her father left their home and began the trek up through the city to the palace with tired circles around their eyes. He had his duties to attend to, magnified as they were because of the storm. Storm's Quarry now sat like a rock in a bowl full of water. Outside the tightly shut gates and the fifty pace wall that surrounded everything, thirty paces of water lapped against the stone. More was added to it every moment by the steam pumps, continuously working to rid the city of the last of the rainwater.

Kesali predicted all that water would be gone in two months, Nadya thought as they passed the first ration line. *I hope she's right.* For the first time since their kiss and the announcement of the betrothal, the thought of Kesali did not squeeze her lungs, robbing her of all but the most painful of breaths. Duty was something the Nomori were ingrained with, and now Nadya could not be more grateful for it. With Storm's Quarry in danger, duty must come first, and that numbed her heart, at least a little bit.

Nadya had convinced her father to let her come, hoping to speak to one of the prisoners that was being held there. With Mirela in the care of one of their neighbors, he reluctantly agreed.

They dodged Erevan traffic as they made their way through the narrow streets of the second tier, heading toward the stairs that would eventually take them to the palace. There were few people about. Erevans stumbled in and out of alehouses. They didn't have money to spend and the barkeeps watered the beer, but food was already getting scarce and there was no work to be had. Nadya kept a wary eye on every man who passed them, but Shadar's uniform limited any harassment to cursing and spittle.

As they rounded a sharp turn, the thin predawn crowds turned into a roaring wave of flesh. Hundreds filled the streets. Nadya stopped. *Where did all these people come from?* Shadar grabbed her shoulder, pushing her behind him. He drew his rapier.

The putrid scent of sweat hung thick in the air as more bodies crowded into the narrow street. Nadya held her stance firm and held on to her father's free arm to keep them both from being bowled over. Men pushed past them, men with wild eyes; Nomori men, she realized with a sick feeling.

There was no reason for this many Nomori to be in the second tier, in a district such as this one. No reason, except the news of Jastima's death that had spread like disease throughout the Nomori tier. And angry and frustrated from the storm, they had come for justice.

Glass shattered as fire billowed out the second-story windows of one of the buildings bordering the streets. The crowd cheered. One shout could be heard above the rest: *Avenge the Nomori blood that has been spilled!*

More fire licked the walls of the building—the most popular alehouse on the second tier. Screams of an entirely different nature came through the windows intertwined with smoke.

"Nadya, get out of here," Shadar ordered. He waded into the sea of angry Nomori men, rapier held aloft. Nadya put a hand to her belt pouch, reaching for a cloak that wasn't there.

She cursed. How was she to do anything without her disguise? Vowing never to leave home without it again, Nadya followed her father. She kept her head down. Several Nomori men made a move to intercept Shadar. She grabbed the backs of their vests and yanked.

She couldn't see what was happening. Bodies pressed in around her, and smoke hung just above the crowd. She shoved through the Nomori rioters, spotted a one-story bathhouse that smelled of piss, and leapt. Her boots hit the roof hard. Nadya turned, and she had an unobstructed view of the street below.

Nomori men hurled rocks and garbage into the windows of the rundown alehouses that lined the street. Any Erevans, drunk or sober, who were unfortunate enough to be caught in the riot were downed and beaten within seconds. Nadya saw one Erevan pull a pistol, but before she could jump down to stop him, the nearest Nomori caught his arm, wrenched it down. The pistol dropped from paralyzed fingers, and the Nomori caught it. In the same fluid motion, he brought it up and fired between the drunk's eyes.

Blood blew out the back of the drunk's head, spattering those who stood behind him with a crimson rain.

Nadya turned away. Her stomach churned as she tried to form a plan. How was she, without a disguise to hide behind, to stop this madness before it became a bloodbath?

A low pounding underscored the gleeful shouts of the Nomori men, finally getting back at those who had ill-treated them for so long. It grew louder. Nadya looked up from the riot.

Hundreds of Erevans ran through the narrow streets straight at the crowd. They carried makeshift weaponry and old muskets. More came out of buildings, joining in to expel the Nomori from their tier. Some of the Nomori turned from their assault on the alehouse to ready themselves to face the oncoming tide of fighters.

Nadya froze. She did not know what to do, and doubt tore at her like a wild animal.

Over the angry shouts of both sides, she heard her father yelling to the pitifully few others wearing the uniform of the Duke's Guard. "Keep them apart!" he shouted, thrusting his rapier toward the empty stretch of street poised to become a bloody battleground as he shoved men aside to reach it. The other guardsmen did the same.

As the Erevans rushed in toward the Nomori, a thin line of the Duke's Guard held the two races apart. They held firm—the Nomori guardsmen with rapiers and the Erevans with barrels of muskets—as Shadar yelled for order.

Nadya leapt off the roof and into the fray. She shoved through the sea of bodies until the red uniforms came in sight. Careful to stay away from her father, she joined the guardsmen in pushing the two sides apart.

It was not easy. The Erevans were filled with drunken anger and cared little for their lives. The innate fighting skill of the Nomori made them much more formidable opponents, even for their own kind in the Guard. Nadya was soon out of breath as she ducked swings and retaliated with restrained blows to slowly push the Nomori back. Behind her, Erevan guardsmen did the same for the other side.

Two men converged on Nadya, intent on breaking through to get revenge for Jastima's death. She ducked the first punch. The second man's fist hit her in the stomach. He gasped and recoiled, rubbing his knuckles. She dove between them, grabbed the first man's arm, and wrenched him off balance. He fell. Nadya whirled around, blocking a blow to her head with her arm. Her other fist came up and hit the Nomori man squarely in the chest. He flew backward and disappeared in the chaos.

"Have you no respect for Jastima's memory? Will you lie down as a dog while these barbarians slaughter us in our beds?"

A guardsman and a rioter, two Nomori men, rapier poised against a long piece of wood, faced each other not far from Nadya. The one who had spoken parried the guardsman's rapier and swung down at his head. The guardsman brought his weapon up. Their faces were close enough to taste each other's breath.

"We are the barbarians if this madness is the legacy of the Nomori," the guardsman said.

Their weapons flashed again, and soon their fight was lost in the pandemonium of the riot.

Nadya drew a ragged breath. She caught a Nomori man who had broken through the line of guardsmen with one hand, and pushed him into the cobblestones. She wiped smoke from her eyes with grimy hands. This could not continue. The Duke's Guard was barely holding back a slaughter. Someone had to end this.

"Enough!" Her father's shout echoed off the walls of alehouses and up and down the narrow street. He stood on the roof of the building opposite from where Nadya had surveyed the scene, rapier at his side. Blood streaked across his face, but his stance gave him the power to grab the attention of the rioters.

The action at the frontlines slowly came to a halt. Hundreds of eyes turn to Shadar, anger in their tired depths. He returned the stares. His eyes swept over the rioters, seemingly staring into the soul of everyone there. Nadya ducked when he turned to where she stood.

"Under the Duke's rule, this city will not succumb to blood-letting and mayhem. It is over."

Angry murmurs turned into shouts up at him. Shadar dodged a few rocks that were thrown, and leapt down. He landed hard, grimacing. Slowly, he paced the neutral ground the Duke's Guard had cleared. Nadya readied herself. The instant he was in trouble, she would act.

"You Nomori scum came into our tier and starting looting and killing. We were protecting our own," one man yelled. When Shadar turned to look at him, a group of Erevans closed in around their fellow, protecting him from her father's wrath.

"And the matriarch of a proud Nomori family was murdered last night." He turned and looked at his own people. "There cannot be blood for blood here. If Storm's Quarry is to survive these floodwaters, there must be peace. Attacking a citizen of this city, Erevan or Nomori, is against the Duke's law. And any who break that law will face the Guard and the Duke's justice." He looked to the rest of his men. "Round them up for processing."

"We're not going anywhere with one of your kind." An Erevan pushed through the crowd. Five others followed him, forcing their way past the Erevan contingent of the Duke's Guard, who immediately aimed their muskets at them.

Shadar shook his head, and they lowered their weapons. Nadya bit her lip. What was her father doing? The Nomori looters watched silently from behind the barricade. Some bore small smiles.

"If you have a grievance, bring it to the Duke's open session this week. Until then, you will follow my orders," he told the Erevan who challenged him.

"Your Nomori witches have the Duke in their grasp. He's a puppet, nothing more," the man spat. His group moved until they completely circled around.

Shadar reached up and wiped his cheek. When he spoke again, it was in the low tone that had always frightened Nadya when she was a child. "You have insulted my Duke, to whom I have sworn loyalty. Watch your next words carefully." He looked around at the five other men who encircled him. "Get back in line. You'll regret it if you do not."

Their leader smiled. "Nomori scum don't know the meaning of loyalty." He swung his fist at Shadar's head.

Nadya cried out. The man was even taller than her father, and Shadar was outnumbered, six to one. But he had ordered the other guardsmen off, and none of the Nomori made a move to help him. She took a step forward, but one of her father's men stopped her. He did not seem to recognize her as he said, "Wait, child, and watch."

He was right.

Clearly, these men had never faced a Nomori swordfighter in his prime. Her father might have been forty-three, but he was still in top fighting shape.

Faster than Nadya could have thought, he dodged the fist, coming up around and grabbing the man's arm. In a swift movement, he used the man's own momentum to flip his upside down and bury his face in the dirt.

Two other men rushed him. Shadar waited for them. He ducked their blows, and then sank a fist into each of their stomachs. Wheezing, they crumpled to the ground.

He did not wait for the final three men to attack. Leaping into the air, he smacked one in the chest with a solid kick. His fists took out the remaining two, and suddenly her father was surrounded by six moaning forms on the ground. He straightened his uniform and looked up at all those who watched him. He said nothing, but the message was clear.

"Show-off," Nadya muttered, but a weight fell from her shoulders.

Shadar looked down at them. In one quick movement, he drew his rapier and touched it to the nose of the man who'd instigated it all. "I had the right to kill you in that fight. I spared you out of pity for your stupidity. You will join the rest of those here, both Erevan and Nomori, who believe that fear and death are suitable ways to get what you want." He sheathed his blade and stepped out of the ring of groaning bodies.

"The Duke's Guard will regret this day!" The shout came from the rooftop where Nadya had stood. A figure in ratty clothing balanced on the edge, his voice carrying over all who were present. Nadya frowned. She recognized the Erevan man—he had been the zealot at the market, preaching the wrath of the storm gods.

The zealot continued, "This is proof of the darkness that has festered in Storm's Quarry. Blood will rain down upon you. Nomori filth has infiltrated the once-proud Guard, and the storm gods will purge it with fire. The Guard will burn!"

Shadar shook his head. He looked at a nearby guardsman, saying, "Get him down from there. We have no need to listen to the empty threats of a madman."

A horn split the air. Reinforcements from the Duke's Guard streamed in, cutting off both sides from escape. Shadar barked orders at other red-uniformed men. The riot was slowly diffused as arrests were made. The zealot disappeared before anyone could lay a hand on him.

Nadya ducked the outreached arm of a guardsman and sprinted down an alley. She would go home, as Shadar had asked her to before the entire mess started. As she ran, her mind replayed his fight with the six men. He could have killed them, even with his rapier sheathed, but he was in control of every move he made. She wished she could do that.

She wished she could ask him to train her as he trained Lord Marko.

CHAPTER ELEVEN

The Guardhouse resembled an anthill, red uniforms skitter-ing around in the aftermath of the second tier riot. Nearly one hundred men, Nomori and Erevan, were brought up for processing. More were sent directly to the prison on the bottom tier. Shadar hadn't stopped bellowing orders since it happened, and Nadya was grateful when she could finally slip away. She sneaked into a nearby corridor. Keeping her head down, she went down the hall to the stairs that led to the holding cells below. She had made a trip back to her house to pick it up her cloak before meeting her father here. The riot reminded her not to go anywhere without it.

Most of the guardsmen she hurried past didn't even glance at her. With each step, she grew more confident, and the images of being strung up in a cell faded.

"Business here, miss?"

She tripped to a stop, biting back a curse. A lone guardsman stood at the head of the cellblock. Thankfully, he was Nomori. She put on what she hoped looked like a shy smile.

"Running an errand for my father. He's got me sprinting all over this rat maze."

He stared at her for a moment before his eyebrows shot up. "You're the captain's daughter?"

Nadya bowed her head. "Yes, sir. Nadya. Pleased to meet you."

"Private Ferka. It sure must be busy for him to send his daughter all the way down here."

"Well, you heard about all the rioting this afternoon. I suspect he'll be here the night. He and Mother have started lecturing me on taking more responsibility for the family and all, so I guess this is just one of the ways I'm to do it."

"Well, I suppose it's fine then." Private Ferka stepped aside. "Just be quick now. The captain does not like to be kept waiting."

"Yes, sir." Nadya almost melted with relief when she walked past him and into the short row of cells where those awaiting trial were kept. Most were bare. It smelled musky down here, with a pungent undertone that made her wonder if some poor animal had crawled in one of the vents and died.

She found Duren in the last cell. A few innocent questions to her father over the past days confirmed he had not yet been executed. The former personal guard to Jurek looked like the life had been leeched out of him. He stared at her with wide bloodshot eyes. His cheekbones looked sharp enough to cut. When he spoke, his voice cracked. "Shadar's daughter...Nadya, right?"

She swallowed and nodded.

"What poor fate has led you down here?"

There was little point in hiding anything. If Duren were to speak of it to anyone, she could always deny it. "I need some answers about the night your master was murdered," she said quietly, hoping Private Ferka would not be able to hear.

Duren's half smile faded. "Go home, girl. This is not a place for you."

Nadya stepped closer to the bars. "I know you are innocent."

"Try convincing anyone else of that. You had your chance, too."

The words stung. "I am trying now." She took a deep breath. "I saw you that night. I know someone else was there."

"In the middle of the night in the fourth tier?" Duren snorted. "I've a hard time believing that."

"Something happened to you. Something strange, something you cannot explain. Whatever it was, it was the last thing you remembered before waking up with your master's blood on your clothes."

"How do you know that?" Duren whispered.

She wasn't about to tell him of the black eyes that linked him and the other Nomori murderer. "Tell me about it."

"It...it was darkness. I can remember turning around to see Master Jurek's guest, a man I saw little of and knew littler about. Then there was darkness. I felt..." He shivered. "Every terrible thing I have done played through me. Like a weight. The darkness held me down. When I awoke, I remembered nothing else. It must have been me who killed him, but I cannot remember making the killing blow." Duren looked up at her. "Does that give you what you seek?"

"Thank you. I can't guarantee your freedom," Nadya said truthfully. "Not many will listen."

"I don't expect anything of the sort." Duren stood up and came to the bars. He stared right into Nadya's eyes, and she struggled to hold his hollow gaze. "I heard about the theater, about Jastima. Stop it, if you can. That's all I ask."

Nadya gulped. "I'll try."

He returned to his bench. She stayed another moment before leaving. Nadya knew she would not see Duren again. He had survived this long because of the storm. Soon, though, the formalities would be finished, and he would be executed.

His words confirmed what her grandmother said. There was someone with strange abilities at the heart of this, and the *nivasi* Drina had spoken of had something to do with it, she was sure.

"Miss Gabori," Marko stammered as he nearly walked into her in the hall. He recovered and straightened his tunic. "What are you doing here?"

"My father, I was visiting him. I wanted to make sure he was all right." The lie came easily.

"I met with him not an hour ago. You should know by now, Miss Gabori, that it will take more than a handful of drunken rioters to hurt your father. I still have bruises from our training sessions to prove it." The bit of humor didn't reach the fatigue in his eyes.

"I supposed that's true," she said, looking at her boots.

Marko gestured down the hall. "Walk with me, Miss Gabori?"

"Nadya," she corrected automatically as they headed toward the front doors of the headquarters. As if he were her friend, not the heir to Storm's Quarry and not the one who was taking Kesali away. When he looked at her, she blushed. "I'm not a *miss* of anything, milord. Just Nadya is fine."

"Well, then, just Marko is fine, too."

"But you're the Duke's son."

"And you're Kesali's friend."

Kesali's friend. *Yes, and you're her betrothed.* She bit the words back, and they tasted like sea salt.

"Besides, we are in the trenches together now, trying to keep this city safe. I think we've earned the right to call each other by our first names." He stopped, his smile uncertain. "Unless you're uncomfortable with it."

Nadya paused, wondering what would come if she voiced the thoughts running through her mind, the thoughts of Kesali, of their kiss, of the harsh glow of Kesali's betrothal necklace. Finally, she shook her head. "No...Marko." She forced a lighthearted tone. "Although, the same does not apply to my grandmother. Call her by her first name, and I won't be able to save you."

He actually laughed this time, and she caught the sparkle in his eyes, the way his posture relaxed just a bit, lifting the weight of the city's future from his shoulders for a moment. Nadya swallowed hard. He was as tied by duty as Kesali was, as she was. Try as hard as she might, in that moment Nadya could not bring herself to hate the Duke's son.

They walked in silence for a bit, before Nadya stopped. She tilted her head, listening to the faints shouts that were growing louder by the moment. Masses of voices seemed to be heading toward the Guardhouse.

"Is something wrong?" Marko asked.

Before she could answer, two guardsmen sprinted through the double doors and skidded to a halt in front of them. They bowed. "Lord Marko," one said, breathlessly, "there's a mob coming straight for us. A thousand souls at least, gaining more every moment. Most of our men are out on patrol. I've called the Guard in, but it'll take time."

Nadya watched as Marko's face flashed with emotion. Her own chest filled with squirming snakes. So soon after the afternoon's riot?

Things were escalating in the city. Marko stared down at the floor, then looked up and all that was written on his features was cool command. "Get everyone who is here outside. Maintain a perimeter around the headquarters. Do not attack unless provoked. I'll try to reason with them."

They bowed again and ran off.

Marko sprinted toward the exit, Nadya carefully at his heels. He flung open the doors and they both saw the encroaching mass of people carrying torches, rifles, and crude homemade weaponry. The Duke's son let out a stream of curses. He turned to her. "You need to get somewhere safe. I cannot spare any men to take you home. Go—"

An explosion cut him off.

She hit the wall of the headquarters hard as the ground trembled. The thunderous noise raked across her ears. Nadya covered them, eyes squeezed shut, until a hand touched her arm.

She jerked, and Marko jumped back. "Sorry. Are you all right?"

Her ears throbbed, but she said, "Yes. How did they—?"

Another explosion rocked the street, more violent than the first.

Nadya slammed into the wall, and several chunks of brick broke loose. Her ears shrieked, and when she put a hand to one, her fingers came away dipped in blood.

She coughed. The air was now smoke, tinged with fire. Her eyes watered as she tried to peer through the gray to see what had happened.

A moan came from fifteen paces away, and with a start, she realized it was Marko. She ran to him and pulled him up. He seemed shaky, but he gave her a grateful nod. Blood dripped from a cut above his eyes.

"What was that?" Nadya said again. Her voice sounded faint and far away. She turned around and saw the smoke rising out the windows of the headquarters. Flames licked at its stone foundations. Her chest went cold. *The Guard will burn,* the zealot had said.

"Gunpowder. A lot of gunpowder." Marko frowned. "How in the gods' name did a mob obtain it?"

A guardsman hurried over, despite a pronounced limp. He saluted Marko, then said, "They're attacking the other side of the building. We're holding them off, but unless you give the order to kill, we won't be able to do so for long."

The blood left Marko's face. "Why? Who? Do they have a purpose? Do they want something?"

"Citizens, Erevan." The guardsman, who was also Erevan, made a disgusted face. "They were protesting our inclusion of Nomori, saying the Nomori guardsmen let their kin get away with murdering us today. One man showed up and starting shouting about killing all the Nomori, and it got violent. Don't know how they got ahold of the explosives. Right now, the crowds are out of control. Dozens of men are trapped inside, and the building's aflame. A call's been put in for the fire patrol. We're trying to reach them, but we have to keep the crowd from killing us."

Her father was in there. The realization was a bucket of ice water over her head. Nadya's hands turned to fists as Marko issued orders she didn't hear. Shadar had been reporting in to the Guardmaster before being relieved of duty for the day.

Marko grabbed her. "Nadya, get to safety. You need to leave—"

She wrenched her arm away. "I've got to go." She took off sprinting so fast that no one would be able to follow her.

It was her father trapped in there, and she could not let anything happen to him.

Even if it meant revealing her abilities.

She ducked into a culvert alley between two storehouses. Her belt pouch was torn as she frantically ripped out the cloak. It swirled around her shoulder, and she fastened the scarf across her face. The fabric smelled terrible, like damp and fish, but it kept out the worst of the smoke.

She gripped the edges of stones and climbed up the side of the building. Her fingers dug into the cement between the stones, chipping it. She climbed faster. Her ears throbbed, masking the sounds of what was going on. Between the loss of hearing and the endless smoke, Nadya felt blind.

She crawled onto the flat roof and stood, shakily. To the east, the three-story building that housed the headquarters of the city's guard was in ruins. Its stone walls had crumbled in places, and smoke billowed out the gaps, escaping the golden and ruby flames that licked hungrily at the edges. Shadows of hundreds of people moved under the smoke. She spotted several crimson uniforms trying to restrain the masses. Others, blackened, dove into the headquarters and emerged, hacking their lungs out, with comrades over their shoulders.

Nadya could not see her father.

She made sure her scarf was fastened tightly, touched her seal and sent a prayer to the Protectress, hoping that this once she might answer, and jumped. She sailed over the crowd and the guard and landed on the crumbling roof.

Nadya yelped as the stone gave way and she dropped into the building, followed by a sizable chunk of the roof. Rubble filled the air and streamed out the windows and gaping holes in the stone. Flames roared underneath her feet and smoke encircled her throat. Nadya kept her breaths short and fast. The heat didn't bother her much, and her cloak was fire resistant. She gathered it around her and began looking.

This eerie hell no longer looked like a building. Stones glowed cherry red as flames licked at them. The wooden planks over the dirt floor were all but gone, reduced to sinister piles of ash. Smoke formed phantoms that darted around corners, taunting Nadya into thinking she saw a person. She dashed through what remained of a doorway. This room looked like it could have been an office. A wooden table sat in the center, looking as if it had been dipped in liquid flame. All around it, the remains of books clattered off burning shelves.

She turned, an arm over her mouth, but a whimper came through the wreckage. Her father's name was on her lips, but she stopped herself. If it was her father, he couldn't know who it was wearing this gray disguise, standing in fire without being burned.

She rushed over to the remains of the desk. A form moved under fallen debris. She lifted a piece of wooden ceiling support off of him, and turned him over.

It wasn't her father, but Nadya didn't hesitate. She lifted him up and threw him over her shoulder. Carrying him was awkward, since he was two heads taller than her, but she grunted and maneuvered his body on her shoulder so she could walk.

She moved as fast as she could, back the way she'd come. As she raced under the doorway, the stone above her collapsed. Nadya swore and dropped the man, shielding him with her body. Stones hit her back, red hot from the fire. She screamed and heaved upward, and the stone clattered to the ground.

Her back ached, but she hoisted the man up again and continued. He wouldn't survive for long, breathing in the smoke. Nadya trudged through the wreckage as fast as she dared until she tasted damp air. It still stung her lungs with smoke, but the cloying heat was gone, and Nadya dropped to her knees. She dragged the man off her back as gently as she could, and laid him down on the cobblestones.

"The Guardmaster," someone nearby shouted.

Nadya blinked. She was surrounded by crimson uniforms. One bent down to check the pulse of the man she had rescued. She searched for her father, but he wasn't there. Just beyond them, a line of guardsmen tried to push back the mass of the mob. Shouts and screams filled the courtyard, as thick as the smoke.

"Who are you?" one asked, but she was already up and running back into the building. Both the guardsmen and her back protested, but she thought of her father, and that made her legs go.

"Let him go," another voice said. "Maybe he can save some of them. It's too dangerous for the likes of us."

He wasn't wrong, Nadya thought as she plunged through the gaping stones, nearly tripping on the loose ones on the ground, and back into the inferno. Heat twisted around her lungs, but she ignored it and followed the faint cries she heard.

The man it led her to was not her father, but a boy not much older than her. He was unconscious, with blood dripping down a wound in his head. She thought he was dead for a moment, until a faint pulse beat under her searching fingers.

The men outside ran over when she brought him out. They were coughing, their uniforms blackened. Nadya realized the healthy ones had all been dispatched to the front line of the protests. One of the men nodded at her, then took the youth and started pumping his chest to get him breathing again.

Nadya dove back into the flames. She was not the only one. The city's fire patrol had arrived, grim-faced citizens wearing blue fireproof suits. Some created a chain of buckets from the nearest well to try to douse the flames. Others followed her example and looked for survivors in the building.

Ignoring them, Nadya searched through the entire building, going painstakingly slow. She didn't find her father, but she pulled out half a dozen men. One of them was Duren. His cell door was white-hot by the time she reached it. She tugged it free, burning her hands. He gave her a long look before letting her carry him out through the flames.

The fire had grown so hot that now she was finding bodies instead of men. No normal person would be able to survive the flames for more than a few moments, and those men were smart enough not to try. Even the men of the fire patrol had given up their searches and instead doubled the efforts on the bucket chain.

She jumped down through a flame-ringed hole in the floor to the basement. Remains of bunks tottered on flamed-consumed supports and crashed in front of her, sending flames shooting up through the ceiling. Nadya leapt back. She might be more protected than most, but even she couldn't stand in the middle of a fire and be immune to its effects.

There was rustling to her left, and Nadya whirled around, expecting to see another form lying prone on the ground.

It was her father.

They stared at each other. Nadya's limbs froze. She wanted to reach up to check to see if the scarf still covered her face, but she couldn't move. Shadar's face was blackened under the scrap of cloth he had bound around his mouth. Blisters covered his hands. He turned from the wall of rubble he'd been trying to tear through.

The basement was silent but for the crackling of fire. In the quiet, Nadya heard scraping. She winced. It sounded like fingernails against stone, coming from behind the wall of rubble.

"What are you doing here?" her father snapped. "It's not safe. Get out of here!"

With a pang of pride, she realized her father was helping to get his comrades out despite the danger. That broke through her paralysis. She rushed over to the wall. Shadar put a hand out to stop her, but she brushed past it easily.

She put an ear up to the rubble.

"What do you think—"

Nadya drew back and slammed her fist into the mix of stones and wood and char. It went through. She opened her hand, yanked it back, bringing half the wall down with her. Shadar's voice faded when he saw her drag the body of a man, still alive, from behind the rubble. He narrowed his eyes, but remained silent.

The building creaked. The fire was eating away at its supports. It wouldn't be long before the entire thing collapsed. She dodged a piece of stone that fell from the ceiling. The stairs had long deteriorated under flame.

Nadya crouched down, securing the man over her shoulders, and leapt. The back of her neck slammed into the ceiling of the second floor, but she came down on stone. The entire building shook with the impact, more rocks crumbling from the floor, falling to the basement.

She dropped the man and looked down for her father. He was tight up against the basement wall, away from the collapsing ceiling. She glanced back at the injured guard, then knelt on the hot floor and stretched her hand down. Her bronze skin, untarnished by flame, shone in the flickering light.

Shadar's mouth opened, and for a terrible moment, Nadya thought he was going to refuse her help. Then, with a limping run, he launched himself in the air.

His fingers brushed hers, and she grabbed him, hauling him up with one hand.

Shadar dropped her grip as soon as he found himself on the first floor. His gaze hadn't displayed any trust. Nadya took the injured man back onto her shoulder. He was coughing up blood and needed to get out of the building.

She pushed through the remains of walls and stairs, her father not two steps behind her. Nadya almost cried when a cool, damp breeze washed over her.

The wounded guardsman was wrenched from her grasp, and Shadar rushed toward his comrades, ignoring his limp and a blistering burn that raced up his left leg. She was too tired to protest, but seeing her father alive filled her with relief. Nadya wanted to sink to the ground and tear off the oppressively hot cloak, but several slightly wounded members of the Duke's Guard watched her closely with suspicion.

She gulped. She needed to get out of there before anyone started asking questions.

Shouts broke through her fatigue, and Nadya realized, as the damp air dispersed the smoke and the headquarters collapsed behind her, that she recognized the voices. One belonged to Lord Marko, barely restraining fury. The other belonged to the zealot.

Nadya blinked through the smoke. Marko, flanked by red uniforms, stood before the zealot, who wore a filthy tunic. He had over a thousand men at his back, all riled up and thirsty for blood. Only the guardsmen kept it from becoming a complete bloodbath.

"Your captain should have listened down in the second tier. The Duke's Guard has fallen to the Nomori, *milord*," the zealot spat, the title an insult. "Those animals have allowed their own kind to kill indiscriminately, and the Guard does nothing." At his words, the crowd roared.

A trail of dried blood ran down the Duke's son's forehead, but his voice was strong. "That is nothing but a fantasy intended to stir up a crowd. Those who started the riot today are being held in the prison. You have gone beyond a simple protest, zealot. People have died. Erevan and Nomori. My Guard. You will pay for this."

The crowd behind the zealot roared to a fury when two of the Guard approached to arrest him. "You have no proof that was my doing, princeling. The storm gods are angry. They have shown their power, and it will only get worse unless the city is returned to them." He pointed at Marko, who raised a hand to stop his guardsmen. "Marko Isyanov, I give you the ultimatum of the storm gods. If the sea has not receded by the solstice, as your witch has predicted, the storm gods demand her as a sacrifice. Only then, will our city be freed."

Marko took a step back.

"Arrest me. Kill me, even, but you will not stop those who are loyal to our gods, to Storm's Quarry." The zealot turned and was swallowed up by the crowd. The guardsmen tried to force their way after him, but the sheer number of bodies repelled them.

Nadya sank to her knees. She watched with numb limbs as Marko stumbled back to the rest of his guardsmen. His face was white, and his hands trembled. Nadya felt sick. The zealot couldn't be serious. The Erevans didn't believe in their storm gods. They wouldn't kill Kesali.

But if none of them believed, then where did these rioters come from?

"There he is. He came out of nowhere, hiding his face." A harsh voice made Nadya look up.

She was surrounded, and none of the faces showed gratitude. One man said, "Remove your mask, Nomori."

Me? She wanted to shriek in their faces. *That man just threatened the life of Kesali, and you want to harass me for saving your comrades?* But she bit back her anger and slowly rose until she crouched on the balls of her feet.

"Take off that scarf," Shadar ordered.

She couldn't look at him. Nadya put all the strength she had left into her tired legs and leapt. She soared over their heads, and several pistol shots echoed behind her. She hit the side of a nearby manor, shattering stone. Her bloody hands clung to the side, and Nadya pulled herself up.

She made the mistake of looking back once. Shadar's rapier was pointed up at her, and behind him, Marko stood silently, all color and hope drained from his face.

CHAPTER TWELVE

Nadya didn't care if anyone saw her. She bounded from roof to roof, carrying the sickly smell of smoke with her. Hot wind rushed past her. The buildings disappeared into a blur of gray underneath her as tears streamed across her face.

Her father was alive and safe, and that was all that should matter. But the weight of the zealot's ultimatum pulled her downward, threatening to crush her. The pain of Kesali's betrothal paled against this. That had twisted her insides, but the zealot's words turned her limbs to stone and swept her down into a Great Storm of her own. She drowned as she fled toward home.

If she had any doubts that the betrothal would change her feelings toward Kesali, for good or ill, they vanished.

With a grunt, she leapt over the white marble wall separating the second tier from the Nomori tier. Nadya landed with a thud on the roof of the bathhouse. Her hands slipped in beads of moistures as she slid down its wall. When her boots touched the ground in the culvert alley, she tore off her cloak.

She sprinted through the streets with it clutched under one arm. She wanted to throw it away, but Nadya knew with cold, gut-clenching reality that she'd need it again before the sea receded.

This neighborhood of the Nomori tier was quiet, unusually quiet. Wives and mothers peered out of doors, waiting for their husbands and sons to come home from the Guard, watching the smoke rise from the other side of the city.

She stopped in front of her house, breathing heavily. Gripping her cloak, she went into the culvert alley and began climbing the outside wall. There was a small gap between the wall and roof, and Nadya shoved her cloak in.

When she opened the door, Mirela rushed up to her. "Are you all right? Where is your father? I saw—"

"He's alive. He will be fine," Nadya said hoarsely. Her throat burned from the smoke, but she did not dare let on. "The Guardhouse was attacked by a mob. Some were killed. I don't know how many."

Mirela hugged her, whispering, "I feared the worst. The Protectress truly was watching over you." She stepped away and pulled a cloak from its peg on the wall. "I must go and tell the others. They need to know what happened." She paused, eyes roving over Nadya.

She tucked her burn-covered hands behind her back. "Go. I will be fine." Nadya managed a smile as her mother gave her a quick kiss on the cheek before rushing out. She stood there for a long moment in the empty house. Then she walked over to their barrel of boiled water and ladled some into a bowl. Soaking her hands into it, she sighed. What she had done was stupid and dangerous, but she could not be gladder she'd made the choice.

Nadya had bandaged up the burns and was sitting up in her loft by the time her mother returned a few hours later, coughing. Not ten minutes later, her father walked through the door. He dropped his soot-covered jacket on the floor without a word.

"Welcome home," Mirela said, embracing him.

Nadya bounded off her ledge. "Papa!" She joined them both. Her father smelled of ash and sweat, and though he managed a weary smile, it didn't reach the grimness in his eyes.

Within a few minutes, Nadya had a new pot of tea on, and Shadar was seated on the floor cushions, sipping a glass of water. He kept shaking his head. "I thought I knew this city. I was sorely mistaken."

"Surely it's nothing but the fear of the floodwaters," Mirela said, stroking his arm. "Two months is a long time for our city to be shut down. People are scared that food will run out, nothing more."

"It is not fear that demanded the head of the Stormspeaker," Shadar said. "And it's not fear that killed sixteen of my men. It was pure evil. It has festered here for twenty years, and now the floodwaters provide a rich breeding ground."

"More good than bad has come of our people entering Storm's Quarry. I have to believe that."

"I fear that good is about to be undone." Shadar thanked Nadya with a nod as she handed him a cup of hot tea. "First a murder that solved itself, yet I still cannot explain it. Then a suicide bomber at the theater. More murder. Riots. An attack on the very headquarters of the city's military force. And now a masked man with the strength of twenty men leaping across rooftops."

Nadya felt very odd. She stood quietly to one side as her parents spoke, not really sure what to add to the conversation. When her father called her a man, relief whooshed through her. He hadn't recognized her, and with the image of the cloaked figure as a man planted in his mind, it was likely he wouldn't see the truth unless she revealed herself.

"What? Nadya didn't mention that," Mirela said. "How is that possible?"

"I don't know. All I do know is that he very probably saved my life and the lives of half a dozen guardsmen. But it was like something I had never seen before. He wore a cloak, hood, and a mask across his face, all gray. He walked through fire as if it were only fog."

Maybe it looked that way, Nadya thought as she glanced down at her wrapped hands. But it certainly wasn't a stroll down to the square.

"He lifted me up with only a hand. Hit through solid brick. Mirela, it was nothing of this world."

"Was he Nomori?" Mirela asked.

"I believe so, though I couldn't be sure with the smoke."

Nadya's chest buzzed so hard she thought it might explode. Now she would have to watch herself even more. Perhaps forgo her nightly escapades altogether. Her parents might not suspect her, but they now knew there was someone like her out there, and

Nadya needed to distance herself as much as possible from the gray-cloaked figure.

"Well," Mirela said after they were both silent for a while, "at least he appears to be on your side. He saved lives, and for that I could not be more thankful to him."

Nadya's face grew warm and she looked down. It had been some time since she'd heard her mother speak like that about her.

But Shadar grabbed Mirela's hand. "Don't be so quick to hand him a hero's crown."

"What?" Nadya said before she could stop herself.

"I know you want to give this man praise, and perhaps he does deserve it. But temper your gratitude. A man of that power can only mean bad things for our city."

"But he helped you," Nadya protested. Her throat had gone dry. "Papa, he saved your life!"

"And he is out of my control, and the control of the Duke. It doesn't matter whether he means good or ill. He's like a storm, a Great Storm, every bit as dangerous as that zealot."

Nadya could not reply. Her lungs felt deflated, like a rock sat her on chest slowly forcing the air out of them. She was not like the zealot. She would never...*I'd die before putting Kesali in danger,* she swore to herself. It didn't matter how angry she got at the Stormspeaker. *I will die first.*

"I need to take a walk," Nadya said finally. When her parents started to protest, she added, "Don't worry, I'll stay within the block. I just need some air."

Shadar nodded. "Return home the instant there is any trouble."

After leaving her house, Nadya struck out at a fast pace down the street. The damp air had little effect on soothing her nerves. She passed more than one home with the door bolted and windows nailed shut. The entire tier had a distinctly unfriendly atmosphere. The few people who walked the streets kept their heads down, their hands close by their sides.

The attack on the Guardhouse sent a message loud and clear to the city, one that could not be overwhelmed by the Duke's reassurances. *If we can do this to the military stronghold of the city, think of what we can do to you.*

Nadya imagined it would only get worse as the solstice drew near and the city's resources dwindled.

❖

She couldn't be sure where it started, whether a couple of Nomori guardsmen swapping stories on the way to the public bathhouse, or an Erevan guardsmen speaking too loudly after his third glass of ale, but Nadya first heard the name a week after the attack on the Guardhouse, while she was in the market buying ingredients for more soothing tea for her mother. The store was picked over, everything remotely fresh gone from its shelves. Shoppers moved quickly, casting narrow-eyed glances at everyone else as if it was a race to see who would get the last bunch of yellowed carrots. In a few weeks, it very well might be.

For the past week, Nadya had wrestled with herself about visiting Kesali. She was still very angry at her friend for keeping the betrothal from her, for assuming that things could continue the way they were between the two of them. But Kesali had received a very serious death threat, and if Nadya were in her place, she'd want the comfort of her oldest friend.

She could always make the excuse that it was too dangerous to travel to the palace. Small fights, riots, were becoming a daily occurrence. Though none did the damage of the attack on the Guardhouse, the city's hospitals were slowly being overloaded. Few people went far beyond their street without a weapon.

A couple of old Nomori men, retired guardsmen from their stances, stood in one corner of the store, sharing a cup of weak tea. "Haven't caught sight of him since, the lieutenant told me," the taller one was saying.

"Have they set out on a manhunt yet? Can't be too many places in the city for someone like him to hide."

The first man shook his head. "From what I was told, they have more than enough to keep them busy without chasing around some lunatic in a cloak."

Nadya took her change, avoiding the gaze of either man.

"Good. Seems to me they can spend their time fighting the real threats, those filthy Erevans, and let the Iron Phoenix keep saving lives."

The Iron Phoenix? Nadya hesitated, biting her lip. She wanted to ask, but it might look suspicious, so she quickly left the store.

It was not the last time she heard that name.

The railbox she took up to the Guardhouse later that afternoon to bring her father his lunch was full of people chattering about the incident at the Guardhouse—nearly all Erevan, they avoided sitting near her at all costs. But Nadya heard their conversations plain as day. They filled her chest with an odd, sour feeling.

"He has powers no man should possess."

"Of course the freak is Nomori. Ask me, they haven't been honest about just what they're capable of, and this fellow proves it."

"My father was saved by the Iron Phoenix. He said he punched through rock like it was water."

Nadya kept her eyes low and counted her breaths until they reached the top tier of the city.

When she made it to the palace storehouse that was the temporary headquarters of the Duke's Guard, Shadar was not pleased to see her. "Do you realize how dangerous it is now, to be out in the city?" he said as he browsed over forms on his desk.

"Do you want your beef roll or not?" Nadya asked, crossing her arms.

Shadar sighed and took the linen bag from her. "You have too much of your mother in you. Thank you, Nadya." Like the rest of the city, the Guard was tightening its belt, and Shadar always went without rations before his men, preferring to bring his own food over taking it from the depleted stores the Guard had. His other officers did the same.

A smart knock on the door, and a guardsman entered. "Here is the sketch of the Phoenix you wanted. I'm having it printed up and hung around the city, but I'm afraid it won't do a lot of good."

Shadar gave a nod of thanks, and the guardsman left. Nadya caught a glimpse of the paper before he shoved it under the pile. It had a sketch of a figure in a gray cloak, only his eyes visible. She swallowed. It did not look like her, but it also did not overly *not* look like her.

"Phoenix," her father muttered. He riffled through the lunch sack. "The entire city is talking about him. Do you know that they've named that masked man? The Iron Phoenix. Because he wore a gray cloak, and when he jumped away from the flaming Guardhouse, the men said he looked like a great bird who rose out of a blacksmith's fire."

"Oh." Nadya stared at the ground. The Iron Phoenix. It was beautiful, in its way. A good name for a worthy cause. She didn't care what her father said. She wasn't the zealot, and she was not dangerous. She was here to help. If she could not save the city as Nadya Gabori, perhaps she could save it as the Iron Phoenix.

Chapter Thirteen

Nadya had to suspend her nightly runs since the Duke's Guard was out in force. Without those outings, however, the days passed with excruciating slowness. She spent most of her time helping her mother, doing chores around the house, and buying food, which proved more difficult with every passing day. Half the shops in the Nomori tier had already closed their shutters, having no stock to sell.

Her morning walks with Kesali were a thing of the past, of a time when waves did not choke Storm's Quarry and Kesali did not wear Marko's betrothal necklace. Whenever the dull emptiness threatened to overwhelmed her, closing off her throat, she concentrated on the city. Kesali always put the needs of Storm's Quarry first, and now Nadya threw herself into doing the same.

Every morning, she listened for news about the floodwaters. If her father was at home, a rare occurrence these days, he gave her the disappointing update. "The Mark of Recession is still buried far below the waters, too far down for any to see. The waters have yet to lower by a fraction."

The Mark of Recession was a sun chiseled into the outer wall of Storm's Quarry. When the Kyanite Sea went down enough for it to be seen, it was safe to open the gates and resume trade. As the days ticked by, Nadya read in her father's expression what he did not say: if the waters were truly to be gone by the solstice, they should be receding more rapidly.

On the twenty-fourth day of the floodwaters, Nadya cracked her eyes open and yawned. It was barely after dawn. Hot, damp air filled her loft. She sucked in a deep breath and immediately started coughing.

"Oh, good, you're awake. Come down, Nadezhda. We were just talking about you."

Nadya jerked up and hit her head on the slanted ceiling. She was so used to it by now, though, it barely hurt. Donning a vest, she then slipped on the least-wrinkled pair of trousers she had. She suppressed a yawn and slid down the ladder.

Her grandmother was standing there. Nadya suppressed a curse. Early light filtered in from the gap in the stones that served as a window. She blinked at it grumpily. She'd stayed up half the night, thinking about the murders, the mysterious circumstances that connected them, and how she might go about finding the truth behind it all. She came up with little. Nadya still didn't know if the murders were connected to the attack on the Guardhouse.

If not, she thought as she grabbed a stale roll from the pantry, then it was only an aftereffect.

She paused. That hadn't occurred to her in her sleep-addled state. Perhaps it was, and more importantly, perhaps it was the intended effect of the murders: rouse everyone into a violent panic and cause as much chaos as possible.

She frowned and gulped down the roll in two bites. But how were the rioters and the zealot able to get that much gunpowder?

"You look half-asleep," Drina said, rousing Nadya from her ruminations.

"She's had a lot to worry about lately," Mirela said. She smiled at Nadya from where she sat swathed in blankets, drinking from a clay mug. Nadya's nostrils twitched. The drink smelled of the stubborn herbs she'd bought yesterday, the ones that only her grandmother could bend to her will.

"Well, worrying never solved anything." Drina sat herself down on the edge of the pallet.

"How are you doing, Nadya?" her mother asked. "You haven't been yourself lately."

"I'm fine," Nadya mumbled. Her mother was right. She jumped at every mention of the cloaked man, the Iron Phoenix. "How are you?"

Before her mother could answer, Drina broke in. "She's doing better, thanks to some traditional Nomori tea. A cure-all, in my opinion. None of that Erevan physician nonsense."

Nadya forced a smile.

"Well, sit, Nadya. I hope the events of this week didn't scare you too much. Your father is a strong man, you know. He can survive a lot worse than a fire." Drina scowled, massaging the joints in her left hand. Nadya sat on the damp stone obediently. "Erevans can't be patient. No Nomori psychic is ever wrong. The sea will retreat on the day the Stormspeaker predicted."

"Let's not dwell on such thoughts. The sun has made a small appearance today." Mirela gestured to their window. "Dark words have no place when the sun is shining."

Drina snorted. "You inherited your father's optimism, darling. There's enough darkness in this city to reach every crevasse, even down here. Did you know that Iron Phoenix man, he's Nomori?"

Nadya froze, her bread halfway to her mouth and forgotten.

"Shadar did mention something like that. He seems to think the Iron Phoenix is more dangerous than helpful."

Nadya set her bread down. She wasn't hungry anymore.

"I trust that husband of yours in these matters. Any Nomori who hides his face like that is someone who should be treated with the highest suspicion. What is his agenda, hmm?"

"To save those guardsmen," Nadya mumbled.

Drina's iron gaze turned to her. "I think that's a pretty naïve interpretation. How do we know he didn't start the fire in the first place?"

"Mother," Mirela began, "you have no reason to be so harsh."

Nadya's voice betrayed a bit of her anger as, ignoring her mother's words, she said, "Why set a fire just to save its targets? It was the zealot and those rioters who set the fire, and that man was probably just trying to help. He saved Papa, after all. And the Guardmaster." Nadya's voice wavered, but she met her grandmother's eyes.

"No one can know what goes through the mind of his like. The things I've heard about that man." Drina shook her head, and Nadya suddenly remembered those muttered words, *the work of one of the* nivasi. Her hands were ice cold, and she rubbed them, staring at the dirt caked between stone tiles on the floor.

"But since you have so many opinions, perhaps you'd be willing to give them on a different subject." Drina smiled, and that chilled Nadya even more. "I've been talking to the others heads of some good families, nice women all of them, and I have a good selection of their eligible sons and grandsons for you to choose from. You'll need to choose a good husband to carry on your name by your eighteenth birthday. It's not too early to start."

Nadya almost wished they could go back to talking about the Iron Phoenix. "I…I don't know."

"Of course you don't," her grandmother went on, oblivious to the heat that rose in Nadya's face. "You haven't met them yet. I'll set up the first introductions. Don't worry. You'll just go into their homes for a bit. You'll eat a nice meal, and talk to the young men. You won't even have to ask any questions. I've taken care of it all. I know which ones come from good procreating bloodlines—"

"Grandmother!" Nadya said in a strangled voice. The last thing she wanted to think about was the procreating efficiency of a future husband.

"I know how important this is," her mother said. She set down her cup of tea. Some of the color had returned to her cheeks. "But this kind of decision, it shouldn't be made lightly. With all that's happening in the city, shouldn't such things wait? It's only another month until the solstice."

Drina frowned. "Our lives cannot be put on hold for floodwaters or zealots. That's just what they want. She needs to meet all the suitors and carefully consider her choice. This will affect the rest of her life and the future of the family name. It must be made with the utmost care."

"Then why don't you make it yourself," Nadya snapped.

As her grandmother's sharp gaze rounded on her, she immediately wished she'd been able to bite her tongue. "Love can't be factored in here, Nadezhda. Love is for those who will not someday be the head of their family. You need a strong husband to stand beside you. I know you have this little crush on some Nomori boy, but you cannot let that cloud your judgment."

Little crush could not even come close to describing it, and Nadya's anger flared at her feelings being described in such a frivolous way, as if they didn't matter. She stood. "I'm needed at home. Besides, our city is on the brink of civil war. I will not make this decision now. If that's what you want, then you should leave."

Drina's mouth fell open. She struggled to her feet. "How dare you speak to me like that? I will remain here, caring for your mother, because that is a duty you have sorely neglected these pasts months while chasing a boy who will never be your husband."

Guilt devoured her fury, and Nadya stared down at her shaking hands.

"Perhaps feelings are running too high to discuss this now," Mirela said quietly. She hadn't moved from her position curled up against the wall in a brightly embroidered quilt. "Besides, Mother, weren't you saying earlier that you wanted to visit some of the men who were discharged from the infirmary with smoke in their lungs."

Drina sighed and nodded. "Foolish Erevan physicians. You can't drain someone of blood and think that will cure them. Herbs, burned and taken in through the lungs, that's the only way to expel the smoke. But that isn't in their fancy books, so they just sit around, staring dumbly at one another while their patients suffer." She started collected her things in her belt pouch, muttering about the ineffectiveness of the city's doctors, then left after kissing Mirela on the cheek and giving Nadya a long look that said *this talk is not over.*

She stood stonily for a long moment. Eventually, the city would be saved, the sea would recede, and she would have no more excuses to avoid marriage. Would she be forced into some loveless match with a Nomori boy? Did she have any other options? Ever since the announcement of the royal betrothal, the future she'd hoped to have had turned to sand, blown away on the icy winds of reality.

When the door shut, Mirela sighed. "I believe your grandmother got all the stubbornness and strong personality in the Gabori family." She held out her hands. "Come, sit with me."

Nadya crawled onto the pallet until she was cradled against her mother's frail frame. She didn't like that she could hear the slight rattle with every breath her mother took.

"So, you're chasing a Nomori boy?" Mirela asked with a playful smile.

"Um…"

"I know you're not for sharing, now less than ever, but I'd like to know what romance your grandmother sensed that has her so flustered."

Nadya stared at her knees. "I don't really know. It's not—"

"You're worried for Kesali, aren't you?"

"What?" Nadya squeaked. She looked anywhere but her mother's face, struggling to keep the shock from twisting her expression. If Mirela suspected, if she knew… "I mean, yes. I couldn't bear to think of anything happening to her. She and I were such good friends, you know." Good friends, nothing more. Nothing then, nothing now, she reminded herself.

"Ay. You were inseparable at the evening gatherings, giving the Elders heart pains by your easy acceptance of Erevan customs. I thought your grandmother was going to faint at the last Arane Sveltura festival with the two of you dancing." Mirela laughed quietly. It turned into a cough. "Have you spent time together since the announcement?" she whispered, her eyes watering.

"I've been busy. Here. Where I should be." Her mother's words from the morning of the ballet, which now felt so long ago, still stung.

"Yes, you have responsibility to this family. But that responsibility is not meant to be an excuse to do nothing else. If you don't want to see her, do not hide behind your family duties." Mirela stroked her braid, tucking a stray wisp behind her ear.

Nadya swallowed. The faint sunlight streaming through the window seemed to intensify, as if the clouds were parting just for this moment. "Mama, I have to tell you something." When Mirela waited, Nadya gave a silent prayer to the Protectress, out of habit more than faith, and said, "What Grandmother said, about being in love..."

"Your grandmother is rarely wrong about such things."

"I know. And she wasn't." Nadya's thoughts went back to jumping into that burning building in search of her father, and she took a bit of the courage her gray cloak lent her and said, "But it's not some Nomori boy. It's Kesali."

The silence stretched out. Mirela's eyes stared dead ahead, her face a mask. Nadya heart began to race. She couldn't bear to be forced to choose a husband, not now with the pain of Kesali's betrothal so recent, and she needed her mother to understand. Such relationships, like the love she was proposing, weren't spoken of among the Nomori. She didn't think they existed. Maybe they couldn't. Maybe this was as much as a travesty as being born with an unnatural gift.

Tears squeezed out of the corner of her eyes. Nadya drew a slow, rattling breath, ordering herself under control.

Mirela's voice was soft and even. "Among the Nomori, love like that isn't allowed. Women choose husbands and marry them, and have children to carry on their family name."

A tear leaked out of Nadya's defenses.

"It's different with Erevans. Men make all the choices and stand at the head of the family. They choose their wives, but sometimes, they don't take wives. Sometimes, women aren't married to husbands. Your grandmother would call their ways barbaric. The Nomori ways are different." A small smile crossed Mirela's face. "But I've never been considered a good Nomori."

Nadya's breath caught in her throat as her mother wrapped an arm around her, drawing her close.

"Oh, Nadya, I've known for some time. You might be able to hide it from your father, thick like he is in matters of love, and even from your grandmother, but you can't hide the spark in your eye when you talk about her. I was just the same at your age, sneaking out, ignoring my duties to spend just another moment with your father."

"Mama," Nadya whispered, and suddenly she was crying into her mother's shoulder as Mirela's hand stroked her back. Each touch anchored her, building a shield between Nadya and the storms that plagued the city and her heart. She let herself go. Tears stained her mother's vest. The scent of oils and stone, of bread, of safety enveloped her, and for a moment, everything dark in her world vanished.

"It's all right." Mirela raised Nadya's chin with delicate fingers. "Look at me. This will be all right."

Nadya sniffed and wiped her nose. She huddled against her mother, who now seemed like the strongest person she'd ever met. "You aren't angry?"

"My daughter is in love. How can I be mad?"

"But it's Kesali. It's a woman, and it's the woman who is betrothed to the Duke's son. It can't…"

Her mother took her hand. "You're right. Too much rides on their betrothal. Kesali has made her choice, and it could save the city from itself. To be in love is to bear heartache, something you already know. Not even the Protectress can shield us against it."

Nadya nodded, but hearing the truth in her mother's soft tones didn't lessen the pain.

"But to be in love is also the most beautiful thing this life holds for us, and it is beautiful no matter what form it comes in." Mirela kissed the top of her head.

In that instant, Nadya almost told her mother her secret. She opened her mouth, and Mirela's soft expression urged her to divulge everything. The first time she realized she was different. The first time she realized her abilities were destructive. The lies about being able to sense the truth. The truth behind the Iron Phoenix. There, curled up next to her mother on the bed, she had never desired anything so badly. She would have given twelve years of her life to be able to make the words come out.

They didn't. The flashes of Shay's parents, their denial of ever having a daughter—the denial of the entire Nomori community of her existence—stopped Nadya's tongue.

Mirela did not see the war within her. "Kesali will be safe. You, Lord Marko, and your father will see to it. The Protectress will watch over you all, and the pain will go away until only the good memories remain."

I hope you're right, Mama, Nadya thought as she sat there, listening to the shaky rise and fall of her mother's chest. She did not believe it.

Chapter Fourteen

Mirela persuaded her to go visit Kesali, to make things right between them. The next day, Nadya reluctantly made the trip up to the palace. After stating her business and being checked for weapons in front of the enormous iron gate, she was allowed in.

What was she even going to say? She was still angry, and the more she thought about it, the more she doubted Kesali needed any consolation. In fact, her friend probably brushed the danger aside, chalking it up to doing her duty as both Stormspeaker and soon-to-be royal. So Nadya made it her mission to convince Kesali to be careful.

Servants and courtiers alike rushed through the marble halls, though not as many as usual. The rising tensions between Erevans and Nomori, between the Duke and the zealot's followers, meant that those without rooms at the palace were boarded up in their homes with their plentiful supplies of food waiting out the floodwaters.

She managed to find her way to Kesali's quarters, but she was not there. Nadya frowned. She knew the palace about as well as she knew the lands beyond the Kyanite Sea. That is to say, not at all. Wintercress to the west, Shikra to the east, and the South Marches were little more than names to her, just as the palace was nothing but a nice view atop Storm's Quarry. She had been there only once for a ceremony when her father was promoted to captain.

The men and women who streamed through the halls ignored Nadya's questions, so she resigned herself to try the main reception room. Perhaps she would run into Lord Marko, and he could point her in the direction of his betrothed. The main hall was quite a walk from the back corridor, and when she arrived, it was unguarded.

The great metal door, painted with the Duke's insignia of a blazing sun expelling the floodwaters, stood in the empty hall of the palace. Nadya's frown deepened. Without guardsmen in front, it was unlikely Lord Marko was within, but it was her best guess. Tomorrow was the Duke's open session. Shouldn't this be guarded, at least?

She realized her thoughts had been foolish when she tried the metal ring handle. The door did not budge. It was locked tight, and not even a battering ram could get through. Even if she could break it, anyone inside would be hard-pressed not to notice the enormous lock breaking. She gritted her teeth, raised her hand, and knocked twice on the enormous door.

This is a very bad idea, she told herself. *What am I going to do if the Duke is in there?*

The two thuds echoed throughout the hall. Nadya ducked her face when a few servants stopped in their duties, staring curiously at the Nomori girl who was knocking at the throne room.

For Kesali. To warn her to be careful.

Against her thoughts, Nadya was about to back away and find another path in when the doors slowly slid open. Her breath caught in her throat as the throne room was laid out before her. No one stood in the entrance. She started walking forward. If no one was here who could direct her toward Kesali or the Duke's son, she'd try one of the servants' doors behind the throne.

"Aren't you a little far from home?" a familiar voice remarked, and the throne room became cold.

Huge marble columns lined real carpet that led up to a simple metal chair set on the ground, at the same level as those who would come to see the Duke with their grievances. Lamps in glistening brackets hung on the walls every five paces, separating fine paintings and tapestries. Large ornate vases stood under the lamps. Beneath the entire splendor, though, was the scent of chemicals and sweat and effort spent on keeping this facade up. It burned her nose as nerves raced up and down her back, making the tips of her fingers tremble.

Levka Puyatin, the magistrate, rose from the writing desk, off to the left side of the throne. "I'm just finishing up a scroll. Can I help you with something, Miss Gabori?" His voice echoed in the emptiness.

Nadya inwardly cursed at her bad luck, but she forced herself to walk toward him. In the lamplight, his pale face and brown hair flickered with a darkness she might have imagined. "I'm looking for Kesali Stormspeaker. Or Lord Marko. I haven't been able to find either of them."

"And they just let you loose on the palace? Shoddy guard system, if you ask me."

She didn't ask him, and her feeling of uneasiness intensified. He was staring at her again with a look of scientific curiosity mixed with something feral, and her hands trembled.

He can't know, she told herself. *There is no way he knows who I am.*

Levka spread his hands. "Well, they're not here. Is there something I can help you with? Or the Head Cleric? I hear he has been mentoring the young Stormspeaker. I can take you to him, but I don't know the two lovebirds' whereabouts."

Nadya winced. "No, thank you. I can find them on my own." She was not truly a psychic, but she wondered if this was what having a normal Nomori gift felt like, all her nerves, her thoughts screaming at her to get out of there.

"Of course you can." Levka stepped out from behind the desk and walked toward her. Nadya held her ground. Nothing about him was overtly threatening, but that didn't shake her bad feeling. *Calm down,* she told herself as he drew level with her. *You're ten times stronger than him, and you're alone. He cannot hurt you.*

"You're one of Lord Marko's closest friends, and he does not have a lot of friends. Anyone here would be happy to help you. They'd think it would garner favor with the Duke's son." Now, as he kept walking in a circle around her, he stood between her and the door. It was innocent enough pacing, but Nadya didn't like it.

"Then I should be going," Nadya said.

"It is interesting, however," Levka kept talking, "that he should choose you before the courtiers and scholars. Even if you are his mentor's daughter." His tone was friendly, as if he was just making conversation.

"Because I'm Nomori?"

"Because you're a murderer." His voice took a hard edge.

Her heart stopped. "What...what?" How could he know? Before the night of Jastima's death, she had never seen this man in her life. She had barely spoken to him. Why was he looking at her like a piece of rancid prey he had just caught?

"You hide it well, my dear. From the Duke's son and his betrothed. From your parents even, and I don't doubt your father the captain is a very hard one to trick. Though we are most blind about the people closest to us." The magistrate smiled. "Don't you think so?"

"I don't know what you are talking about," Nadya said, her voice shaking. "But I won't stand here and be accused of murder."

"Resolve, just like the rest of your people." He spat out the last word. "How adorable. But no, you are not going to leave. Not until I have said my piece. I have to say, your timing is impeccable. You've saved me the trouble of tracking you down."

Nadya tried to swallow, but she couldn't. "What do you want?"

"Stay away from things that are beyond your ken. There are powers at work in this city that you cannot understand, and I don't want you fooling around in them."

"The murders?" she asked. "Jurek, the ballerina, Jastima. That was you?" It didn't fit, not in her mind. Levka was not the figure she had seen outside Jurek's manor. His stance, his walk were all wrong.

"No, although I'd like to thank those lowlifes for getting their hands dirty. It certainly made things easier. My work, or rather my funding, went toward a bigger project. A couple dozen kegs of gunpowder, for example," the magistrate said.

"You were behind the attack on the Guardhouse?" Why was he telling her this? Her hands curled into fists. Damn the answer, he nearly got her father killed!

"Yes, and believe me, that was just a prequel. But I want you to stay out of it—all right, Miss Gabori?"

"I'll tell Lord Marko," she whispered. Her mind was racing, trying to fit the pieces together, trying to figure out why this man was confessing to her, and why his smile had not wavered.

"Is that so?"

"Yes," she said in a stronger voice. "I'll have you arrested for the sixteen men that died. Then I'll find out who's behind the murders, and I will make sure this city doesn't destroy itself before the solstice." She took a deep breath. She hadn't meant to say it all, but her words carried a weight of conviction behind them.

But instead of bristling with rage, the magistrate laughed. "You can't prove anything. Moreover, you won't prove anything. Because you are not going to tell anyone about this." Levka grabbed her arm and whispered, "I know what you are."

Nadya jerked back, knocking him to the ground. The magistrate slowly got to his knees, coughing, as she backed away. Every nerve in her body was on edge. Did he actually just say those words? Maybe he meant that she was Nomori, though that was obvious to anyone with a pair of eyes. The door was in front of her, not twenty paces away, but her legs were rooted to the carpet as if bolted down by metal that even she could not break. She could do nothing but watch Levka get shakily to his feet.

He rubbed his elbow, turning to her with that awful smile. "Seeing it is one thing, but experiencing it is another. You are an unnatural creature, aren't you, Nadezhda Gabori."

"No." It came out a whisper. He didn't know anything. He couldn't prove anything. That thought gave Nadya enough strength to say, "I don't know what you're talking about." All desire to goad him into spilling the truth disappeared as the game of words had turned on her.

"Of course you do." He said it so matter-of-factly.

"I'm going to report this all to Lord Marko." Nadya didn't know if she wanted to cower in fear or throw Levka across the room. She needed to get out of there, but she needed to make sure he wasn't going to do anything rash. *You could stop him, you know.* That awful thought froze her. *No one is here.*

As if he read her mind, Levka spread his hands out and said, "Why let Marko handle it? You could take care of it yourself. Why not string me up by a hand and snap my neck?"

A cold sheen washed over Nadya. Her breathing was suddenly very difficult, as if something incredibly heavy had settled on her chest. Her chest rose and fell fast, but she couldn't get any air.

Levka nodded. "So, we can drop all pretenses now. You will leave the palace and go back to your own tier. If and when you see Lord Marko or your father, you will not repeat any of this. To anyone. You will stay at home like a good daughter, and the Iron Phoenix will not make another appearance. If you do, I'll be sure to reveal the secret you have tried so hard to keep, to tell the entire city of the true murderous nature of the Phoenix."

"They won't believe you," she whispered.

"I am a magistrate in service to the Duke. You are a Nomori girl. Who will be believed?"

If he revealed her secret, she would be cast out of her family, her people. Nadya was left without a choice, except to obey. Finally, she nodded.

"It'd be so much better for you if you had the heart of a killer, Nadya, as you did once." He walked past her, disappeared through one of the servants' doors, and let it slam behind him, shattering the silence.

Nadya drew a deep rattling breath. She looked down and realized she was bleeding. She had gripped her fists so tightly that her fingernails on her right hand punctured the tough skin. Several drops of blood fell to the red carpet, disappearing into its softness.

Standing alone in the throne room, she didn't know which was worse, that Levka knew her secret and could set the entire city on her at his whim, or that she had a solid lead to the perpetrator of the riots, to saving Kesali, and she couldn't tell anyone without losing everything.

For the first time since she discovered her abilities, Nadya felt well and truly helpless.

CHAPTER FIFTEEN

"Nadya?" The voice echoed about the servants' hall. She jerked up and whirled around to see Kesali standing just beyond the double doors that led into the palace kitchens, hands raised in the air. Her chain of betrothal rubies glimmered in the dim light.

"I didn't mean to frighten you."

Nadya swallowed. Was she cursed to be looking over her shoulder for the rest of her life for that smirk and those haunting words, *I know what you are*? She wiped her eyes and straightened. "You didn't. I'm fine."

"What are you doing here?"

"I…I wanted to make sure you were okay."

"And you came here to find me?" Kesali smiled. "We need to work on your reasoning skills." When Nadya did not return her grin, her tone changed. "What's wrong? Did something happen?"

"No." The Stormspeaker was not the only one who could keep secrets. Nadya still couldn't put what had occurred in the main hall into words. Her entire world had been thrown into chaos. In the past hour, she'd learned her secret was no longer her own and saving Storm's Quarry now came with a heavy price.

"Don't lie to me."

"Then don't ask me questions I cannot answer," Nadya snapped.

Kesali sat down next to her. "I'm not accusing you of anything."

Neither had Levka, in so many words.

"I know I'm the last person you probably want to confide in. I'm happy you came to see me. But I've noticed things. You keep pushing me away, and I know it's not just because of the betrothal."

Nadya's heart stopped for a moment. *Watching me.* Had she seen something? Did she know? She couldn't handle Kesali finding out, not right after Levka gave his ultimatum.

"I know you, Nadya, and I know you're hiding something."

Nadya gulped, staring at her knees. "What makes you think that?"

"Coming and going at night. You don't speak to me anymore. Well, recently, I know why, but before that. You always look scared. I had to practically order you to attend the theater with me, something we both regret. When you do reveal anything of yourself, you seem very hesitant, like any single word could expose you." She put a hand on Nadya's knee. "Tell me what's going on."

"Is that an order from Lady Kesali, princess of Storm's Quarry?" Her words came out carrying the bitterness of her heart that had festered since the betrothal announcement.

Kesali removed her hand. "No, it's a request from the girl you danced with in the public square, angering the Elders and not caring. The girl you kissed—well, or maybe who kissed you. Who you didn't push away, regardless. From just Kesali, and if you can't answer…" She didn't finish the sentence, and she didn't look at Nadya.

Nadya closed her eyes for a moment, thinking through all the possible lies she could tell her. But she was tired of lying, and in the oppressive damp heat breathing through the kitchen doors with the day's events and revelations hanging over her like stone weights, she was too tired to come up with a lie. "I can't. And I wish I could."

"What kind of answer is that?"

"It's the only answer I can give." Nadya laid a tentative hand on Kesali's thigh, ignoring how natural it felt, and waited until Kesali looked at her. To reassure herself that her dearest friend did not see the monster Levka did.

For a moment she thought Kesali was going to pull away and stand up, accusing her of treason and lies. She thought Kesali would call her out for being the Iron Phoenix, and bring the Duke's Guard here, led by Shadar, to lock her up.

Instead, Kesali put her soft, callused fingers underneath Nadya's chin. She leaned in, neither of them breathing, and gently kissed her.

Nadya stiffened. This was wrong. Her hands opened and closed at her sides, not knowing what to do. But as Kesali pulled her into an embrace, Nadya stopped fighting against her better judgment. Her hands stilled, coming to rest on Kesali's waist, then tracing a line along the seam in her vest up to the back of her neck. Her eyes closed, and she melted into the kiss. It was warm and soft and tasted like wine and spring. Kesali's scent filled her nose, overpowering even the damp. Kesali's heartbeat, separated by nothing but two thin layers of cloth, thundered in her ears.

They pulled apart. Nadya took a deep breath and blinked. *Fool,* she told herself. "We can't," she said. "I told you, we can't do this."

Kesali rose. "You're right, and I'm sorry. But I think we both wanted that."

"People like us," Nadya said, staring straight ahead, "rarely get what we want."

She did not turn, even when Kesali's footsteps echoed across the hall. Going after her would only bring more pain. She swallowed, but she could still taste Kesali's spice. Worse, she did not regret it.

❖

Nadya tried to bury the memory of that kiss over the next few weeks. It was not easy, as the only other thing to think about was the seawater that trapped the city. Storm's Quarry rose like a pale rock in the middle of a pond. The sun rarely showed its face, and the waters did not recede. Food had become harder to find. The Nomori tier had long run out of new stock. Its citizens lined up every morning at the ration stations. Lines circled around the warehouse, clogging streets. More often than not, the Guard's presence was required to keep the peace. Day by day, as the floodwaters showed no signs of relenting, fewer believed the Stormspeaker had spoken truly. As people gave up hope, fear took its place.

Nadya feared for her city.

As she walked past the ration line one morning, she overheard the mutterings of two guardsmen as they wheeled out yet another box of hardened nut bread. "These won't last much longer."

"The city wasn't meant to be able to withstand a siege, whether by armies or water. It'll run out of food by the solstice, mark my words."

Despite the damp, their conversation gave Nadya's shivers. Later, she asked her father if it was true.

His answer was the long sigh of a tired man. "The palace storehouses are nearly depleted. If it continues this way, on the morning of the solstice, the people will go to the ration lines and find no food."

"There will be riots," Nadya said.

"If we are lucky, that is all there will be."

As the city tightened its belt and the violence grew worse, she began to understand what Lord Marko had said the night of Jastima's murder. As much as she wanted to solve the mystery of the murders and the enigmatic man behind them, it all really seemed inconsequential compared to what the city faced now.

She could not shake the feeling that had those people not been killed, Storm's Quarry wouldn't be ready to devour itself in civil war.

Just days before the solstice, a sharp rapping on the outer stone wall of their house roused Nadya from a fitful sleep. She glanced down over the ledge and saw her mother sleeping alone on the pallet. Her father must have stayed on duty all night.

Nadya leapt down, landing quietly on the balls of her bare feet, and padded around her mother's bed, through the workshop, and to the door. She opened it. The early morning's dampness, thick enough to touch, hit her in the face, and it took her a few moments to realize the cloaked and hooded figure standing outside her home was Lord Marko.

"Good morning, Nadya," he said cheerfully, and she blinked again.

"Um...good morning." She rubbed her eyes. "Is something wrong?"

"No, I was just out for some air."

She frowned. "Out for some air...in the Nomori tier. When the city is practically ready to rip itself apart."

"Okay, so I came to see you. Do you have a few minutes?" His eager expression, nearly hidden in the shadows of the hood that covered his brilliant red hair, didn't exactly give her room for an answer. She didn't think it was anything serious, or Iron Phoenix related, but she had to be cautious.

The memory of Kesali's lips filled her mind, and she could not look him in the eye. The kiss on Arane Sveltura was one thing. Nadya hadn't known then. In the palace, she knew about the betrothal, she knew how much it would hurt, and she did it anyway.

She had not seen the Stormspeaker since.

Nadya shook her head. "My mother's asleep."

"The morning is cool, if damp. Would you join me on a walk?"

She bit her lip, scrounging for an excuse. But her mother was feeling better since taking the Erevan medicine, and Nadya was not needed to sit in their house and watch her sleep. She nodded and was about to step outside when she realized she was still dressed in only a nightshirt. Marko was making a valiant effort to keep a straight face, and her ears started to burn.

"Give me a moment," she mumbled and shut the door in front of his face. As quickly and quietly as she could, she crept round her mother, jumped to her loft, and donned a vest and trousers. She sniffed them and muffled a groan. She would need to wash them soon.

Marko was lounging up against her house when she came outside. He straightened and offered her a hand. Nadya stared at it.

"Never mind," he said. "Beautiful day, isn't it?" He started walking. Instead of heading toward the marble stairs, he walked in the opposite direction, farther into the Nomori tier.

Nadya matched his step. "It's damp enough to scoop it out of the air and bottle it. The sun hasn't come out from behind the clouds, and it smells like rat droppings and wet fur. Lovely day. Haven't ever seen better."

He laughed. "If only my father's courtiers spoke like that during meetings. They would be much less dull."

She blushed again. "Sorry, mi—Marko."

They stayed on the main cobblestone street that ran around the entire island like a snake circling its prey. On either side, stone shops stood with doors sealed and men holding knives guarding the windows, warning off any looters. Through the narrow alleys and side streets, the rest of the dwellings that the Nomori lived in could be glimpsed. Most had wood boarded up over their doors, the windows dark. Nadya kept one eye on the ground as they walked, dodging the numerous puddles that remained weeks after the storm had ceased. They had become home to buzzing insects that laid their eggs and attacked any, Nomori or bug, that invaded their territory.

Hundreds of Nomori passed them, all headed to some form of work. Most of the men wore uniforms of either the Duke's Guard or private security or the whites of a weapons tutor. A few desperate ones with reddened eyes wore the overcoat of a miner. The women carried baskets and tools, employed as everything from lady's maids to engineers on the steam pumps that could still be heard through the stillness. No one spoke, either not wanting to draw attention to themselves or not wanting to bring voice to the tension in the air.

"The sea hasn't gone down," Marko said suddenly. "A couple of brave souls actually rappelled off the walls to measure against the Mark of Recession. Not even a fraction." He sighed. "It's been six weeks. It should have lowered by now."

Her stomach sank. It was less than a week until the solstice and all that day would bring. Nadya swallowed her panic down and tried to make light. "All the more reason that you shouldn't be here alone," she said sternly. The Nomori they passed did not give them more than a passing glance, but if Marko's identity were exposed, the sheer number of people could give them trouble.

"I won't tell Kesali if you won't." Marko glanced over at her. Nadya tried to keep her face a mask.

"I am worried about her," he said, dodging a couple of women pulling a wagon.

"We're all worried. But nothing will happen. The rioters won't win, and the zealot will be found and the Kyanite Sea will return to its bed," Nadya said quietly.

Marko laughed, but this time it was hollow, echoing across the desolate stone buildings they passed with wide-eyed Nomori children watching them with hands outstretched. "Is that for me, or you?"

"Both of us."

"I just hate feeling useless." He stopped, and Nadya had to pull him out of the flow of workers to keep from being trampled. Marko didn't even seem to notice. "I can't do anything, anything to protect the city, anything to save her. Your father is busy searching for factions of rioters and keeping the peace. He actually ordered me out of the temporary headquarters yesterday, saying I was just getting in the way." He sighed. "I was."

"Sometimes we have to leave things to those who know them best," Nadya said without believing it.

He looked down at her. "That's pretty wise for someone so young."

She snorted. "I'm only two years younger than you."

"My point." He sighed. "I know your father was right to kick me out. He knows far more than I ever could."

He started walking again, and Nadya followed. "That isn't all that's bothering you."

Marko sighed. "My father is holding an open session today, against the wishes of his son and his deputy Guardmaster. Were you planning to go?"

She shook her head and lied, "No, I need to look after my mother." She had made her plans last night. Such an event was a tantalizing target for the zealot and any others who wished the city ill. Something might happen, and Kesali would be there. Nadya decided the Iron Phoenix would be as well.

"He says that now, more than ever, the family needs to show openness to the city. He thinks he can quell the unrest with diplomacy, with peace." Marko shook his head. "My father has always been the peacemaker. It's worked so well for him that it's narrowed his mind. Sometimes...sometimes all someone understands is the bullet or the blade."

There was a finality in his words that Nadya didn't like. "You think that of this zealot and his followers." She couldn't help but think of the magistrate. She had a sinking feeling that Marko was right, and there was nothing short of violence that would stop him.

"Don't you? Or," he paused, "maybe you don't."

"What is that supposed to mean?" Now it was she who stopped, backing into a culvert to avoid the thinning crowds. The sun had risen behind the clouds. It lit everything in a gray glow. Water splashed up around her boots.

Marko leaned against the stone wall. "You don't really have gods."

"And you have gods that no one actually believes in, until a madman riles them up enough to spill blood." Nadya took a breath and said in a softer tone, "Just because we don't have shrines or make sacrifices, do not think we don't pray. Who do you think the Protectress is?"

Marko leaned forward. "I guess I've never really known. The Nomori I know rarely talk about her other than invoking her name."

She hesitated. This was a question better suited for an Elder, not a Nomori girl whose very life was blasphemy. But something in her chest pushed her to answer, so she considered her words and began, "The Nomori were nomads for a thousand years. We traveled the waterways from one end of the world to the other. During those centuries, we faced plagues and barbarians and swords and pistols and animals and elements." The history in the Elders' songs came to her now. "We didn't need a pantheon of gods to appease, not like those who originally built Storm's Quarry needed someone to blame the storms on."

She took a deep breath and reached up to touch the seal, hidden under her shirt sleeve. "The Nomori did not need gods. We needed a protector, and we received a Protectress."

"Like a goddess?"

She shook her head. "A Protectress. That is what she's called, and that's what she is. She looks after my people, listens to our prayers, and protects us. In years gone by, it was from the dangers of a nomadic life."

"And now it's from the dangers of living in a city with Erevans," Marko finished. His expression was unreadable.

"Ay." She paused. "She is not better or worse than your storm gods. She's merely different."

"But you believe in her."

She did not know how to answer. Once, her belief in the Protectress was stronger than the great marble walls of the city. Now, she never prayed. "Yes," she said finally. "Every Nomori wears her seal." It was not a lie. She still believed in the Protectress, in her curse. But Nadya did not have her faith anymore.

"Kesali never told me this."

"Perhaps she was waiting for you to ask."

Marko grunted and started walking again, cutting through the culvert to loop down a side street, heading back toward the marble stairs and the upper tiers of the city.

Nadya tried to cheer him up. Despite his relationship with Kesali, she did not wish to see him upset, not with the unrest in the city and him bearing the burden of its future. "It's really a private thing, not something we talk about."

"You talked about it."

"Because you asked me. Have you ever asked her about it? About any Nomori custom?"

The red that crept over his ears, barely hidden by the hood, was answer enough. "Sometimes I think we've been betrothed forever, and sometimes it feels like I don't know her at all." He looked down at Nadya. "You've been friends with her for years. Tell me about her."

It wasn't an official command from Lord Marko, the Duke's son, but the request of a man in love, Nadya realized with a sour taste in her mouth. This was why he sought her out this morning. The worry about the riots and the open session, while genuine, was a simple cover to be able to talk to her about Kesali.

The kiss was too fresh in her mind. Nadya wanted to remain silent, but one glance at Marko's hopeful face, and she knew she had to say something. "Kesali...Kesali is the best person you'll ever meet."

"I know that."

Do you feel how strong her heart beats when you kiss? "Do you know that she likes to dance?"

He frowned. "I thought the Nomori didn't approve of such activities."

Nadya shrugged. "Kesali likes it. She always shocks all the Elders by prancing around to their songs."

"That sounds like her." Marko smiled. When he spoke again, he stared mistily over the heads of the Nomori they passed, all the way to the edges of the tier that could be seen. "I'm lucky. I always knew I would marry for political gain. I thought it would be a princess of one of the neighboring nations who wanted a larger share of our mine's output. Wintercress, most likely, but one of the Marchlands if I got lucky. But I never imagined someone like Kesali. I love her."

Bile rose in her throat, but Nadya forced herself to smile. "I'm happy for you two."

"I know we're engaged already, but I want to propose to her in the Nomori fashion."

Nadya almost tripped over her own feet. Marko continued speaking, drilling her with questions on Kesali's likes and dislikes and different methods of performing a Nomori proposal. He insisted she tell him in detail how the man brings a loaf of bread to the woman's house. If the woman accepts his offer, and most Nomori women of good families had multiple offers, she cuts a slice and they share it. Marko looked like an eager child, absorbing all of Nadya's bitter words.

She was relieved when the front of her house came into sight. Marko bowed when they stopped at her door. "Thank you, Nadya. I should return to my father, but thank you. You've eased my heart." He bowed again and left.

He shouldn't have been so cheerful, not with the city teetering on the edge of chaos and starvation. But then again, he was a man in love and nothing stood between him and his betrothed. Marriage meant forever, one of the few things the Erevans and Nomori agreed upon. She wondered what it felt like, knowing he would wake up to those soft eyes, that eager smile every day for the rest of his life. She swallowed back her jealousy and went inside. Any thoughts she'd had of a romantic future always involved Kesali. She tried to see someone else and found nothing past Kesali.

Shoving back the raw thoughts of what wouldn't be, she checked to make sure her mother still slept soundly, then climbed up to where the gray cloak that belonged to the Phoenix was stowed. Surveying the roofs of the Nomori tier from her own, Nadya saw nothing standing between her and protecting Kesali at the palace.

Chapter Sixteen

The damp seemed to close in, choking her as Nadya sped through the narrow streets to the rail. She ignored the angry looks and grunts that were thrown at her as she barreled past people. After she knocked one guardsman to the ground by accident, she tempered her speed slightly.

A whistle blast screeched through the air just as she reached the base of the stairs. Nadya leapt over the edge of the slow-chugging railbox just as it departed. She got one or two stares from its other passengers, but settling into a seat at the far end, she did her best to look average.

The gray cloak, rolled up and secured to her back with twine, felt like an anchor and a brand.

The Iron Phoenix might not take precedence with the Guard over rioters, zealots, and murderers, but she would be a fool to think any of the Guard would just let her masked persona waltz by. With the increasing tension between Erevans and Nomori, guardsmen were everywhere. Wearing the cloak and scarf painted a target on her back, but the thought of not wearing them was even worse.

If she was needed to step in to save Kesali, the Iron Phoenix would be there. If she wasn't, no one would recognize the cloak as belonging to the man who was either a hero or a villain, depending on who you spoke to.

A bell rang throughout the tier, marking the beginning of the Duke's weekly open session. Chatter and boot steps filled in the silence after it, punctuating stern shouts from guardsmen and the creaking of the palace doors.

Nadya stepped off the rail platform. She carefully pushed her way through the throngs of people. The cobblestoned square of the top tier was full of people from all walks of life. Courtiers in their fine clothes and huge amounts of gaudy jewelry that looked heavy enough to snap their necks walked alongside muddy beggars from the second tier. Nadya peered through the crowd. She saw one or two Nomori, but no one she recognized. The two races gave each other a wide berth and dirty looks. Red uniforms stood out from the milling people, more than Nadya had ever seen at an open session. They walked through the crowd, checking faces.

Looking for the zealot or his rioters, she thought, then realized with a pang of sickness, *and the Iron Phoenix, if he's foolish enough to show.*

At the huge metal doors melded into the imposing white marble walls of the palace, a troop of the Duke's Guard stopped everyone before they entered. They dug through bags and parcels, raking along peoples' limbs despite the outraged cries of the citizens. Then the guardsmen waved the group through the small gap in the doors and called the next few dozen people forward.

Nadya had no weapons, but that didn't stop her pulse from pounding in her ears as she weaved her way through the disorganized line to the front and the guardsmen. She kept her head down. Only one was Nomori, and she kept well away from him. The Erevan who searched her did it with rough hands that lingered too long over her backside and her chest. He touched the cloak, and Nadya bit back a surge of fear. She forced herself to breathe as his hands rifled through it looking for the butt of a gun or the hilt of a rapier.

"Go on, now," he said gruffly, and Nadya hurried through the door.

The crowd was restricted to the throne room with queue of the Duke's Guard on either side, directing them forward along the velvet carpet. The astonished cries of children, their wonder at the splendor of the palace, were the only noises to be heard over the constant hum of suspicious murmurs. No one was here because their life was good.

Nadya could hardly believe, as she walked through the sun-painted doors, that she had encountered Levka in here just the day before. It felt like a lifetime ago, with a lifetime's regret and hardship settling on her shoulders ever since. She wished more than ever that she could go to someone with her new knowledge of Levka's involvement in—well, she still didn't know what. Supplying explosives to the rioters, perhaps. All she knew for certain was there was a lot more to the magistrate's quiet looks and confident demeanor. It masked a man who wasn't afraid to watch a city fall to chaos and see its streets run red with blood.

She had considered the consequences of an appearance by the Iron Phoenix. If Levka planned something for the open session and she got in the way, he very well might reveal her identity to everyone.

As much as that thought made her sick, the thought of Kesali's lifeless eyes staring up at her was worse.

The marble pillars now stood like sentries, guiding the crowd down the center aisle. Nadya had to restrain herself from clapping her hands over her ears. Every little sound, from the woman who lectured the Duke on the food shortages to Marko's sigh to the dozens of heavy footsteps, echoed in here, coming back like a tidal wave to her sensitive ears.

She slipped out of the crowd as soon as one of the uniforms who patrolled its edge had to wade into the mass of people and separate a Nomori woman from an Erevan one.

Nadya quietly walked backward until she melted into the shadows and cobwebs in this back corner. The frames of the gilded paintings that hung back here were dusty, and the sole torch in the corner had gone out. None of the meager light that came in the hall's stained glass windows reached this corner, and for the first time since leaving the Nomori tier, Nadya let herself breathe easy.

Sitting in an unadorned wooden chair atop three steps of gleaming marble, Duke Aleksandr Isyanov presided over the hall. He was handsome enough...for an Erevan. His flaming locks were dimmed by gray strands. He wore a rich purple tunic and an ornate jeweled collar—the signet of the ruler of Storm's Quarry, a sun with brilliant rubies and more subtle opals. Nadya, a hundred paces away, saw the rings around his eyes. Yet he still listened to the woman who raged about the food shortages and her children's hunger with attentive eyes.

On the Duke's left side, Marko stood in formal purple and jewels that he did not look very comfortable in. Beside him, Kesali stood in her traditional, almost stubborn, Nomori vest and trousers. Like the ones she had worn to the theater, they were made of expensive cloth and richly embroidered. There was no mistake of the message she was sending to the entire city. She wore the necklace of rubies. Nadya's heart ached when she saw the pair of them holding hands.

She was there to protect Kesali from anything that might happen. That was all there was. That was all there would ever be, watching her and Marko hold hands, and the sooner she accepted that, the happier she would be.

Nadya stayed in her corner, unmoving so as not to be noticed by the guardsmen. If any saw her, they ignored the young girl standing there quietly and turned back to the citizens who were causing trouble. The mass of people slowly moved as each citizen got their few moments before the Duke. On his right side, several scribes worked away at the writing desks, copying down his every word. More often than not, he ordered extra rations to be given to families. Nadya wondered if the city could spare them, or if the Duke was dipping into the rations saved for his own family. Sometimes he resolved a dispute between two parties, but mostly, he just listened. As she watched, Nadya realized what Marko hadn't. The Duke was right to continue with the open session despite the growing turmoil in the city. These people needed to see their leader, and most came away happy, or at least no longer glowering. If they found a compassionate leader who listened in the Duke, they would have no need to go to the zealot.

After almost an hour, Nadya started to believe that her worry was unjustified. Her mother would be wondering where she was. There was always something that needed to be done around the house. She did not yet need to scavenge for food, though. The

Erevan shopkeepers would still sell to them, even if they tripled the price of the already overpriced food.

She felt it as she turned to leave, a tingling between her shoulder blades. It was nothing more than a fancy, but Nadya had learned to trust her instincts. They had been right about Levka. She swept her eyes over the proceedings but saw nothing suspicious. The Duke's Guard was doing a fine job keeping order. She saw her father once or twice but always looked away before he could meet her eyes.

She thought she had imagined it, until she glanced directly across the hall, to the other abandoned corner that no one was paying attention to.

Someone was there.

Nadya sucked in a breath. She stared, trying to pick features out of the semi-darkness. A man, tall with indeterminate skin color and fair hair. He turned and looked at her with black Nomori eyes.

Nadya fell back against the wall. The painting beside her shuddered. She swallowed. It was the same man she had seen in the fourth tier and again at the theater. She squinted, her face growing warm under his fierce gaze. Every instinct told her she was right.

He smiled once more, and Nadya's hands went cold.

"Death to the Duke!" A feral shout ripped across the already noisy throne room. Silence reigned for one moment. Then the screaming began.

Chapter Seventeen

Nadya winced and clamped her hands over her ears as she surveyed the chaos. Guardsmen shouted to one another, drawing weapons as they directed the stampeding crowd back out the metal doors. Nadya's heart nearly stopped. Five men, peaceable citizens a moment before, had drawn pistols out of the ornate vases and now approached the Duke with wild eyes. Somehow, they had been able to use trickery, or far worse, to get the weapons past security.

The men shot and reloaded, their first bullets going wide and ricocheting off the walls, nearly hitting Kesali.

Kesali.

Nadya let out a guttural roar of her own and leapt, cracking the fine marble tile as she left the ground. In midair, she ripped through the twine, letting the cloak billow out, and yanked the scarf across her face. She slammed into the ground, between the attackers and the royal family. Debris and dust flew, and she slowly rose from her crouch.

A bullet slammed into her shoulder. Red swam across her vision. Nadya staggered back, hitting the side of the throne. She clamped a hand over the injury but stayed upright. Pain raced up and down her arm, circling around her neck. Nadya spat and ignored it. She turned to face the men, putting herself between their pistols and the Duke, Marko, and Kesali.

Guardsmen struggled to reach them. Nadya heard her father's shout, but everything faded behind the smoking barrels of the five pistols aimed at her heart. All held by men who were no longer men, but something wild, with solid black eyes.

One man shot again. He ran forward, shooting and quickly reloading, as he tried to get around her to the Duke.

Nadya slammed a fist into his temple, and he collapsed in an instant. Blood seeped out of his mouth.

She turned to the other four. They weren't afraid at all, even after seeing their companion brought down so quickly. She dodged another bullet, her shoulder crying out. Nadya stepped back and shoved the Duke and his son down to the ground. Her hand connected with the signet the Duke wore, and she ripped it off as the Duke cried out. He fell to the ground, and she tossed the jeweled collar aside. Kesali was already lying there, her face white. Their eyes met for an instant, before Nadya roared again and charged the men.

She knocked their pistols out of broken fingers. She should have stopped there. She could have stopped there, but the frightened look in Kesali's eyes as bullets whizzed by her, nearly killing her, fueled a fury deep within Nadya.

The smell of gunpowder and blood filled her nostrils. She grabbed one man around the neck, picking him up like a rag doll, and threw him across the hall. His limp body slammed into a group of guards running to the rescue of their Duke. Nadya whirled on the other two.

The darkness from their eyes faded. They backed away from her. "What…what's happening?" one whispered.

She ignored him. Her boot flashed out, and the sound of dozens of bones snapping filled the quiet throne room. A blow from her fist dropped the final attacker, and then all was silent.

Nadya straightened. She slowly unclenched her fists, and then she felt the warmth. Raising her hand in front of her, she watched as the thick blood raced down her fingers and dripped onto the floor. A tightness gripped her throat, constricting her until she couldn't breathe.

Were they dead? She swallowed, but that didn't stop the bile from rising into her mouth.

The forms of the five men did not move. Nadya blinked and the rest of the throne room came back into focus. The citizens were gone, leaving several dozen of the Duke's Guard converging upon the dais. Behind her, Nadya heard the scraping of boots as people rose from their seats. She slowly turned around. The Duke backed away from her, his collarbone a mass of purple bruises. Marko put himself between her and his father. Kesali's face was pale, and her fingers shook at her side. She looked uninjured though, and for a moment, Nadya felt happy.

Until she glanced down at the ruined bodies of the attackers.

Nadya didn't move for a long moment as a horrible realization curdled in her gut. She had fought. She had used her abilities to hurt, perhaps even to kill. It was a line she'd sworn she would never cross again, and now she had. For Kesali. For Kesali's safety, she had not even considered how she might accidentally kill someone.

The throne room blurred and vanished. She was fifteen, running from a larger, older Erevan boy through the back streets of the Nomori tier. Damp stung her cheeks, mixing with tears as she put on an extra burst of speed. Her pursuer had legs that were twice as long as hers and he caught up to her as she turned down a tight culvert alley. "You're mine," he whispered in his horrible courtier accent, his heavy breaths clogging her nose. Nadya opened her mouth to scream, but he clamped a hand over her mouth and started fumbling with her vest. Something tightened in her chest, and Nadya grabbed his arm, and he was the one to scream as bone cracked under her grip and blood bubbled up over her hands. Nadya raised him up with a trembling grip, and she pushed him away, desperate to get his touch off her. He flew down the culvert, hitting a solid stone wall with a *thunk*, and lay still. Blood trickled out of his mouth, running with water down the culvert and mingling around her boots. She was frozen, staring at his body, then at her hands, and wondering what sort of monstrous creature she had become.

Nadya blinked, and her first encounter with her unnatural abilities and their deadly consequences vanished into the warm glow of the throne room. She swallowed again, but her throat was dry. She could not go near Kesali anymore, not if it meant doing something like this again.

Guardsmen had circled her. Behind her, Marko yelled, "Try not to hurt him."

A burning filled her chest. Nadya crouched. She wanted to, *needed* to wipe the blood from her hands until they glistened like it had never happened. But the ring of crimson uniforms and shining rapiers and pistols stood between her and that delusion. Her father was there, his expression hard.

She leapt, shouts following her, and grabbed hold of a marble pillar halfway down the throne room. Using her momentum, she launched herself up again and through the rapidly closing doors. Guardsmen yelled. She hit the ground running, nearly tripped on the shining floor, then barreled through the group of uniforms blocking her exit.

She propelled herself in the air with the first step she took on the cobblestones and landed on the roof of a storehouse. From there, she kept running, blinded by tears and weighed down by the scent of blood.

She did not go straight home. Instead, her pounding boots took her over the roof of her house and toward the wall. Nadya landed in one of the deep culverts used to hold the runoff rainwater during storms. Above her on street level, steam pumps worked to pump the remaining water over the wall. In this stone culvert, as large as the public bathhouse, the water was knee-deep. She collapsed into it, and the water soaked her to the bone and brought sharp pains to her shoulder. Nadya did not care as long as it washed the red stains off her hands.

An hour passed, perhaps more, before Nadya climbed, sopping wet, out of the culvert. She removed the cloak and rolled it up. Tucking it under her arm, she trudged off toward her house.

She was halfway there when she realized she could not go home, not yet.

Maybe I did not kill them, she tried to tell herself. *Maybe they are just injured, in the prison infirmary by now. I could go there and see.*

The chance was slim, so slim as to be nonexistent, but Nadya grabbed ahold of it like it was a lifeline and she was drowning in blood.

To reach the city's prison, nestled next to the mines on the other side of the Nomori tier, she did have to pass her house, or waste valuable time winding through side streets. She did not go in. Stashing her cloak in the alley, she then ripped off a part of the bottom of her shirt and stuffed it up the vest to stanch the slow bleeding. Every movement hurt, sending more blood through her injured shoulder. The injury wasn't fatal, though.

For anyone else, it would have been.

Forced to walk more slowly than usual to minimize her blood loss, Nadya kept her eyes down. Few Nomori wandered about. News of the palace attack had already begun to trickle down, and everyone knew that a storm of a far different kind was coming. More dangerous than the Great Storm, likely to leave Storm's Quarry a crumbled husk of what it once was. Nadya paused when she reached the great marble stairs. She looked up, her eyesight allowing her to see all the way to the top of the city. For the first time since she could remember, the gates to the fifth tier were closed. A regiment of the Duke's Guard stood on the top five steps. No one was allowed through.

She broke her gaze away and continued on. Miners' Tunnel was open once more, though poorly lit and just as suffocating. She gasped when she reached the other side, trying to breathe in the pale sunlight and rid herself of the darkness.

It was too reminiscent of the eyes of the murderers.

Most of the Duke's Guard was deployed throughout the city, concentrated on the palace, its storehouses, and key places of defense. Only a handful of guardsmen patrolled the thin wire fence that separated the prison from the sealed mining tunnels across the roughly hewn street. It was a matter of little difficulty for Nadya to judge their pattern, wait for an opening, and hop over.

It was a risk going as just herself, but if anyone found her, she could lie and say she was looking for her father.

She broke into the prison building through a window. Intending to go down to the lower cellblock that housed the infirmary, Nadya stopped when she heard familiar voices. Her throat turned dry. She crept along the hall, keeping her ears open for the sounds of guardsmen.

The voice came from the other side of a stone wall. Nadya glanced around. There, near the top, a crawl space meant to filter out the damp air. With a leap, she scrambled into it, and suddenly she was looking down at a meeting room below through a thin vent.

In the chair at the head of the table sat a tired-looking Duke with a hastily bandaged collarbone. Beside him, the magistrate dutifully copied down the notes of the meeting. Nadya began to sweat.

On one side of the Duke, the deputy Guardmaster, a small, lithe Erevan who looked like he could take on a Nomori man in a fight and last, drummed his fingers on the table. On the Duke's other side, Marko sat with tight lips, clutching Kesali's hand.

Nadya barely looked at her except to note that she was all right.

The final figure at the table shocked her most of all. Drina Gabori sat right across from the Duke. She did not pay him the deference due his station with lowered eyelashes and humble looks. Instead, her piercing gaze did not leave his face. Nadya's back twitched nervously. What could be so bad as to bring her grandmother together with the Duke?

Shadar entered the room, closing the door behind him, and bowed to his Duke, before sliding into the seat. "I posted six guards in the hall and two outside this door. No one is getting in here, Your Grace."

The Duke looked around at everyone at the table, then said in a raspy voice, "I would like an explanation as to what just happened in the palace."

The deputy Guardmaster cleared his throat. "For those of you who weren't present, during the Duke's open session, His Grace was attacked with the intent to kill by several of the city's citizens. We do not yet know why they attacked, or what propelled them. Our first focus was getting him and his family to safety. This prison was built to be impregnable, from both sides. A—"

"Short-term solution," the Duke said. "I will not hide down here. Tomorrow, we return to the palace once the proper security has been put in place."

"Of course." The deputy Guardmaster sounded like it was an argument he had tried and failed to win. "Two of the attackers are dead. The other three are in critical condition. They will not be able to be questioned for days."

Nadya swallowed, but the throbbing in her shoulder increased until she swayed with dizziness. She had killed them. She had now killed three people. She was a murderer equal to Levka, to whoever was behind the killings in the city.

"The one called the Iron Phoenix killed the two men, injured the other three and also His Grace, the Duke. We did not yet know what his purpose there was, but I would guess he was somehow involved with the attack." The deputy Guardmaster crossed his fingers.

"Involved? He clearly saved the lives of the royal family," Shadar said.

"And you would give him a medal?"

The captain shook his head. "Of course not. I believe he is dangerous, but I will not let my personal prejudices get in the way of my reasoning."

The deputy Guardmaster stood up. "You go too far. I am your superior—"

"Who will condemn a man and instigate a citywide hunt for him because he does not conform to your ideas of normalcy. You have no proof beyond that. Well," Shadar said, his voice calm, but carrying an undercurrent of poison, "he is Nomori. Perhaps that's all you require."

"How dare you!"

"Enough!" the Duke said firmly. Both men stopped. Nadya held her breath. She had never heard her father talk that way to a superior officer, and his words brought a measure of steadiness to her otherwise collapsing world.

"I brought you all here for answers," the Duke continued. "Here is what I have to say on the matter. If possible, bring the Iron Phoenix in. I would have him questioned. Our city is fragile, and we need certainties, not masked men running about."

Marko frowned. "No offense, Father, but do you think the Guard would even be capable of bringing him in? He took on five armed men and defeated them."

"Five armed civilians who weren't in their right minds. Not five trained guardsmen," the deputy said.

"Perhaps," Levka said, speaking for the first time, "we need to be harsher in our judgments."

A cold sweat broke out on Nadya's forehead. Was he going to reveal her identity?

The magistrate continued, "I know it's not a popular opinion here, but we simply cannot take the risks we might if it wasn't the time of floodwaters. Yes, I want to believe the Iron Phoenix is a hero. But we do not have the luxury of doing so. I think the Duke's Guard should focus on getting this man off the streets. After the solstice"—he inclined his head toward Kesali—"we can look into whether or not it is good for the city to have a masked vigilante running about."

"We have limited resources, Magistrate," Shadar said. "I would tend to agree with you, but I don't think any of our men can be spared."

"Surely a dozen of the Guard can be pulled from the ration lines, or the lower city," Levka replied.

Nadya knew what he was doing and why he did not reveal who she was. If he did, there would be nothing stopping her from focusing entirely on bringing him down. But by keeping it a secret, he insured she still had much to lose, and by setting the Guard on her, she would be too busy to interrupt whatever he had in store for the city.

Simple. Brilliant. She realized with a sour feeling that solving the mystery behind the murders and taking down such a man as Levka might be beyond her abilities. It did not mean, however, that she wouldn't try.

The Duke raised a hand to halt any further debate. "We will look into the man who calls himself the Iron Phoenix, but that will not be at the expense of peace. We will not let anyone, let alone a zealot with rioters at his back, threaten my future daughter-in-law."

Kesali gave a small smile, but she remained silent. Nadya wondered what she was thinking. Was she scared at the ever-nearing deadline of the summer solstice, now only days away? Or were her thoughts back down in the servants' hall, lingering on their kiss?

"Fools," Drina muttered under her breath. Nadya was surprised she had stayed quiet this long.

Shadar went red, but before he could make excuses for his mother-in-law, the Duke turned his gaze to her. "Madame Gabori? Do you have something you wish us to know?"

Drina sniffed. "You have no idea what you are dealing with." She spoke in Nomori, and the deputy Guardmaster glared at her.

The Duke, however, nodded. "Please, I would know what you do. I was not far from the Iron Phoenix during the fight in the throne room, and I saw a bullet pierce his shoulder, fired from close range."

A bullet meant for you, Nadya thought bitterly, and her shoulder throbbed.

"The Phoenix stumbled back but didn't even falter. That should have killed him. How did he not only survive but fight with a strength that is supernatural?"

"Simple," Drina said. "He is...one of the *nivasi*."

All the warmth leeched out of Nadya's hands. They trembled as her grandmother's words from the night of Jastima's murder came back to her: *the work of one of the* nivasi.

"*Nivasi*?" Marko asked.

"It is not something we share with Erevans," Drina said sharply. Shadar leaned over and whispered to her in rapid Nomori that Nadya could not pick up from where she perched. Drina sighed. "But, as I am reminded, these are not ordinary times. You know of Nomori gifts, what our men are born with, and what our women are. Very rarely, there is a third kind."

Nadya held her breath.

"Some Nomori, one in ten thousand, is born with an unpredictable gift. It does not fall in with the psychic gifts of our women or the fighting prowess of our men. It is something altogether different."

A memory flew through Nadya's mind: Shay and the fire she could call. She clenched her teeth hard to keep from being sick.

"What kinds of gifts?" Lord Marko asked.

"Impossible to say. The abilities of the *nivasi*, as we call them, are violent and unpredictable. And far more powerful than normal Nomori. From what I've heard, it seems that this man has incredible strength as well as speed and fighting reflexes."

"Almost a combination of a male Nomori's skills and a woman's psychic gift," Kesali said softly.

Marko patted her hand, and Nadya was too preoccupied with her grandmother's words to feel the usual pang of jealousy.

"Can one of these *nivasi* be stopped by the Duke's Guard?"

Drina's eyes were hard. "Not one in their prime. You do not understand these creatures. But you know of one. Durriken was his name."

A collective gasp filled the epic silence following Drina's pronouncement of that name. Nadya felt a squeezing pressure on her heart. Durriken the Butcher? He was a *nivasi* like her?

You do not know if you are nivasi, *yet. You can't be sure. Not yet. Not without proof.*

"Durriken the Butcher was *nivasi*? So he was Nomori?" the Duke asked slowly, echoing her thoughts. "He killed hundreds of Erevans centuries ago."

"Ay, hundreds and Erevans and even more Nomori," Drina said. "He found his way to this city after slaughtering a great many of our people, running the rivers red with blood. He developed powers that could not be matched. Our histories speak of his ability to rip someone's heart out with his mind."

Nadya tried to swallow the lump in her throat, but she couldn't.

"The Elders wanted him destroyed when he was discovered as *nivasi*. While strong in their gifts, these creatures are weak of mind. Durriken went insane and murdered hundreds." Drina looked directly at the Duke. "Do you now understand what has taken root in your city?"

Nadya couldn't breathe. The room spun around her.

The Duke sighed and was silent for several moments. Nadya heard only her heartbeat, smelled only blood, and was barely aware of his words when he said, "Search the entire city, both for the Phoenix and the zealot. I want them both found and interrogated before the solstice. That is still our deadline. The food stores will not last beyond it." He turned to the deputy Guardmaster. "Can you hold the city against an uprising?"

The confidence vanished from the man's drawn face. "No, Your Grace. If enough people wish for the Lady's head, even this place will not be safe for her. We cannot question everyone in the city to know their loyalty, and while your Guard will do its best to stop a frontal assault on the palace gates, I fear a knife in the dark might be a greater threat."

His words rang out with a somber reality. Marko finally let go of Kesali, who was pale and quiet. "A civil war, even if we can hold the palace, will ruin Storm's Quarry beyond repair," Marko said. "We have been free of invasion for centuries because the city is defensible to the point that an enemy would have to survive the storms to be able to siege it. But with a war within, I fear that one of our neighbors that covet the gem mines might decide we are weak enough to strike. Wintercress, while always diplomatic, has long desired a larger share of our wealth, and our alliances with Shikra and the South Marches may not be enough to deter them if given the opportunity."

"War with Wintercress, or one of the barbarian tribes to the north, is not something we will survive unscathed. Or even at all." The Duke's words rang out, somber and final. "Find these two men, and do it with all haste," he ordered everyone at the table. "At the same time, have all tiers of the city notified that I am making a public address on the day before the solstice."

"That is exceedingly dangerous, Your Grace," the deputy began.

"My people are hurting, and I must reassure them. Now is not the time for aggression and locked doors. The zealot sent a message. I will send one of my own." Beside him, Marko shook his head, but the Duke either missed it or ignored it. "I want answers. I want peace, and I want this city to survive the coming storm."

Storm's Quarry had weathered tempests from the sea and sky for a thousand years, but Nadya did not think he was referring to rain and lightning and winds. The greatest of the Great Storms would come from hunger and jealousy and the darkness in men's hearts.

The Duke dismissed them, staying back to talk to his son and his future daughter-in-law. Nadya left without looking at Kesali. Their kiss, so beautiful at the time, now seemed like a distant memory as the weight of revelation pulled Nadya down.

She waited until the room emptied to sneak out.

As she made her way slowly home, clutching her injured shoulder, Nadya knew three things.

The murderer was *nivasi*. Her grandmother had said so, and the solid black eyes of all the murderers proved there was some sort of power at work. Nadya knew the mysterious man who watched the attacks was part of it. Somehow, the zealot and magistrate fit into the picture, but she couldn't quite figure out how.

She was *nivasi*. The thought made her heart ache harder than her shoulder. Was her lack of control in the throne room the first onset of madness?

Finally, Nadya knew now what would truly happen if anyone discovered her abilities. The Elders, led by her grandmother and assisted by her parents and the Guard, would try to kill her to eliminate the threat of another Durriken the Butcher.

CHAPTER EIGHTEEN

Behind gray clouds, the sun crept toward the horizon and the city grew darker. Gedeon felt a twinge of sadness. Night was his domain, the shadows his temple, but he could not deny the thrill that coursed through him as he wielded his power during the day. Darkness provided protection, but using his abilities in the light brought a rush of power that was nearly as intoxicating as the cheap ale served in this tier.

He stood on the corner of two narrow streets. Nomori swept past him, heading home from a day of grueling work. They avoided eye contact and did not speak to one another. Cloaked in black with his face covered, he was another potential threat to them, a rioter who could be brought to spark at any moment, and nothing more.

The Nomori girl walked down the street, keeping close to the edge. Her face was lined in pain. One hand clutched her right shoulder where the faintest bit of red seeped through her vest. Gedeon watched as she rounded the corner. Her eyes never found him as they feverishly scanned the crowd.

The magistrate had been right. Gedeon was glad he hadn't simply taken over the man's mind and used him as another pawn in his war of chaos on the city. The magistrate, Levka Puyatin as he had so suavely introduced himself, had sneaked up on Gedeon as he left the palace just after the attack on the Duke.

"Your work is quite impressive, you know."

Gedeon jumped. Not many things could surprise him. He cursed himself for letting the need for a speedy departure cloud his senses. Whirling around, he grabbed ahold of his power, ready to render this man before him into a sniveling puppet.

The man, well-dressed and covered in jewels—such an Erevan fad—held up his hands. "I am not armed, no need to worry. And I'm not here to arrest you."

Gedeon licked his lips. "I care not why you're here, Erevan."

"But I care a great deal why you are, Nomori. My name is Levka Puyatin, and I'm a magistrate to His Grace, the Duke." The man held out his ringed hand.

"If you think a title will save you..." Gedeon glanced around. They were fairly concealed, just behind the main gate to the palace, next to one of the storehouses.

"No, no, of course not. You don't plan to spare anyone, not Erevan, not Nomori. You are something more, are you not?" Levka did not wait for his answer. "I admire what you have done. The way you started before the Great Storm, just one murder. Then another, another. The feat at the theater. Now, an attack on the Duke. You've got the city practically tearing itself to bits." He held up a hand when Gedeon opened his mouth to speak. "Impressive, yes. But a few concentrated attacks can only be the beginning. I can help you sow chaos in every crevasse of the city."

"You?" Gedeon had to admit, he was slightly intrigued. The magistrate carried a certain self-assurance that bordered on suicidal. Amusing enough to let him live for another few moments.

"Yes." Levka's face darkened, and Gedeon found himself wanting to flinch away from the murderous look in the magistrate's eye. "You see, I have a goal, too. One that coincides rather nicely with yours, though it's a bit more focused than simply bringing chaos to the city. From what I can deduce, we both work much the same way. Through surrogates."

This man was clever. Gedeon narrowed his eyes. Cleverness could get one killed.

"What I am proposing is a partnership. I will let you in on my plans, and I think you'll be nicely surprised."

"Why would I work with an Erevan?" Gedeon hissed.

"Because I have the knowledge, wealth, and power to do what you cannot." Levka smiled. "And because I know the identity of someone who might prove very interesting to you."

Gedeon stared at him for a long time. Levka held his gaze. Finally, he said, "Tell me more."

Now, watching the girl the magistrate had pointed him to, Gedeon could not stop the little shivers of pleasure that raced up and down his back. This was the girl who turned what would have been another wondrous display of chaos into a fight that ended in the defeat of the five armed men he had gotten through the guardsmen at the gate. This was the girl who had leapt over crowds as if they were stepping stones, broke bones with bare hands, and walked away after being shot from five paces out.

If the rest of the magistrate's plans were as good as this, then Gedeon did not regret letting the man live.

He watched the girl enter one of the ramshackle dwellings. He stared at the door for long time after she had disappeared within and thought, this was a girl he could use.

❖

Nadya staggered in through the door of her house. Her hand gripped the doorway with white, bloodless knuckles. She tripped and fell through the flap, cracking her knees on the stone floor.

"Nadya? Nadya!" Her mother ran through to the workshop. She crouched next to Nadya, cradling her face in both hands. "What's wrong? What happened?"

She opened her mouth, but words wouldn't come out. Her throat was too dry. She swallowed, and it burned. Everything burned. Her shoulder, her forehead, her mother's soft touch.

"Your shoulder?" she asked, gently removing the hand that clenched it.

The scent of blood, iron and sharp, filled the room, and Nadya threw up. The bile burned her throat, and even after it landed on the stone floor, a pile of yellow and red, she couldn't rid the taste from her mouth.

Her mother gasped when she lifted the edge of Nadya's vest and saw the bullet wound beneath. Nadya glanced down at it. Blood had congealed until it was thick and black, a lump of unnatural ooze spreading from her collarbone to her seal. Mirela touched it with careful fingers, and even they burned. Nadya cried out.

"I'm sorry. If only the hospitals weren't already overrun." She squeezed Nadya's good arm. "We'll just take care of it ourselves. Can you walk to the bed? Come, it's not far."

Leaning far too much on her mother's frail frame, Nadya limped toward the living room. Her mother started to cough, each hack rippling through them and throwing off their careful rhythm. "Mama, I can do it. You don't have to—"

"I'm fine," Mirela said quickly. She guided Nadya over to the bed and slowly sat down with her. "I need to take your clothing off, to be able to clean it. This might hurt."

Nadya bit her already injured lip against the tiny fires that ran up and down her arm as Mirela struggled to get first the vest, then the shirt underneath off without jostling her arm too much. She wore only her breast band now, but it was stained red and black on one side, and yellow with sweat on the other. Mirela removed her seal of the Protectress and Nadya bit her lip. But her mother just set it on top of the bloodied vest showing no signs that she had taken a psychic reading of it.

"Nadya, what happened?" Mirela asked again. She rose and went over to their water pitcher, lighting the kiln as well before returning with water and a soft cloth.

Nadya looked at the ground. When she wasn't stumbling in delirium and pain, she had considered this question on the way back. "I...I was attacked on the third tier." Her voice trembled. "I went to get more medicine."

"Oh, Nadya, you shouldn't have." Slowly, Mirela dipped the white cloth into the cool water and began dabbing the thick dried blood away. Nadya's back straightened, but she refused to let the pain get to her.

"I know you're running out." She bit back a yelp as Mirela touched the leaden bullet. "The floodwaters have not receded any, and the solstice is so soon." She gasped at the pain.

"Such a risk is not worth it."

The water in the pitcher was now a light shade of translucent red, the cloth dyed nearly black. Her skin was now visible under the mess, and Nadya regretted looking. Spider tendrils of muscle underneath shot out from the green-tinged center that contained a black lump—all that remained of the bullet intended for the Duke.

"A group of Erevans. They had muskets." Her voice choked at the memories of the men she had killed, and her mother was there, embracing her and whispering words of strength into her ear.

"You will be fine. It's over now. You made it."

Nadya swallowed. "I was so scared."

"I know, love, I know." Her mother returned to her work. Every time she touched the bullet, Nadya jerked. "They must have been far away when they fired, else this would be have a fatal shot."

The image of the smoking pistol in front of her flashed through Nadya's mind, and she shivered.

"This will hurt, Nadya, but it must come out. Its poison has already begun spreading. If we leave it in longer, it will only get worse." Mirela's voice was calm and confident, but Nadya heard her thundering heartbeat. She wasn't sure her daughter would be all right. If Nadya wasn't unnatural, she wouldn't have been.

Mirela left her for a moment, going to fetch pliers from her workshop. She dropped them into the kiln for a few moments to sterilize their sharp edges. Nadya's stomach threatened to revolt again.

"I'm here. It will be over in a moment, I promise." Mirela gave her a hand to hold as the other deftly angled the pliers toward the bullet. As soon as their edges touched the lead chunk, Nadya dropped her mother's hand to avoid breaking every bone in it. She dug her fingernails into her palms, her teeth clenched, as fire ripped from her shoulder and spotted her vision.

"It's out now. Are you still with me? Nadya?"

She blinked, and her mother slowly came back into focus. Blood flowed freely from the wound now that the bullet had been removed. Mirela smiled and began dabbing at its edge again with the red cloth. "You were lucky. This should be far worse. The Protectress truly was watching over you."

The Protectress does not watch over creatures like me, Nadya thought as tears sprung to her eyes. *The Protectress shields the rest of you from me.*

Mirela gently cupped her hands around a mug of tea. "Here, drink this. It will help calm you down."

Nadya obediently drank the hot tea, avoiding her mother's gaze. She felt as if she was drowning in an ocean of things she did not know, and answers, straight answers, were her only way out of the clinging waters.

That man, the one who controlled the murderers with their black eyes, knew what it was to be a *nivasi*. She could get answers from him, to know if she was to go mad like Durriken the Butcher.

A few minutes after taking the tea, Nadya fell into a dark sleep.

When she woke, her bandages had been replaced and tied neatly, a small loaf of hard bread waited on a plate next to her, her seal of the Protectress was gone, and her mother was not in the house.

Nadya did not stop to wonder about it. Sleep had pushed back the pain in her shoulder. An iron resolve built in her chest. She scarfed down the bread in three bites, put on a shirt, then left the house. She stopped in the alley to pick up her disguise. Despite the spots of dried blood that dotted the damp cloth, it went into her belt pouch. She would walk to the stairs leading up to the city's top tier. No need to provoke the Duke's Guard—not yet, anyway.

Today, the Duke would stand before his city and offer reassurances. Nadya, like Marko, did not think such an approach would work, but if anyone could bring peace to Storm's Quarry by talking, it was the Duke.

Nadya wasn't headed there to listen to lies thinly veiled as hope. The solstice was tomorrow, and the very future of Storm's Quarry could be at stake. The Duke's Guard were spread thin through the city, trying to quell riots as they started. At their numbers, they wouldn't be able to save the city from chaos, but the Duke might.

The mysterious man, the *nivasi*, would be there, and Nadya would find him and question him. Whatever he did to those men to start the fire in the Guardhouse, he could not do it to her. She was too strong for that.

The Nomori tier was nearly deserted. She heard whispers as she passed. The floodwaters had not receded at all, and now even the Nomori doubted the psychic powers of their own Stormspeaker. Doors were clamped shut and windows barricaded as the Nomori prepared themselves for the storm tomorrow would surely bring.

Nadya would do anything in her power to prevent that, and that started with finding the man at the root of it all. She needed to know how the *nivasi*, Levka, and the zealot all figured into this, and what their final plan was. She was the only one who could do it, because she was the only one who knew enough of the truth to see past the lies.

Erevans in the second tier watched her with shielded eyes and dark scowls. One man, corralling a woman and a small child through the empty market, shouted at her, "Go back to your tier, Nomori filth. You're not welcome here."

Nadya bit her lip and ignored it. However, when another grabbed at her injured shoulder, she cuffed him slightly in the gut. He doubled over, wheezing and unable to speak. No one bothered her after that.

From the fourth tier, Nadya could see the regiment that guarded the palace gates. It was a show of both strength and humility on the Duke's part, conducting the meeting in the city, away from his palace.

Nadya slipped in through the crowds of people. The gap between the races ran as wide as a river, down the center of the tier. At its head, the Duke stood with three dozen guards at his back, Marko at his side. Kesali was nowhere to be seen. Both royal men were dressed in their finest, their jewels sparkling in the faint sunlight let in through the clouds.

"This city belongs to the Nomori as well as Erevans," the Duke was saying. "If it wasn't for them, if it wasn't for the first Stormspeaker, the city would have been overrun by the sea twenty years ago. The deaths that sparked the violence our city has endured these past weeks were the work of wicked men, not gods that we have forgotten the names of."

Nadya let his voice fade into the chaos of the crowd as her gaze swept around. Her heart pounded in her ears. She didn't know if she would even recognize the man, let alone if he was even here.

There—on the rooftop of a nearby manor. Its doors and windows were bolted shut and hired guards stood outside just within the front gate, rapiers drawn. Balanced on the slanted, shingled rooftop stood a familiar figure with dark, bottomless eyes and a thin scar. He watched the proceedings with a slight smirk that Nadya could see across the distance. He was *nivasi*, and he was going to sabotage the Duke's address.

CHAPTER NINETEEN

Nadya kept her eyes on the strange man as she ducked back through the crowd until she could step into a culvert alley. The gray cloak, now bloodstained, smelled of iron and gun smoke. Nadya gagged, but she put it on. Her fingers found purchase in the wall of the manor, and she scrambled up, the gray scarf tight across her mouth. Her shoulder throbbed and cried with every upward motion her right arm made, but the tea and the bandages had worked wonders. Deep down, though, she knew it was more than her mother's skill in healing. It was her abnormal gift, her unnatural strength.

Her *nivasi* blood.

Nadya crawled onto the top of the manor, slipping and sliding along its slanted shingles. She squinted. It was nearly two hundred paces across the cobblestoned square to the next manor where the mysterious man watched the proceedings and plotted. She slowly backed up until her boot heel hit the far edge of the roof. Her first few steps were long lopes until she found her footing on the slanted roof. Each time her boot struck, shingles were crushed, their pieces skittering down the roof to fall to the drain below. When she reached the edge, Nadya crouched and leapt in one fluid movement. She sailed over the crowd below, hearing their shouts and exclamations. She kept her arms tight at her sides, resisting the urge to thrash like a duck avoiding slaughter. Wind rushed at her, pulling wisps of hair from her braid.

Nadya's arms started flailing on their own accord. She was headed down, and the manor wasn't quite there...

Her hands hit the top edge of the roof. Nadya cried out as fiery pain raced through her shoulder. Grunting, she hauled herself up. Her body fell over the raised edge of the roof and onto hard stone.

Wincing, she got to her feet. The mysterious man didn't turn at her clumsy entry. He watched the Duke's address, a smirk that reminded her unpleasantly of Levka pasted across his face—one that meant he knew something she did not.

Nadya checked her mask and walked over to him with purposeful steps. She stopped fifteen paces from him, the fronds of a nearby potted plant brushing her arms and sending shivers down her spine.

"You seem to like watching important events," she said. "And those events almost always take a nasty turn."

He turned, and Nadya's fists were up and clenched.

"I was wondering when you were going to show up." Her fighting stance didn't seem to bother him. "I couldn't make my presence much more obvious without commissioning a print shop for a sign."

His voice was deep, but smooth. He wore black, a simple tunic and breeches that no doubt allowed him to blend in anywhere. His hair was dark brown, his skin light for a Nomori, and his eyes...

Nadya swallowed. She looked just above them, focusing on his forehead as if a target had been painted there. Something about their black depths unnerved her. Not solid black like his victims, but unnatural all the same.

The man laughed. "So, the Iron Phoenix is a girl, a Nomori girl. I was told, but now I see it. Not exactly what I was expecting, especially after watching your performance in the Duke's throne room yesterday. So, what's your name?"

Nadya didn't answer, and for some reason, the man found that incredibly amusing. "I'm called Gedeon. We should get to know one another."

Her ears burned. "You're behind this. You were at the manor when Duren killed Jurek. You were in the throne room when those five men attacked the Duke. I don't know how you are doing it, taking control and changing their eyes to black, but it's happening by your hand."

"What is?"

She swept a hand over the tense conference below. "The murders. The tension between Nomori and Erevans. The whispers of civil war. Have you been living here for the past two months? If it isn't resolved by tomorrow, the city will run out of food and demand the Stormspeaker's head."

He shrugged and turned back to the scene below. "It seems to me like most of that is the Stormspeaker's doing. She shouldn't make a false prediction. People get angry at that kind of thing."

Nadya bit back a curse, quelling her instinct to defend Kesali. Gedeon was like those sleek black panthers they imported for circuses and rich courtiers, slippery and cunning. She didn't know where his powers lay or how much, or little, of an upper hand she had. Until she did, she had to treat him like the wild animal he was.

"You're *nivasi*, aren't you?" Nadya took a step closer. "I learned of Durriken the Butcher's true nature. I know what you are capable of. You are *nivasi*." She tried to say it with conviction, but the last syllable still turned up like an unasked question.

The edge of Gedeon's mouth twitched. "You should not ask questions that you already know the answer to."

In front of her, Nadya's hands began to tremble with energy. She had come here for straight answers, and so far, Gedeon was not forthcoming. Her eyes narrowed. That would change, one way or another.

"Doesn't matter. I know what you are capable of, and I am going to stop you from hurting anyone again."

Gedeon turned back, and the slight smile, the knowing curl to his lips, made Nadya shiver. "If you knew what I was capable of, you would not be standing on this roof with me."

Nadya swallowed. It was an empty threat. The man looked as if he had never picked up a weapon in his life. Even his fingernails were perfectly clean. He might be a Nomori man, but since he was *nivasi*, he lacked the preternatural fighting skills her father and all the others had. She would be able to handle him in a fight.

Her matter-of-fact attitude toward fighting someone made her stomach squirm, but Nadya pushed it away for another time.

She had one more question before she knocked him out and delivered him to the Duke's Guard, before all this could end and the ultimatum of the zealot would be thwarted and Kesali would be safe.

"I need to know something," she began.

He raised an eyebrow.

"How do you know if you are *nivasi*? I mean, am...am I one, too?" The question almost got stuck in her throat.

Gedeon's smile vanished, and his face looked almost pleasant for a moment. He looked her up and down, Nadya struggling not to fidget under his gaze, until he finally said again, "You should not ask questions to which you already know the answer."

She nodded numbly. She knew it. She had known it, deep down, since her grandmother's whispered words in that alley: *the work of one of the* nivasi.

Nadya swallowed down a Great Storm of emotion before it could overwhelm and drown her. There would be time for that later. Now, she had to deal with Gedeon and stop him before he did something to destroy the Duke's address.

"None of that matters. You are coming with me. To the Duke's Guard. You need to answer for what you've done."

Gedeon's expression was unreadable. "Is that so? And what exactly have I done?"

"Why do you ask questions to which you already know the answer?" she said, meeting his eyes squarely for the first time.

"Humor me. What do you think I've done?"

"You took control of innocent people and made them kill, all to create strife and light a fire between the Nomori and Erevans."

He shook his head. "You are foolish."

"Doesn't matter. Either come with me willingly, or I'll drag you to the Duke's Guard myself." Nadya's fists tightened in front of her. "You won't be able to get away. I am far stronger than I look."

He smiled again. "So I have seen. You took a bullet from five paces away yesterday, and yet today you are leaping from building to building. You withstood a roaring fire and carried out grown men twice your size. Not to mention, you faced down five armed men and knocked them out in under a minute, killing two of them." He slowly walked away from the edge of the roof and toward her. Nadya held her ground. "Your abilities are incredible. You should be thankful. Although, turning me in to the Duke's Guard might be difficult, as some of them are pretty hungry for the blood of the Iron Phoenix. You shouldn't bother with the likes of them."

It was her turn for a patronizing smile. "Are you going to ask me to join you in tearing this city apart? Because I will tell you now, I have no interest in working with scum like you." She bridged the gap between them with one step, her fists hovering a hair from his chest.

"You are already a murderer." He shrugged. "It's not exactly a huge jump from where you're sitting to where I am. After all, we are both *nivasi*."

She stared up into those bottomless black eyes. "That was an accident. I am nothing like you, and I would never help you destroy the people I love."

"My dear, who said anything about giving you a choice?"

Before Nadya could take a step back at the horrible matter-of-factness in his voice, his black eyes expanded until they were everything she saw. She was drowning in a dark well of ink, her voice choked off by an invisible hand. She tried to move, to thrust one of her fists up and into where she knew Gedeon's chin had been a moment before. But the black torrent that surrounded her closed in, and Nadya could not move. The blackness rose, bound itself around her, as images of the teenage boy she'd killed two years ago mingled with the wide eyes and pleas and prone forms of the men who attacked the Duke yesterday. She didn't have to look down to know her hands were the only pinprick of color in this black, brilliantly red and stained forever with blood. Nadya tried to scream, but even her voice was cut off by the hammering of her own heart. She closed her eyes against it all.

The black contracted and snapped back into Gedeon's eyes. It took a moment for Nadya to realize she was no longer drowning. Faint sunlight filtered in through the clouds, and Gedeon's eyes were nothing more than the dark eyes of a killer.

He was smiling again. "Like I said, you shouldn't have come here. You are not as strong as you think."

Nadya was ready to show him just how strong she was, but when she tried to move her arm up to punch him square in the chest, it wouldn't go. Panic seized her throat. She tried again, but nothing. She tried to speak. Her mouth didn't work. She tried to walk, to back away from this man—she was just starting to realize she really had no idea of who he was or what he could do—but her legs remained calmly rooted to the roof as if bolted there.

"You're starting to panic right about now." Gedeon turned back toward the peace conference. Shouting had broken out in the crowd, and the curt orders of guardsmen tried to bring peace once more.

Nadya struggled against her invisible bonds. Why wouldn't her body work? What had this man done to her? He had frozen her somehow, probably to keep her from interfering with his plans for this conference. Nadya cursed her stupidity of jumping in to confront him without better information.

She jerked. Her body had started walking toward Gedeon. Nadya ordered it to stop, but she kept moving. She couldn't even turn her head to look from side to side as her body came to a rest beside Gedeon. The movements weren't spasmodic either, but smooth, as if she commanded them.

She, or someone else.

A terrible thought occurred to her, so awful that Nadya forced it back down. Gedeon started speaking again, his eyes on the Duke as he passionately made a case for the future of the city and Kesali. "When I first saw the Iron Phoenix, I could hardly believe my fortune. Not only did you direct the attention of the entire city and the Guard to yourself, but you presented me with a weapon to throw at them.

Nadya screamed silently as she struggled to rip herself free.

Gedeon looked her over as if he had heard. "Don't worry. I won't keep you forever. I rather like the reactions of my puppets once their strings have been cut and they see what they've done. And because you're *nivasi*, you will get to remember it all."

She cried as her body jumped off the roof and down into the crowd of people listening to the Duke's address.

CHAPTER TWENTY

Nadya kept screaming, but her mouth was a tight line of indifference. Her feet slammed into the cobblestones after the five-story jump. Stone flew away from her, and she stood up in a deep circular depression. The people around her edged away uneasily.

I am wearing the scarf, she thought with the tiniest bit of relief. Her body calmly walked out of the hole and into the crowd. *No one will recognize me.*

Nadya willed herself to stop, but she was powerless. The world flashed before her like a painting, and she was only an audience to it, not a participant within the frame. For a hopeful moment, she thought that Gedeon merely wanted the Iron Phoenix to make an appearance, to disrupt the Duke's address.

She hung on to that thought until her fist shot out and through the chest of a frail, old woman. Nadya shrieked as she withdrew a blood-soaked hand, and the woman crumpled to the ground, a gaping hole in her chest.

Before she could comprehend what she had just done, her leg flashed out and snapped the neck of the man who went to his elderly mother's rescue. The sickening crunch of her boot colliding with bone filled Nadya's being. She railed against her invisible bonds, trying to take back control of her body, but she might as well have been trying to hit air.

She watched as the realization of the deaths spread through the crowds. Some people already had run away in terror, but most hadn't yet realized the danger. Her ears picked up whispers of *the Iron Phoenix*, and she tried to scream at them all to run, to escape before the automaton that was her body destroyed them all. Her voice didn't work, but Nadya continued to yell until her spirit was exhausted. Then she yelled some more.

Her body, outside of her control, waged war on the citizens of Storm's Quarry. Both races died under her hands. Men. Women. The elderly. The newborn. Nadya wanted to throw up as her body wrenched a baby away from its mother.

Her disguise, gray cloak billowing unmistakably in the wind, was drenched in the blood of Erevans and Nomori alike. When she came upon a group of Nomori youth, boys who were almost men, at first, their expressions were hopeful. This was their hero after all, one of their people who had saved their fathers from the fire and the Duke from bullets. Those looks of wide-eyed adoration slowly changed to confusion when she grabbed the first of them, a tall boy Nadya recognized as a trainee for the Duke's Guard. Her fingers dug into his back and snapped his spine. He didn't have time to even whimper before the life left his body, and she dropped his corpse to the ground. The four other faces turned from confused to terrified.

Run! Nadya shouted at them.

As if they had heard her voice through her body's sealed lips, they took off. But her cursed gift made her far faster than them, and two died with uncompromising blows to the head before they took three steps. The others shrieked and begged for their lives. Nadya cried internally as her hands crushed the light out of their eyes.

The address was in complete uproar. People were running left and right, trying to escape the deadly rampage of the Iron Phoenix. She did not have to chase after them. Her body walked, almost strolled, through the chaos and death, reaching out and snuffing the life out of the unfortunates who crossed her path.

Nadya wished for death. She prayed to the Protectress that some stray bullet would strike her between the eyes and end it all before another life could be taken. Perhaps this was a prayer the Protectress could answer. But then there was the final cry of a father desperately protecting his children. Then the silence of those children, then the shriek of a man who ran to their aid who was nearly torn in half by the calm-faced automaton that was once Nadya.

She tried to close her eyes, to even blink to get a moment's respite from the nightmare she now walked through. But any control was beyond her grasp, and Nadya had no choice but to watch and memorize every face screwed up in horror as they died.

Shouts that weren't screams of panic came to Nadya's ears. The Duke's Guard had arrived. Her body turned. Several hundred paces ahead, a regiment of guardsmen closed in around the Duke and his son, hustling them up the marble stairs and to the safety of the palace. Nadya prayed that she would not pursue them. If she killed the Duke, the city would fall. If she went into the palace, she might kill Marko.

She might kill Kesali.

Dozens of guardsmen, their uniforms as bright as the blood that coated her arms and fists, closed in around her in a clawlike pattern. Muskets aimed at her heart, steady in the hands of the Erevans. Rapiers were drawn by the Nomori. Nadya did not see her father, and she prayed she wouldn't.

Kill me, she shouted silently to the grim faces of the men who circled her. *Kill me now and end this.*

"Fire," a voice called out, and a rain of bullets closed in on her from all sides.

Nadya waited for death to take her.

Her body did not. The automaton flipped backward, dodging the first dozen bullets. She corkscrewed in the air. Several grazed her arms and legs. Nadya cried out, a reflex, but her lips didn't part. None of the wounds came even close to fatal. She slid down on her knees, bending backward so far the back of her head grazed the wet ground. In an instant, she was up and right next to the first group of guardsmen.

They were a dozen men, mostly Erevan. The automaton dodged to the right, as four bullets ripped past her. The men stopped, unslung their muskets, and furiously began to reload. Her mouth twitched into a smile, and Nadya wanted to cry. Her body smashed through the sea of red toward the men.

One dropped his musket altogether. He was young, a new recruit who thought the most he would be facing was an argument in the ration line. The plea on his lips was stopped by a blow that snapped his head back. He crumpled to the ground. The others leveled their muskets at her, bullets forgotten. The bayonets affixed to the long barrels glinted in the sun. One stabbed for her, and her body twisted around, then grabbed the barrel of the gun and shoved it back. The butt went right through the man's chest and out the other side.

A sharp pain throbbed in her torso, and her gaze was directed down at the bayonet stuck into her right side. She looked back up to the grim-faced man who held it.

More guardsmen poured in around her, firing. Several bullets hit Nadya squarely, forcing her to the ground. Inwardly, she cheered despite the pain. *Kill me! Kill me, and stop this slaughter.*

Red uniforms and rapiers and bayonets pressed in from all sides. Nadya's body went stiff went she felt the cold barrel of a pistol against the back of her neck.

Pull the trigger, she screamed. *Pull it!*

The guardsman's finger crept backward as time slowed. The automaton brought her elbow up, despite the pain in her shoulder, and rammed it into the man's knee, shattering it. In the same movement, she leapt to her feet, forcing the blades back. Metal snapped under her fingers as she grabbed at swords and bayonets and thrust them back to their owners. More than one man crumpled, his weapon protruding from his chest. She jumped aside as bullets whizzed past the bridge of her nose, and she whirled around, taking down two men with a kick.

Nadya sobbed without crying. For a moment, she believed it was going to end. How was she capable of this much destruction? Before, a single bullet and five men had nearly brought her down. What had Gedeon done to her abilities?

"It ends here, Phoenix."

Her body turned from the bodies of the slaughtered guardsmen. Six Nomori guardsmen, their rapiers drawn, faced her. Their reflexes could match her own, and their battle experience, judging from the hard looks in their eyes and the scars that crisscrossed their faces, far outweighed hers.

Nadya allowed herself to hope as she stepped out of the circle of carnage to face them.

There was no hesitation in their movements. They came at her all at once, their sword points moving in perfect unison.

The automaton dodged the first swipes, but the swords were there again, one ramming through her injured shoulder, and pulling back out, the blade dyed a deep crimson. The others stung her like angry hornets, none of them landing the fatal blow. When Nadya lunged for them, the men were suddenly gone, ducking and rolling as she had, out of her grasp.

Her face remained passive, but inwardly Nadya was screaming for them to finish her quickly. She wasn't an opponent that could be worn down.

For a long moment, she hoped that the skill of the Nomori swordsmen could overcome her unnatural strength and speed. For a moment, the automaton believed it, too, frowning in frustration at the speed and skill of the men who faced her.

A rapier shot forward toward her throat. She leapt to the side, grabbing the metal blade and snapping it. Without pause, she hurled the broken sword into the face of the man who dared think he could challenge her. It went clear through him, and he collapsed.

The tide of the fight turned.

Nadya's mind grew cold as she realized the awful truth, watching the Nomori men fight to the death in order to stop her—to stall her even—for as they fought, the final few civilians were running out of the square and down the stairs or toward their opulent manors and locking the doors. She tried to shut her eyes once more, knowing it was futile, but not wanting to see the truth.

Gedeon hadn't done anything to her abilities. This was Nadezhda Gabori in peak form, not caring about hurting those she fought. This wasn't the work of a malevolent *nivasi*. This was what she had been capable of all along, if she had embraced her power rather than shied away from it.

It scared her to her core.

The final body dropped to the ground, its spine eviscerated by the man's own blade. His eyes were wide and empty, and Nadya realized how quiet the square had become. The rest of the Duke's Guard had retreated, up to the marble stairs that led to the palace. They watched her with white faces, their muskets gripped in trembling hands.

Nadya looked away.

She could move.

Comprehension made her fall to her knees. Blood soaked into the fabric of her trousers, still warm. The rapier fell from numb hands. Nadya tried to breathe, but the scent of blood was too much.

Someone was laughing. After an eternity, she managed to raise her head to the roof of the manor. It was Gedeon, his smile plain and blazing in the noon light. He turned and left Nadya standing in the middle of her personal nightmare, a graveyard of people she had murdered.

Trembling, she rose to her feet and began to run. Buildings and stairs and people blurred past as she ran. She ran until her feet were numb, until her legs screamed with the dozens of injuries they had received. She ran until she thought it would kill her, and then she ran some more.

Her legs gave out underneath her in a culvert alley in the darkest part of the Nomori tier, not far from the gem mine. The trickle of water that ran down the stone was stained red as she collapsed into it.

For what seemed like a thousand years and not nearly long enough, Nadya sat there, leaning up against a stone cold wall, and sobbed.

CHAPTER TWENTY-ONE

The darkness of night gave way to translucent sunlight, filtered through clouds, marking the dawn of the summer solstice. Under the overpowering smell of blood, Nadya caught the scent of putrid water and salt tears. She did not need to look over the walls to know the sea had not receded, and she did not need the hammering of her heart to know what that meant for Storm's Quarry, for Kesali.

She sniffed and wiped her eyes. All night, she had sobbed until there was not a tear left in her. From the early hours of dawn until now, she'd stared at the wall on the other side of the thin culvert, not seeing anything.

Slowly, she unclenched her hands from her knees. They were covered in dried blood, with bits of bone and sinew stuck under her fingernails. The cloak had dried around her into a hard, caked form that barely resembled the original gray disguise she had bought.

Nadya stared at her hands.

The events of yesterday still did not fully register with her. It was simply too terrifying, too horrifying to have actually happened. But it had, and now dozens, perhaps even a hundred, souls now wandered the land, cut off from their lives by her hands.

These hands.

She swallowed. She tasted blood, metallic and acrid as it burned its way down her throat.

Her hands that had held Kesali as they danced, that had tangled with Kesali's fingers, that had run up and down smooth skin as they kissed and pretended tomorrow would not come.

Bile surged into her mouth and she threw up. What she might have done to Kesali…how could she had believed herself harmless, safe?

Nadya creaked to her feet, and with one violent movement, she tore off the cloak and let it fall down to the culvert. Her boots were encrusted with blood all the way up to her thighs, but she felt slightly better without the cloak's suffocating closeness. It reminded her too much of her imprisonment by Gedeon within her own body.

It had been her fault. Gedeon might have pulled the puppet strings, but Nadya had confronted a powerful *nivasi* with only half a plan, believing that she was infallible. That she was too strong to lose. The crunch of bones echoed in Nadya's ears. She winced. It would haunt her nightmares for the rest of her life, however long that was.

A thunderous roar split the quiet air of morning, and the stone underneath her feet quaked. Nadya slammed into the wall of the building in front of her. Shingles and stones rained down on her head. One caught her eyebrow with its sharp edge, cutting into flesh.

Rallying cries filled the stillness in the aftermath as the sound of hundreds, no thousands, of footsteps descended into the Nomori streets. Screams of men, women, and children echoed through the small alley as Nadya stood there, frozen.

"The mines!" One voice wailed as a woman ran past the alley's mouth. "They've taken the mines and destroyed the gate." She shrieked. "Get your filthy hands off me! I would rather die—"

Nadya acted without thinking. She sprinted out of the culvert, splashing through water, and onto the street.

If yesterday was her personal nightmare, then this was the terror-filled dream of all of Storm's Quarry.

Smoke rose from every crevasse, mingling with the gray clouds above. The bright orange of flames could be seen throughout the Nomori tier and up into the fourth tier. Above them, a wild black mass of a raging mob stormed the gates of the palace, calling for the head of the Stormspeaker. Bodies lay strewn in puddles. Insects buzzed over them, they alone glorifying in this new feast.

An Erevan man had the Nomori woman by the throat as he tried to rip her vest off. An old musket topped with a rusty bayonet was slung over his right shoulder. His mouth opened wide when Nadya, bloodstained as she was, emerged from the alley.

She stared at him, and he let the woman go, backing away. The Nomori woman was about the same age as Mirela. She bowed in thanks and turned, probably going to find her family, and with a jolt, Nadya realized that her mother was home and at the mercy of rioters.

Dodging looters as she sprinted to her house, Nadya knew the truth would finally come out. She needed her mother. She needed Mirela's guidance and wisdom, but most of all, she needed her mother's arms to wrap around and tell her that this nightmare would end and everything would be all right. The bloodstains would fade, Kesali would be saved, and their home would not succumb to civil war.

Her mother wasn't there.

Nadya stood in the workshop, staring at the two objects on her mother's stone workbench. A note, just starting to curl with damp, and her seal of the Protectress. With trembling fingers, she picked up the note.

It read: *Nadya, checked in quickly last night. I'm all right, the Phoenix didn't hurt me. Stay inside, keep the door shut. Don't trust anyone. Wait out the storm. Your mother left suddenly for Drina's. Don't know why. –Shadar*

She put it back down and grasped the metal band. Her seal, the most prized possession that she or any Nomori had, and the best piece of jewelry for her mother's gift to read.

She knows everything.

Nadya's grip tightened until the metal bent slightly. She dropped it as if it had turned white hot.

She knows, and she left.

A peculiar buzzing filled her chest.

She is afraid of me.

It was anger.

Nadya calmly walked through to the living quarters. She stripped out of her bloodstained clothes, leaving them in a pile. Using the water basin, she scrubbed the dried blood off her skin until it gleamed bronze. She climbed the ladder to her loft, bringing back a clean change of clothes and her gray blanket. She dressed, then tied the blanket around her like a cloak, ripping a hole in it for her eyes.

The anger only intensified as she worked silently with the sounds of chaos outside echoing through the room. She stopped by her mother's workbench once more, gingerly picking up her seal and fastening it on her upper arm, underneath cloak and shirt.

If she could not be the dutiful Nomori daughter for her mother or the steadfast partner that Kesali deserved, then she could be a weapon, the hardened blade that stood between them and the worst the solstice could throw.

Nadya left her house, probably for the last time, and headed to the palace and to the one who had a hand in unleashing this madness on Storm's Quarry.

A mass of rioters, several hundred in number, had broken through the gates and in to the top tier of the city. The few men of the Duke's Guard left in the top tier boarded up the gates of the palace. They stood before the portal with white faces and sweating hands, clutching muskets and rapiers.

Nadya was careful to skirt around them after leaping to the top of the city on rooftops and breaking into the palace through a window. She kept to the shadows, quietly padded down the hall and to the sun-emblazoned doors of the throne room. She knew he would be there.

With a heave, she tore open the locked metal doors to the throne room. They closed behind her, shutting out the sounds of the riots and leaving Nadya alone to face the magistrate. He stood calmly by his little writing desk, flipping through the pages of a record book. In three seconds, she crossed the velvet carpet, still strewn with parcels and bits of this and that from the crowd that had abandoned belongings in the rush to escape two days before. Levka did not look up.

"You missed a lot of the excitement." His voice was calm, as if he was speaking to a servant or child, chiding them. "Everyone was shouting, terrified. They dispatched most of the Duke's Guard into the city to keep order and find the Iron Phoenix. After what happened in the public square yesterday, who could argue? The Stormspeaker and the Duke have been locked up here with a hundred guardsmen stationed throughout the palace. I'm sure you ran into some on your way here."

Nadya didn't say anything.

"It's beginning," he continued, closing the book. "The Stormspeaker was wrong. People went to the ration lines this morning, and there was nothing to give them. This city is about to get torn in two through civil war and panic. Her head will be demanded, and the Duke and his Guard will be powerless to stop it." He looked up at Nadya. "How is the Iron Phoenix faring now, with the blood of the innocent on her hands?"

She grabbed him by the throat, knocking the writing table on edge, and thrust him up against the nearest pillar. His feet dangled just above the carpet. Nadya kept her grip loose, so as not to kill him. Yet.

"How do you think she's doing?" she hissed. "I want information."

Levka's voice rasped out, "You're not going to kill me. Why should I tell you anything?"

Her fingers tightened, and he coughed violently. Bruising started to spread out from her hand, making spiderweb patterns around his neck. "That animal Gedeon and his little puppet act have cured me of much of my squeamishness for hurting people."

She wasn't lying, and Levka must have seen it in her eyes. Instead of being terrified, however, he started to laugh. It sounded like a croak, and Nadya dropped him, stepping back. He straightened and rubbed his neck.

"I always knew you were a killer," he rasped, the honey in his voice gone. "Gedeon only revealed it. I have to say, I am glad I pointed him in your direction." Levka glared down at her. "Your hands have been drenched in blood for two years, and now you've finally realized that you can't walk through life pretending otherwise. You are a murderer, Nadya Gabori."

"Two years?" she asked, watching him. Her fists clenched and unclenched at her sides.

"The Erevan you murdered in a back alley two years ago. I was there. I saw everything."

"He attacked me—"

"And you threw him into a building, breaking his back and killing him." Levka drew a rattling breath. "His name was Valiar. He was my brother."

Nadya took a step back from the hatred that sparked in Levka's eyes.

"I wondered where my brother went every night, so I followed him. I watched him confront you." Every word came quickly and smoothly to him, as if he had spent two years rehearsing this speech. "Was it disgusting? Of course. But instead of running away or knocking him out, like you were more than capable of, you killed him."

"I didn't mean to. I had no control," she started to say.

Levka interrupted her. "I don't want to hear your excuses, *nivasi*." At her flinch, he smiled. "I know what you are. I've always known. You see, after I saw a small girl of fifteen kill my older brother with one blow, I started searching for answers. I got access to the city's histories, and it only took a few innocent questions for that doddering old cleric to tell me everything I needed to know. Everything to eliminate the threat that Nomori bring to my city."

Nadya breathed slowly. Why was he telling her all this? What purpose did it serve his scheme, two years in the making? "For someone bent on eradicating the *nivasi*, you keep strange friends."

He shrugged. "It wasn't hard to figure out who was behind the murders. He's a brute, but he takes suggestion well. His vision for the city was so limited. It did not take much persuasion to bring him around to aid my plans."

Flashes of the dark well, the blood spatters, and the screams of the innocent made Nadya look away.

"He is a tool, nothing more. Nothing like the power of the *nivasi* to show this city how dangerous the Nomori really are. By this time tomorrow, every Nomori will either be dead or forced out into the sea."

"How could you?" Nadya demanded.

"I am trying to save Storm's Quarry. That demands certain sacrifices." He glanced up at the ornate clock above the throne and smiled. "It should be nearly time."

"Time for what?"

"Lord Marko is headed to the edge of the Nomori tier and the wall. He has a contingent of guardsmen with him, intent on finding the zealot and taking him into custody. Reports of sightings of the Iron Phoenix also helped to draw him there."

"What did you do?" she whispered.

Levka continued as if she hadn't spoken. "Of course, he's not the only one there. His betrothed went. She was supposed to stay with the Duke, but that Nomori girl is smarter than her predictions make her look. Not to mention more stubborn than a horse in the rain. With a few carefully dropped hints by yours truly, she realized one of the *nivasi* was at the center of all the murders. *He* also happens to be at the wall. She's on her way there now."

Nadya flung herself at him, forcing him back up against the marble violently. Levka cried out. His ribs snapped under her grip as she laid one arm flat against his chest, pinning him to the pillar.

"Where are they?" Her voice was low and deadly, and left nothing to the imagination as to what she would do if he refused to cooperate.

"At the north gate. You can hardly miss it. The zealot has gathered all his followers, numbering in the tens of thousands." He spat blood. "They invaded the Nomori tier, demanding the head of the Stormspeaker. Someone tipped them off that she was no longer in the palace. They mean to lure her there with the blood of her kinsmen. She's too brave to stay away."

"Braver than you'll ever know," Nadya hissed. "Why tell me this? What's your plan?"

He smiled again, that horrible smirk that said he knew something she did not. "Because, Phoenix, you are not going to leave this room."

She whirled around, dropping him onto the carpet. He coughed again, and the scent of his blood wafted up to her nose.

Nadya paid no attention. While all her focus had been on the magistrate and his words, the throne room had slowly filled with red-uniformed guardsmen. They stood, six to a row and two deep, in front of the metal door. Rapiers drawn, eyes hard, staring at the one who had murdered so many of their comrades. She frowned. Twelve guardsmen was hardly an army, probably all that could be spared from the city and the Duke. Where did Levka's confidence come from?

Shadar drew his rapier and said, "Phoenix, you are under arrest. Resist, and we will kill you."

The answer to her question hit her straight in the heart. She couldn't move. Kesali was headed into a trap, toward a malicious *nivasi* who was nothing more than a mad dog bent on hurting as many as possible. She needed to get out of here, to run to save Kesali before she was killed by Gedeon or the zealot's mob. The life of the woman she loved was at stake.

She started forward, ready to knock them all out and burst through the door. Her father would never have to know the truth about her.

Nadya swung at the first man, breaking his sword in two as her fist smashed into his shoulder. Bones cracked. She stumbled back in horror, and the rapiers advanced. She still had no control over her strength, and she didn't wish to kill these men. Nadya dodged blades, weaving in and out of the guardsmen. She broke every sword she could get her hands on, using the momentum to toss the men out of her range. She did not trust herself to actually hit them. The last thing she wanted was more blood on her hands.

Shadar faced her. Nadya gulped. They were alone. The rest of the men lay unconscious in a widespread circle around them, their weapons broken. Only her father's blade was whole, and it was pointed straight at her heart.

"You fight me, Phoenix."

I don't want to fight you, Papa, she shrieked inside, a low whimper escaping her lips. But Kesali needed her.

He swung at her head, moving so fast that Nadya barely ducked out of the way. His blade clipped her hood as it sailed over her. She dropped to the side before he could come back with a stroke at her heart. But Shadar was a step ahead of her, and as she rose to her feet, he was there, his sword thirsting for her blood.

The blade snaked out. Nadya jumped backward. The rapier came to rest a handbreadth from her chest. Shadar drew it back. He wasn't breathing heavily. He was, after all, the finest swordsman in the city, and in that moment, Nadya didn't think she could get around him without killing him.

And like any Nomori, he would fight to the death.

Shadar lunged forward. She dodged and grabbed the tip of his blade, breaking it off and dropping it. He frowned slightly. Was he wondering what had happened to the bloodstained murderer who had been present in the fourth tier yesterday?

She leapt toward him and wrenched the other half of the rapier from his hands. Her father staggered back but caught himself. "I can fight you without a weapon, Phoenix."

He dodged to the left, using his momentum to jump into the air. His leg shot out as he spun, coming down to crack into Nadya's jaw. She stepped back. Her skull buzzed with pain, but her father's wide-eyed stare indicated that the strike had been meant to take her down.

Sweat dripped down the back of her neck under her hood. She did not know how much time she had before Gedeon or the zealot's army got their hands on Kesali. She couldn't afford to waste any more.

A fist came at her from nowhere. Instinctively, she dodged and grabbed the arm. A moment before she snapped the bone, Nadya caught herself. She let go and backed up.

"Are you afraid to kill me?" Shadar spat. He held up his hands in perfectly balanced fists. "I gave you the benefit of the doubt, once, to my great shame. No more. The Duke is being transported to safety as we fight. You'll never find him."

He was willing to give his life to buy time for the Duke to get away.

Nadya dropped her arms. Out of the corner of her eye, she saw Levka laughing, and she knew what this was about. He knew she could not win against Gedeon. Yesterday proved that. The only reason he told her everything was so she would go after Kesali and Marko, so that she would have to face her father.

So she would have to choose between keeping her secret and saving Kesali.

This wasn't part of a great plot to destroy the Nomori. No, this was solely to hurt Nadya as she had hurt him two years ago. Her stomach clenched. Was there another way? She scrambled for an answer, for anything but the choice the magistrate forced upon her. But it was simple. Kesali's life was more important than her secret. It was more important than anything right now. Kesali and Marko were the only ones who could bring the city back together. As she faced her father, her thoughts grew fuzzy. She was tired. Tired of secrets and sneaking around and lying to those she loved. Now Kesali needed not the Nomori psychic she pretended to be, but the *nivasi* she was. The Iron Phoenix.

"Fight me!" her father yelled, and she tore off her disguise.

CHAPTER TWENTY-TWO

S torm's Quarry burned.

From atop the great wall that encircled the city and its chaos, Gedeon watched with a satisfied smile. The smoke stung his eyes, but he didn't shut them. Ash rose from the fires that consumed the bottom two tiers of city. Stone buildings glowed red as the flames devoured their innards. Screams echoed off the bloodstained streets as looters and rioters seized what they wanted.

On a building on the outskirts of the Nomori tier, not far from where Gedeon stood on the wall, the zealot yelled encouragement to his soldiers of chaos. "Take back the city. Find the Nomori witch, and bring me her head. They were warned. Now, with the powers of the storm gods, they will be punished!"

A charming man, Gedeon thought with a smirk. If the city had been harder to take, he might have utilized the zealot. As it was, however, Storm's Quarry did not need his aid to fall.

"Sir!"

Gedeon turned at the voice. A guardsman, his eyes full black, saluted him. Nine others fanned out behind him, securing this part of the wall. Normally, Gedeon struggled holding so many under his control, but he found guardsmen to be particularly...malleable.

Two came forward, holding a squirming Nomori woman between them. She spat at Gedeon.

He wiped the spittle away, studying her. Her eyes, however, were on the destruction below. They filled with tears. Good—he would be able to use that. Gedeon had never seen Kesali, Stormspeaker of the Nomori and betrothed to Marko Isyanov, as more than an exotic ornament at the Duke's son's side. Her trousers and vest, once immaculate purple silk, were stained by dirt and ash. Cuts marred her pretty face, and the expression she wore was anything but nice. Hurt and anger twisted her features in a battle mask.

She was the seal on Storm's Quarry's fate. He had ordered her brought to him so he might take control of her, and give Storm's Quarry a show it would not soon forget. Gedeon's mouth twitched. Not even Durriken the Butcher could boast of such an act.

"How? How can you do this?" She turned to stare up at Gedeon.

"Because no one is able to stop me."

Gedeon reached for the power and sent it crackling out and into Kesali's eyes. He searched for the source of her tears, for the guilt that was sure to be plaguing her over the city's fate, for something to provide a gateway into her mind.

The power snapped back. He stumbled, catching himself on the edge of the wall.

"Will you kill me? Or are you too cowardly to do it yourself? Will you send me down there to be slaughtered by the mob?" Kesali demanded.

Gedeon barely heard. He swore. She had to be one of the few who would not provide a passage into her mind. His power needed a weakness of the mind in order to take root and give him control. Those he normally preyed on had that in spades—uncontrollable anger, guilt, fear. It never mattered how virtuous they were. Strength of mind was not a product of good or evil. But this woman was different. Her mind was a tight drum that his power bounced off.

Nothing, however, was without weakness when pressed.

Straightening, he walked up to her and grabbed her shoulder, digging his fingernails into her flesh. His eyes were level with hers as he whispered, "I will find a way in. And then you will bring about the end of Storm's Quarry."

❖

The cloak drifted to the ground, coming to rest a few paces from Nadya. Cool, damp air caressed her cheeks as she locked eyes with her father.

Shadar's eyes widened, and the corners of his lips trembled. He had not dropped his fighting stance. "Nadya?" It came out as a croak.

"Papa, let me explain."

"It was you all this time? You were the one yesterday, in the public square?" If there had been anger in his voice, it would have hurt less. The disbelief, the pain in his eyes as he stared down at her made Nadya want to disappear.

"I don't have much time. Kesali is in danger. So is Marko." She stepped toward him, and he backed up into the door. "Papa, it was one of the *nivasi*, a man named Gedeon. He was behind all the murders. He can take control of a person's body."

"So it was you." He looked away from her.

"I went to stop him yesterday." Her ears burned as she tried to make him understand. "I shouldn't have. I thought I could, but he took control of my body and made me—" She couldn't get the words out. "Papa, you must trust me. I know I have lied to you. I am...*nivasi*. I'm not a normal Nomori. The things I can do—but I never meant to kill anyone. I just wanted to save you from the burning building, and it all started there with the Phoenix." Tears flowed freely down her cheeks.

Shadar said nothing, but he looked at her with a scrutinizing gaze she could not read.

Desperation tore at her voice. "Papa, Levka the magistrate sent Marko to the wall, and Kesali, too. He supplied weapons to the zealot. The *nivasi* is there. If I don't get there, they will die. All of our people. You know what's happening out there. I think I can stop it."

Her father drew a slow breath and said, "Go." He stepped aside.

"Thank you. Papa..." She reached for him.

"Go!" And there was the anger.

With numb fingers, Nadya gathered up and donned the cloak. She opened the door and risked one last look at her father. He was touching the seal of the Protectress on his belt, shaking. She didn't know whether it was in fury or grief, or both.

"I love you," Nadya whispered, and left, sprinting down the palace hall.

Storm's Quarry was in flames when she left the safe marble confines of the palace, jumping over the troop of guardsmen protecting its doors, and headed down to the lowest tier. The hastily tied blanket around her face kept out the worst of the smoke, but still her eyes stung. She blamed her tears on the smoke and the wind that ripped by her as she sprinted and leapt from building down to building.

In the fourth and third tiers, where most people had barricaded their doors and windows, the light of lamps peeked out through the bolts. The streets were deserted. Not even the rats dared to go outside on the solstice.

The inferno began in the second tier.

Nadya skidded to a halt, spraying shingles. Fire roared up in front of her. It exploded out the shop's front, and several men ran away, their arms laden. She couldn't tell if they were Erevan or Nomori. At this point, it didn't matter. She ran around and jumped to the next store. Only a slight wisp of smoke curled out of its windows. She hoped no one was inside.

Nadya leapt across the narrow street. She came to the edge of the tier, looking down on the Nomori tier and the wall.

The noise alone overwhelmed her. Shouts mingled with explosions and screams and bloodcurdling cries. She clamped her hands over her ears as she surveyed the smoky remains of the place that was once her home. It took her a moment to realize that she was looking directly down on the Nomori square.

Its stone benches were smashed, the ashes in the fire pit scattered. Nomori men, women, and children ran screaming across the square, pursued by a ragtag group of Erevans. Nadya squinted through the smoke and realized that they carried muskets and pistols, new by the gleam of the flames off their barrels. Levka's gift to them, no doubt.

Men ran in and out of burning buildings. Some rescued the poor souls trapped inside. Some plundered what was left before letting the roofs collapse on the inhabitants. Fires roared along the tier, lighting up the cloudy day in a ring of flames. Smoke filled the streets, smoke and screams of helplessness and the mob.

Nadya judged there to be at least five thousand rioters, smashing storefronts and gutting any Nomori unfortunate enough to cross their path. The worn cobblestones were stained in blood—the only scent underneath the acrid smoke—and for a moment, Nadya swayed. She was back in her invisible bonds watching her hands paint the square red. She fell to her knees and clamped a hand over her nose, struggling not to vomit. Death was everywhere. Women lay strewn next to their children, ripped naked and bruised. The bullet-ridden corpses of the men who had tried to protect them lay near them in heaps. So did the bodies of some rioters, the price of confronting a Nomori fighter.

The mob had numbers, however, and superior weaponry provided by the magistrate. She swallowed. This had to be stopped, and she did not know if one person could do it.

Marching boot steps echoed under the sharp blasts of muskets and the screams of the dying. Red uniforms emerged from the smoke, led by—Nadya's stomach twisted—Lord Marko, who carried a rapier. Its tip shone red. Rioters scattered before the discipline of the Duke's Guard, but there were only several hundred guardsmen and thousands of rioters.

A yell broke through everything. "Do not let them intimidate you. We have the power of the storm gods on our side. Take up your weapons, brothers, and fight for your city!"

It was the zealot. Nadya took a moment to locate him, as the rioters slowly backtracked out of the nooks and crannies they'd been running to. More men joined them, until the angry citizens stretched down the street and disappeared around the curve of the tier.

There he was, standing atop a building not far from her. A ring of men holding pistols protected their sacred leader. The zealot had not changed his attire. Ash stained his already filthy tunic, but it did not stop his cries of encouragement to the rioters—cries, Nadya realized with a sinking feeling, that were feeding their frenzy and gathering more men to them by the second.

The Duke's Guard now looked hopelessly outnumbered. Nadya saw Marko's pale face through the smoke. He shouted some orders to his men, pointing his blade at the zealot.

Nadya stood. There was a root cause to all this madness, and she needed to find it. Gedeon would be here, and so would Kesali. She swept her gaze over the scene.

Marko shouted a rallying cry, and the crimson tide rushed into the rioters, pushing them back with deadly accurate bullets. While the gunmen reloaded, the swordsmen—the Nomori fighting for their homes, their families, and their very lives—moved in and cut down more of the mob.

But some guardsmen remained with Marko. His rapier was now pointed at her. He had seen the Iron Phoenix, and he was leaving the zealot alone in order to deal with what he judged to be the greater threat.

She leapt down from the building. She could not afford to remain a standing target.

"Get the Phoenix!" Marko shouted.

Nadya dodged the first volley of bullets and ducked underneath an overturned wagon, the hay inside starting to crackle with fire. She forced down the pain of all her old injuries, remembering how her automaton-self was able to call up the depths of her powers to a point where her shoulder hadn't even bothered her. Nadya breathed slowly, and the pain receded.

That's when she heard it.

"Look down there! Look, and see the sea's height. You predicted it would retreat by now. You are the reason for all this death, all this chaos. You are at fault. Have you no shame?" Gedeon's voice was loud, with a frantic undercurrent Nadya had not heard from him before.

She staggered up from the wagon. The voice had come from above. There, on the top of the wall, stood a cluster of figures. Nadya dodged a few rapier strikes, her gaze fixed on the group. Most wore crimson uniforms—guardsmen Gedeon had under his control. One was dressed in black, pointing out to the sea. And next to Gedeon was a tall young woman wearing a smoke-stained vest and trousers.

Nadya's heart stopped for a moment. Gedeon's hand was on Kesali's back, and he could have pushed her out over the wall to her death.

"This is your fault, this chaos! She has deserted you!" He kept speaking low and fast to Kesali, whose face remained calm. Somehow, she seemed to be immune to his control. Nadya wasn't.

She jumped on top of a nearby pile of rubble. From across the battlefield, Marko stared at her, and Nadya held his gaze. She breathed low and fast through the fabric of her disguise. Something passed between the two of them, not recognition, but a degree of understanding. She nodded once and looked to the wall where Kesali was held. The Iron Phoenix was the only one who could rescue her, and Marko knew it.

He turned to his men. "Stop the zealot!" he ordered. One of them began shouting to the remaining guardsmen who weren't desperately trying to push back the rioters. The mob's power and numbers seemed to grow by the moment. The pitifully small group of men in red uniforms and Marko in his brilliant purple one started to jog toward the building that held the zealot on its roof. A ring of over a hundred men, clutching their weapons with fanatical glee, stood between them and the leader of the rebellion.

Nadya touched her seal and sent up a prayer. *If you do not look after me, look after them.* Then she looked to the wall and began to run.

Chapter Twenty-three

Nadya's boots splashed through pools of rainwater tinged with blood. Behind her, the tide of the battle between the guards and the rioters was slowly changing as the Duke's Guard was pushed farther and farther back. Nadya only hoped the fight bought enough time for the Nomori remaining on the tier to escape, although to where, she didn't know. There was nowhere else in the city they would be welcome now.

The steam pumps, suspended over the large culvert that bordered the wall around the entire city, had stopped working. The culvert was finally empty. Nadya ran along the narrow wooden bridge that they sat on, leapt over the pump, and grabbed the sleek marble wall.

There were virtually no finger- or footholds, only slight cracks that ran along the slippery surface, showing where the marble blocks had been cemented together a thousand years ago. Nadya's hands screamed as she hauled her entire body up by two fingers. She gritted her teeth and kept moving.

"They call you their Stormspeaker, their priestess, their prophet. They have no idea what you are truly like. If they knew of your darkness and your selfishness, they would have taken your head long ago." The frustration was palpable in Gedeon's voice. Nadya climbed faster. If he acted upon it, if he did something to Kesali...

"If you won't admit the darkness within yourself, then the city will destroy you for it. You, bring her down. Give her to the zealot for his sacrifice. Tell him it is compliments of the storm gods. That fool will believe it. Go!"

Nadya clenched her jaw and kept climbing. Her hand touched the top, and she vaulted over into the middle of the scene. Four guardsmen had taken hold of Kesali, trying to drag her along the walkway down to the nearest guardhouse and the stairs that led to the city below. Nadya's gut twisted. Kesali would not survive a moment on the ground before some fanatic with a knife killed her. Six other guardsmen converged on Nadya. She knocked one out with a blow to the jaw, and another to the ground as she swept his feet out from under him. One got behind her, and before Nadya could react, he tore her cloak off.

"Nadya," Kesali whispered, eyes wide. "How...?"

The way Kesali looked at her now, her fear, her disbelief, seared itself into Nadya's mind, and she would not forget it for the rest of her days.

"Stop." Gedeon's voice rang out firm and calm. He smiled at Nadya. "I've been waiting for you."

Nadya stopped breathing. Those black eyes held her, and she just waited for them to expand and take her over.

"Bring the Stormspeaker back. I have a better idea." He lounged against the side of the walkway. "Oh, and don't think of trying anything, Nadezhda Gabori. If you do, you will be made to regret it." His tone left nothing to the imagination. "I was planning to make Lady Kesali here into one of my puppets and force her to walk to the zealot and renounce her Nomori heritage and offer herself up as a sacrifice to the storm gods. That would stir things up nicely, if only she wasn't so self-righteous."

She didn't know what he meant. "Why?" Nadya managed in a strangled voice. "Why do any of this? Why let Levka control you?"

He laughed. "That whelp isn't controlling me. I was originally going to kill him when he showed up. But he does have a quick mind, and he came up with quite a good plan. Using you and the Stormspeaker. What chaos! The zealot isn't one of mine, you know. A couple of kills, followed by the floodwaters and food shortage, and this city hardly needed my help to tear itself apart."

"Why?" she repeated. Her eyes darted around to the guardsmen. She didn't want to kill any of them. If she pushed them over into the sea, they would survive for at least an hour, provided they could swim. It would buy her enough time to save Kesali.

The glistening rapier at Kesali's throat, however, stopped her from making a single move.

"Because I can. Because I'm more powerful than they are, and once my family realized that, they tried to have me killed for it. So I hate them in turn." He laughed. "I only wish to cause misery, as is my right."

He was insane. He had Durriken the Butcher's madness.

"And I believe that having the Iron Phoenix murder the betrothed of Lord Marko, the Stormspeaker herself, will cause quite a ripple in the city."

Nadya shut her eyes, backing away from him.

"You cannot avoid me."

Someone grabbed her shoulder, and Nadya threw them off. There was a long moment of silence, then a splash below.

"Get out of here," Kesali yelled. "I'll be fine. Go, go and save yourself."

Nadya could not listen. She was here to save Kesali, and Kesali must not die. She and Marko were the only two in the entire city who could heal the rift between Nomori and Erevan. They needed to live so the city would live, and if that meant giving her life for it, then Nadya was happy to make the sacrifice. Not for Storm's Quarry, not for Marko or the Duke. Not even for her parents.

For Kesali. For the dream Kesali had of a united people, and for the love between them that could not be.

Love for love. Making that sacrifice meant she would not live to see the day of their wedding.

She clenched her fists. "Why don't you fight me like a soldier instead of cowering behind your puppets?" Two sets of hands grabbed at her, and the barrel of a pistol settled on the back of her neck. Guided by her senses of hearing and touch, she jerked away, and after a moment, two splashes sounded below.

"You have to open your eyes at some point."

"Only to kill you," she muttered.

"Or to save her."

Nadya heard Kesali's scream. She turned, eyes shooting open, to see a bit of trousers plummet over the wall. Nadya did not think. She turned her back on Gedeon and the remaining guardsmen and leapt off the wall, pushing off the stone edge to give her more speed. Time slowed as the air took hold of her and she fell.

Kesali was flailing in the air, pure terror etched across her features. Nadya put her hands at her sides and willed herself to go faster. Kesali's body loomed closer and closer, but so did the hard stone bottom of the dry culvert.

Kesali reached out for her, and Nadya clasped her hand. She yanked Kesali up, turning her over. In that instant, her mind went to the safest place she knew, and she prayed. *Let us live through this,* she called out silently to the Protectress. Warmth bloomed in her seal, and time resumed.

She slammed into the bottom of the culvert, Kesali on top of her. Stones cracked and gave way underneath her. Dirt billowed out, clogging her eyes with grit and shards of rock. The rumbling did not stop for a long moment. Her back screamed. The air was forced out of her lungs, and suddenly, all was still.

Nadya opened her mouth, croaking. Slowly, her chest expanded with air. It hurt. Everything hurt. Her back and legs shrieked in pain. She was sprawled across a depression in the bottom of the culvert, surrounded by dirt and bits of rock. She blinked away the grit from her eyes. Every breath she took hurt, but Nadya forced herself to keep breathing and not go near the darkness that hovered at the edge of her vision.

On top of her, Kesali groaned.

Slowly, Nadya sat up, cradling Kesali. Bones, bruised and cracked, made popping noises in her back. Nadya spat out blood. She was alive. They had survived the fall, and Kesali…here in her arms, Kesali was breathing.

"Nadya?" she whispered. Her lips cracked open. Blood dribbled out the corner of her mouth. "You saved me."

Kesali sank into her embrace, tears flowing down her cheeks. Soon, Nadya was crying, too, and they sat there in the crater, sobbing.

"You jumped off after me," Kesali said, wiping her eyes with hands dirty with ash. "You could have died."

"I will always jump off for you," Nadya whispered. "No matter what has happened, I will always do it for you."

Their blood and sweat mingled as they held each other through their tremors. Smoke had filtered down as the edge of culvert was licked by flame. It wouldn't be long before someone came to investigate the crash, and she knew she couldn't defend Kesali against a group of rioters, not in her current condition. She tried to stand, but pain exploded in every corner on her body. Nadya fell back onto the dirt, whimpering.

Kesali's lips brushed her cheek, before she slowly got off Nadya. She stood, wincing at every movement. Her face was chalk white as she held out a hand to Nadya.

Nadya was almost afraid to take it, but Kesali's gaze was insistent, and with her help, Nadya hauled herself up to her knees.

"You're hurt," Kesali said quietly, bracing Nadya on her uninjured arm.

"So are you. And it's my fault."

A voice from above called down, "I thought you might have been done for, but you are stronger than you look. Good."

Nadya looked up to the edge of the culvert before she realized who that voice belonged to. Gedeon's eyes trapped her in their black depths, and this time, he wasted no time. The blackness expanded, trapping her.

Nadya tried to claw at her throat, to beat the overwhelming darkness she now drowned in. Everything fell away, even Kesali's touch. The black guilt beast consumed her, and her hands were painted red with the blood of the countless innocents she had murdered under Gedeon's control.

The black snapped back, and Nadya was once again viewing the painting of her life. All the pain faded. Her body straightened, and Gedeon smiled.

Nadya shrieked, though her lips did not move, as she grabbed hold of Kesali with one hand and dragged her out of the culvert. Kesali screamed, her injured arm catching on the edge of jagged rock. The automaton that was Nadya did not even flinch.

"Nadya," she said, breathless, "Nadya, take back control. Do not let him—"

"Silence, Stormspeaker, or I'll have her snap your neck." Gedeon gestured to Nadya with an almost familial love in his eyes that made her sick to her stomach. "Come. This needs to be a spectacle."

Her feet carried her and Kesali across the bloodstained cobblestones to the center of the public square of the Nomori tier. Now it was filled with bodies and rubble and smoke, the sounds of the Duke's Guard and rioters battling not a hundred paces away. Cowards, avoiding the fight, looted the stores that ran along the square. Several buildings down, the zealot's men had cornered Lord Marko and his guards.

Nadya's heart broke at it all. This was her fault. All the death, all the chaos, the ruined city—it all stemmed back to the first time she had killed two years ago.

Gedeon looked at her and the black in his eyes gleamed.

Some men had come to gather around them, licking their lips and readying their weapons. Gedeon paid them no heed. He looked at Nadya, and her soul froze. "Kill her."

Her hand dropped Kesali's shoulder and closed around her neck. Her fingers tightened, and Nadya fought. She fought with every bit of strength she had. Time slowed down as she watched as her fingers slowly curled around Kesali's throat, cutting off her air. She had seconds before bone snapped, and Kesali would be gone.

Nadya screamed and kept screaming, but it did nothing. Her mind was a hurricane of stillness, her heart trapped in its eye. How was she so weak that he could take her like this? Kesali was strong. Kesali was immune. Kesali was—

The answer sank into her consciousness, and tears welled in her eyes. Nadya looked beyond her hand as it slowly killed the woman she loved and to Gedeon's black eyes. They sparked with the power of control.

But as her grandmother had said, no one can seize control of one's mind without a foothold, a foothold Nadya had and Kesali did not.

Nadya looked down at Kesali's face. It grew pale as blood seeped out of her mouth. In the fuzzy distance, she heard Marko's desperate cry. Kesali's dark eyes stared down at her without fear.

She cringed as the images of the innocent, the feel of blood on her hands, intensified. The people at the Duke's address. The men in the palace. Levka's brother, those years ago. All swam around her, threatening to suffocate her.

Not matter her physical strength, she was weak. She was angry and fearful, just like all Gedeon's other puppets. There was no way she could resist him on her own.

I need your help.

She stopped fighting. This wasn't a battle physical strength could win.

Gedeon's eyes widened slightly. "Kill her!" he ordered again.

If you did not curse me, then help me.

Nadya fingers closed around Kesali's throat, and she forced herself to calm. The scene in front of her faded, and she was fifteen again, being attacked by a large Erevan man with hands that groped and breath that smelled of desire and fish. She heard the crack as his body hit the stone wall and slid down, limp.

Gedeon had all the control. But, Nadya realized, she had something far stronger.

You have always protected your people. I have faith that you will protect both of us. I accept the burden you have given me. Nadya felt the words resonate deep in her bones. *I am afraid. Of Gedeon, of Levka, of the future. Of myself. I am afraid,* she thought as her mind cleared and grew stronger. *But I am not cursed, and I will not stand to let this evil continue. For Kesali, I will fight.*

Her seal of the Protectress burned hot. Nadya's fingers snapped away from Kesali's neck.

Kesali fell to the ground, coughing.

Nadya turned toward Gedeon. His hold on her was gone, and now he would pay for what he had almost made her do.

"Kesali!" She heard Marko's cry, but it was distant and fuzzy. All her attention was focused on the man in front of her.

"Kill her!" His scream carried more desperation than authority. His eyes sought hers again, the black trying to consume her once more.

Nadya held her ground as the darkness came and swirled around her. It touched, trying to pry its way in, but the path it had previously taken to her heart was blocked. Her conviction formed a shield around her consciousness, one that the dark power battered against to no avail. The darkness faded, snapping back into Gedeon's eyes, and for the first time, he looked frightened. Sweat trickled down his face. He backed up, then looked wildly around at the rioters.

With a cry, they rushed at Nadya. She batted them aside. They hit the cobblestones with sickening thumps. She closed the distance between her and Gedeon in three steps. Nadya grabbed him by the neck and lifted him up.

"Will you kill me, *nivasi*?" His mouth twisted into a horrible smile, and he looked truly mad. Spittle frothed at the corner of his mouth as he rasped for breath. "Will you embrace the darkness that is our birthright? Will you follow in the footsteps of Durriken the Butcher? Of Gedeon the Chaos-maker? Will you succeed where we have failed, in bringing this city down?"

One week ago, she would have let him go, thumping him between the eyes to knock him out, then leaving him for the Duke's Guard to collect. One week ago, however, she had not seen her city in shambles and her people slaughtered by mindless rioters. She had not taken the lives of dozens of men, women, and children with her bare hands. She had not known the extent of her power, nor the extent of his.

Nadya lowered him to the ground. He spat out blood. "You are weak. I knew you could not do it. You will never—"

She grabbed his shoulder with one hand, and wrenched his head off with the other. The words froze in a throat that now frothed up blood as his body collapsed to the pavement, unmoving. His head fell from her fingers, his smirk forever molded into its features.

Blood dripping from her fingers, Nadya turned around to see Kesali, pale-faced and shaking.

As Nadya opened her mouth to explain what she could not put into words, an explosion of a magnitude that would put fear into the storm gods rocked the city. The earth quaked, the wall fell, and the sea surged down upon them.

CHAPTER TWENTY-FOUR

As water rushed in, thunder roared. Nadya sprang for Kesali. She flinched away, but Nadya grabbed her good arm anyway and hauled her as fast as she could out of the path of the oncoming sea.

Nadya's own pain was temporarily gone in the face of necessity. She grabbed the doorway of the nearest building and hauled herself up. She got to the roof, pulling Kesali up behind her, just as the water hit. With one hand gripping the stonework, she held onto Kesali with everything she had left.

Water exploded around them. One moment, there was nothing but encroaching waves of black, tipped with angry white foam. The next, they were swallowed whole.

In the middle of the swirling monsoon, Nadya could not see or hear anything. The only thing that kept her anchored to this world was her grip on Kesali. That grip was the only thing that kept them from being swept away. She could not think or believe. She could only close her eyes and hold.

The wave roared past them, through them, and suddenly, it was gone. Nadya blinked. She straightened, her chest and back aching. She was soaked. The blood had been washed clear of her hands. In front of her, Kesali sputtered.

She turned around. Three hundred paces down, a gaping hole punctured the wall that had stood for a thousand years. Barrels of still-smoking gunpowder stood around its base as the water continued to pour in, flooding the entire first tier. A great sucking sound filled the air as the Kyanite Sea poured through the gap, into the city, and down into the open mines. The initial wave had passed, but the water was at least seven paces deep, filling buildings and streets. Cries echoed around the eerie stillness left in the aftermath of the wave.

On top of the wall, next to the smoking hole, the zealot stood and waved his arms triumphantly.

"He did this," Nadya said, hardly able to believe it. "To make a point."

"He still wants me dead," Kesali said softly. "He was no puppet of the *nivasi*, only a fanatic who saw an opportunity."

"One given to him by the magistrate." Nadya almost leapt off the building then, ready to take down the zealot, but she calmed herself. Her hands had spilled enough blood, and she was not eager to spill more. She turned toward Kesali. "Go. The royal family of Storm's Quarry needs to bring that monster to justice."

"And the Iron Phoenix?" Kesali faced the hole in the wall. She did not look at Nadya.

"The Iron Phoenix is needed to save lives today," Nadya said, knowing there would be no reply. Without pause, she leapt off the building. Her stomach was a tight knot. Now was not the time for guilt or punishment. Now was the time to save as many as she could.

She dove down into the freezing waters. A man in a crimson uniform floated by. Nadya grabbed him and, with a strong stroke, broke the surface. Hauling him up to the roof of a building, she made sure he was breathing before she dove in again.

After the sixth man was pulled out, half guardsmen, half rioters, she heard a confrontation on the wall. Marko and Kesali and the few members of the Duke's Guard who had been on high ground when the waters hit cornered the zealot. She watched for a moment as the zealot threw himself off the wall to the waters below. After a moment, his body floated up to the surface, tossing limply on the waves like a broken doll.

So much death for so little purpose, she thought, and resumed her rescues.

When she broke surface again, strong hands grabbed the young woman from her and pulled her onto a dry roof. Nadya looked up, treading water, and saw her father. He was soaked in water, sweat, and blood, but to her relief, the blood did not look as if it belonged to him. His face was hard, and he turned slightly, barking an order to another guardsmen. He looked back and offered Nadya a hand.

She took it gingerly and pulled herself to the roof. She was wet to the bone and cold, the pain of her injuries slowly coming back as the power she found to defeat Gedeon faded into fatigue.

He didn't look at her for the longest moment. "I always wondered," he said finally. "You came from a line of such strong psychics, but you never had their power."

Her throat tightened. What was he trying to say?

Shadar tentatively reached out, hesitated, then laid a hand on her shoulder. "I interrogated the magistrate," he said. "With a blade to his throat, he was very...talkative." He pulled her close, and Nadya felt safe for the first time since all this started. There was nothing between her and her father, no secrets, no lies. When she let go of him, he handed her a bundle.

She glanced down at it. It was a gray cloak, soaked through, but clean of blood.

"I saw this ten minutes ago floating out of a tailor's shop. I don't think she'll mind." Nadya took it with trembling fingers, and Shadar said, "You're needed. Talk will come later. Go, and be safe."

She pulled on the wet garment and leapt off the building, but she was warm despite the chill.

The sun sank lower and lower until it was hidden by dusk, and still Nadya worked. She spent hours diving in and out of the seawater that now engulfed the first two tiers of the city after completely filling the mines. Body after body was pulled from the dark waters, some alive, most dead. The guardsmen who took the wounded from her did it with cautious hands and suspicious, even murderous glares. After a while, Nadya stopped looking at them. Her new cloak made it more difficult to swim, as it billowed around her in the water and hung heavy when she emerged onto a rooftop, but she was not ready for the entire city to know the identity of the Iron Phoenix, especially since few would believe the story of a second *nivasi*.

Fires still burned on rooftops and floating piles of wood and rubble, giving the flooded tiers an eerie glow after sunset. Nadya and the Duke's Guard continued their work. She moved slowly around the city, going into every dwelling. Many of the people she had found had been dead before the waters came, from bullets or blades or blunt weaponry. Her insides went numb after the first hour.

The injured were boated up to the third and fourth tiers, where most courtiers opened their homes to the refugees. The rioters were sent to the storehouses on the top tier, where they received treatment and a watchful guard. But without the zealot, their nameless leader who managed to stir their hunger and fear into a murderous fervor, they were scared and trembling. The injured guardsmen who secured them didn't report a single problem.

Nadya saw her father leading her mother and grandmother toward one of the boat stations, across the hastily laid planks that joined rooftops. They looked uninjured, but the smoke that still hung in the air made her mother cough violently. Across the waters, Shadar met Nadya's gaze and shook his head.

Her heart ached, but Nadya turned away and finished lifting rubble off a man's trapped leg. Her mother and grandmother were not yet ready to face the truth of what she was—the mantra of the villainy of the *nivasi* had been drilled into both of them. Nadya swallowed her tears and continued her work.

When the sun rose, the clouds were gone. It sparkled off the seawaters that now occupied the bottom two tiers of Storm's Quarry, turning the entire island into a glittering sapphire. The Duke made an official announcement outside the palace steps. Using the information Shadar had received, he condemned the zealot and the *nivasi* named Gedeon. He mentioned nothing of the Iron Phoenix, and Nadya knew the city did not yet know how to handle her. The death toll for the Blood Sun Solstice, as it would be forever known, was in the thousands, with more bodies being dragged out of the water every hour. Levka was in custody, and she feared what he might say. Marko had returned to his father's side. The city was broken, and it needed its leaders to begin to heal. Kesali, however, did not stand with the Duke for this announcement.

Nadya tentatively walked along the wall. Fatigue chained her every step to the ground. She had worked for twelve hours without ceasing until she had rescued every soul she could. Finally, she had stopped, and that's when she saw Kesali standing on the wall alone, next to the hole.

It was more impressive and terrifying from this height. Marble that had never seen the light of the day gleamed in the sunlight, its ragged edges blackened and as sharp as bayonets. The wall was ten paces thick, and the explosion knocked a triangle out of it, the chunks of marble now submerged in the waters below. Nadya looked out across the Kyanite Sea to the distant sharp edges of the coast. The waters below lapped calmly at the walls, and the Mark of Recession gleamed with moisture, announcing to the world that the sea had receded enough for trade.

"The waters receded on the solstice," Kesali said quietly without turning. "As my vision always showed it. The sea has gone down, disappearing into our city." She looked up at Nadya, her eyes wet. "A self-fulfilling prophecy. My own words caused this."

"This is not your fault. I'm the one with blood on my hands." She did not deserve to be standing up here, next to Kesali.

"I know you were being controlled," Kesali said.

Hearing those words from her should have meant more. Nadya stared down at the ragged marble edge of the wall, knowing the truth. "The public square, yes. The times before that, no. And not here, not with Gedeon." As she spoke of painful memories, the great crushing weight of so many lies lifted.

"And how do you go on?" Kesali asked, looking out over the plains to the mountains in the distance. "After so much that is evil around you, how do you still see the light?"

You find someone who makes you whole, and you fight with everything you have to give them a world of light. But all she could say was, "You learn."

The corners of Kesali's mouth twitched. "Learn not to trust the gift that was given to me at birth?" Her hand clutched her right arm just below the shoulder. Someone had seen to her injuries, and it no longer seemed to be paining her. "I prayed to the Protectress, and she has forsaken me."

Nadya slowly walked closer until they were an arm's length apart. "I understand." Slowly, she dropped her cloak to the ground and rolled up her right sleeve. Her seal, a plain metal band with the flower symbol of the Protectress, shone wet in the sunlight. "I've lost everything. My greatest secret has been exposed to those I care about, and the city thinks I am a murderer." Her voice dropped. "I guess I am. And all the time, I prayed for guidance and protection, and I got none. I thought I was cursed." She looked up and met Kesali's watery gaze. "Until it mattered most, when I dove off the wall to catch you, and the Protectress wrapped us both in her arms and saved us. Her strength poured into me to resist Gedeon. I believe...it will be all right," she said, realizing that, despite everything, she actually did.

Kesali reached out and brushed her seal. She looked down into Nadya's eyes and slowly rolled up her right sleeve. She winced as the fabric gave way to bandages and to a simple metal band around her upper arm with the seal of a flower pressed into it.

"The Elders say that those who wear the Protectress's seal in the same spot are destined for each other." Kesali reached out, and Nadya, hesitating only a moment, met her halfway.

Their hands entwined as they looked out over the ruins of Storm's Quarry. The future of the city was perilous, and Nadya knew it would need both the marriage of Kesali and Marko and the strength of the Iron Phoenix to heal what had been broken. But she relaxed in the warm grip of Kesali's hand, inhaling the sweet scent of the woman she loved that stubbornly clung underneath the day's blood and ash. For that moment, she was not the Iron Phoenix. She was Nadya Gabori, and as she gazed out over the city, holding on to Kesali, she was home.

About the Author

Rebecca Harwell grew up in Minnesota and has since lived around the Midwest, which has given her a love of winter and the prairie. She holds a BA in creative writing from Knox College and is currently pursuing her MS in library science at Indiana University.

Her writing reflects the comic books, space operas, and high fantasy epics she loves to read. When not writing, Rebecca can be found studying, watching *Star Trek* reruns, playing with her rabbit, and staging imaginary battles in her head. She remains unconvinced that unicorns aren't real.

Rebecca can be contacted at rebeccajharwell@gmail.com
Website: http://www.rebeccaharwell.com/

Books Available from Bold Strokes Books

A Touch of Temptation by Julie Blair. Recent law school graduate Kate Dawson's ordained path to the perfect life gets thrown off course when handsome butch top Chris Brent initiates her to sexual pleasure. (978-1-62639-488-9)

Beneath the Waves by Ali Vali. Kai Merlin and Vivien Palmer love the water and the secrets trapped in the depths, but if Kai gives in to her feelings, it might come at a cost to her entire realm. (978-1-62639-609-8)

Girls on Campus edited by Sandy Lowe and Stacia Seaman. College: four years when rules are made to be broken. This collection is required reading for anyone looking to earn an A in sex ed. (978-1-62639-733-0)

Heart of the Pack by Jenny Frame. Human Selena Miller falls for the domineering Caden Wolfgang, but will their love survive Selena learning the Wolfgangs are werewolves? (978-1-62639-566-4)

Miss Match by Fiona Riley. Matchmaker Samantha Monteiro makes the impossible possible for everyone but herself. Is mysterious dancer Lucinda Moss her own perfect match? (978-1-62639-574-9)

Paladins of the Storm Lord by Barbara Ann Wright. Lieutenant Cordelia Ross must choose between duty and honor when a man with godlike powers forces her soldiers to provoke an alien threat. (978-1-62639-604-3)

Taking a Gamble by P.J. Trebelhorn. Storage auction buyer Cassidy Holmes and postal worker Erica Jacobs want different things out of life, but taking a gamble on love might prove lucky for them both. (978-1-62639-542-8)

The Copper Egg by Catherine Friend. Archeologist Claire Adams wants to find the buried treasure in Peru. Her ex, Sochi Castillo, wants to steal it. The last thing either of them wants is to still be in love. (978-1-62639-613-5)

The Iron Phoenix by Rebecca Harwell. Seventeen-year-old Nadya must master her unusual powers to stop a killer, prevent civil war, and rescue the girl she loves, while storms ravage her island city. (978-1-62639-744-6)

A Reunion to Remember by TJ Thomas. Reunited after a decade, Jo Adams and Rhonda Black must navigate a significant age difference, family dynamics, and their own desires and fears to explore an opportunity for love. (978-1-62639-534-3)

Built to Last by Aurora Rey. When Professor Olivia Bennett hires contractor Joss Bauer to restore her dilapidated farmhouse, she learns her heart, as much as her house, is in need of a renovation. (978-1-62639-552-7)

Capsized by Julie Cannon.What happens when a woman turns your life completely upside down? (978-1-62639-479-7)

Girls With Guns by Ali Vali, Carsen Taite, and Michelle Grubb. Three stories by three talented crime writers—Carsen Taite, Ali Vali, and Michelle Grubb—each packing her own special brand of heat. (978-1-62639-585-5)

Heartscapes by MJ Williamz. Will Odette ever recover her memory or is Jesse condemned to remember their love alone? (978-1-62639-532-9)

Murder on the Rocks by Clara Nipper. Detective Jill Rogers lives with two things on her mind: sex and murder. While an ice storm cripples Tulsa, two things stand in Jill's way: her lover and the DA. (978-1-62639-600-5)

Necromantia by Sheri Lewis Wohl. When seeing dead people is more than a movie tagline. (978-1-62639-611-1)

Salvation by I. Beacham. Claire's long-term partner now hates her, for all the wrong reasons, and she sees no future until she meets Regan, who challenges her to face the truth and find love. (978-1-62639-548-0)

Trigger by Jessica Webb. Dr. Kate Morrison races to discover how to defuse human bombs while learning to trust her increasingly strong feelings for the lead investigator, Sergeant Andy Wyles. (978-1-62639-669-2)

24/7 by Yolanda Wallace. When the trip of a lifetime becomes a pitched battle between life and death, will anyone survive? (978-1-62639-619-7)

A Return to Arms by Sheree Greer. When a police shooting makes national headlines, activists Folami and Toya struggle to balance their relationship and political allegiances, a struggle intensified after a fiery young artist enters their lives. (978-1-62639-681-4)

After the Fire by Emily Smith. Paramedic Connor Haus is convinced her time for love has come and gone, but when firefighter Logan Curtis comes into town, she learns it may not be too late after all. (978-1-62639-652-4)

Dian's Ghost by Justine Saracen. The road to genocide is paved with good intentions. (978-1-62639-594-7)

Fortunate Sum by M. Ullrich. Financial advisor Catherine Carter lives a calculated life, but after a collision with spunky Imogene Harris (her latest client) and unsolicited predictions, Catherine finds herself facing an unexpected variable: Love. (978-1-62639-530-5)

Soul to Keep by Rebekah Weatherspoon. What *won't* a vampire do for love... (978-1-62639-616-6)

When I Knew You by KE Payne. Eight letters, three friends, two lovers, one secret. Can the past ever be forgiven? (978-1-62639-562-6)

Wild Shores by Radclyffe. Can two women on opposite sides of an oil spill find a way to save both a wildlife sanctuary and their hearts? (978-1-62639-645-6)

Love on Tap by Karis Walsh. Beer and romance are brewing for Tace Lomond when archaeologist Berit Katsaros comes into her life. (987-1-62639-564-0)

Love on the Red Rocks by Lisa Moreau. An unexpected romance at a lesbian resort forces Malley to face her greatest fears where she must choose between playing it safe or taking a chance at true happiness. (987-1-62639-660-9)

Tracker and the Spy by D. Jackson Leigh. There are lessons for all when Captain Tanisha is assigned untried pyro Kyle and a lovesick dragon horse for a mission to track the leader of a dangerous cult. (987-1-62639-448-3)

Whirlwind Romance by Kris Bryant. Will chasing the girl break Tristan's heart or give her something she's never had before? (987-1-62639-581-7)

Whiskey Sunrise by Missouri Vaun. Culture and religion collide when Lovey Porter, daughter of a local Baptist minister, falls for the handsome thrill-seeking moonshine runner, Royal Duval. (987-1-62639-519-0)

Dyre: By Moon's Light by Rachel E. Bailey. A young werewolf, Des, guards the aging leader of all the Packs: the Dyre. Stable employment—nice work, if you can get it...at least until silver bullets start to fly. (978-1-62639-662-3)

Fragile Wings by Rebecca S. Buck. In Roaring Twenties London, can Evelyn Hopkins find love with Jos Singleton or will the scars of the Great War crush her dreams? (978-1-62639-546-6)

Live and Love Again by Jan Gayle. Jessica Whitney could be Sarah Jarret's second chance at love, but their differences and Sarah's grief continue to come between their budding relationship. (978-1-62639-517-6)

Starstruck by Lesley Davis. Actress Cassidy Hayes and writer Aiden Darrow find out the hard way not all life-threatening drama is confined to the TV screen or the pages of a manuscript. (978-1-62639-523-7)

Stealing Sunshine by Tina Michele. Under the Central Florida sun, two women struggle between fear and love as a dangerous plot of deception and revenge threatens to steal priceless art and lives. (978-1-62639-445-2)

The Fifth Gospel by Michelle Grubb. Hiding a Vatican secret is dangerous—sharing the secret suicidal—can Felicity survive a perilous book tour, and will her PR specialist, Anna, be there when it's all over? (978-1-62639-447-6)

Cold to the Touch by Cari Hunter. A drug addict's murder is the start of a dangerous investigation for Detective Sanne Jensen and Dr. Meg Fielding, as they try to stop a killer with no conscience. (978-1-62639-526-8)

Forsaken by Laydin Michaels. The hunt for a killer teaches one woman that she must overcome her fear in order to love, and another that success is meaningless without happiness. (978-1-62639-481-0)

Infiltration by Jackie D. When a CIA breach is imminent, a Marine instructor must stop the attack while protecting her heart from being disarmed by a recruit. (978-1-62639-521-3)

Midnight at the Orpheus by Alyssa Linn Palmer. Two women desperate to make their way in the world, a man hell-bent on revenge, and a cop risking his career: all in a day's work in Capone's Chicago. (978-1-62639-607-4)

Spirit of the Dance by Mardi Alexander. Major Sorla Reardon's return to her family farm to heal threatens Riley Johnson's safe life when small-town secrets are revealed, and love may not conquer all. (978-1-62639-583-1)